A BIT OF A SHUNT
UP THE RIVER

by Desmond Cory

A BIT OF A SHUNT
UP THE RIVER

DESMOND CORY

PUBLISHED FOR THE CRIME CLUB BY
DOUBLEDAY & COMPANY, INC.
GARDEN CITY, NEW YORK
1974

All of the characters in this book are fictitious, and any resemblance to actual persons, living or dead, is purely coincidental.

ISBN: 0-385-01461-9
Library of Congress Catalog Card Number 73–10800
Copyright © 1974 by Shaun McCarthy
All Rights Reserved
Printed in the United States of America
First Edition in the United States of America

CHAPTER 1

You could regard Bony Wright (and Tracy also) as being a victim of circumstance, though I'm told such an approach is no longer fashionable in criminal psychology. He didn't see himself that way, and nor did his fellow inmates in Strangeways Prison. The nickname they gave him made no allusion to his facial or his skeletal structure, but supposedly invoked the Emperor Napoleon, who Bony had once—perhaps ingenuously—claimed to have attained the peak of the criminal profession and to constitute, therefore, a model to be admired and emulated. Of course Napoleon may be held to have been, like Bony himself, a murderer; but history (a prison record written large) usually seeks to distinguish the slaughter of many thousands from the overenergetic disposal of a night watchman with the butt of an unlicensed pistol in the course of an armed raid on a Bond Street jeweller's store, and this distinction can, in fact, be safely made, since neither the night watchman nor those who died at Waterloo are in a position to argue the contrary case. But Bony, with characteristic naiveté, chose to ignore this distinction.

He was, however, in some ways a famous man. Naturally the death of the night watchman hadn't been enough in itself to make of him a public figure, nor had his capture and eventual trial been very adequately reported by the national press; and his eighteen-month tour of various provincial prisons went, needlessly to say, altogether unremarked. Strangeways, though, was to become his Elba. Like Napoleon, he escaped, and his escape made him famous. Journalists—like historians—worship a winner. They did Bony proud. For days on end they gave him a splendid write-up. They even put his picture on the telly. It made things rather difficult for him, in a way, but he accepted these tributes with a proper stoicism; such, he realised, is the lot of the public hero.

The gentlemen who had arranged his escape—and therefore, in reality, deserved most of the credit for it—didn't view the matter quite so philosophically. Not that they *wanted* the credit for it; their problem was otherwise. They had done a good job, as far as it went. Within four hours of his entering, on a quiet crossroads not a hundred miles from Manchester, an unobtrusive chauffeur-driven Ford Executive, Bony had been installed in a small but comfortable flat in an eminently respectable South London suburb. While he stayed there, his name—he was told—would be Greaves. This information was in fact supplied to him by Mrs. Greaves, who had lived in the flat for some five weeks previously and who would do, throughout the period of his residence there, his cooking, his shopping, and his laundry; since she appeared to be in no other respects a motherly body (and in fact had been—though Bony didn't know this—for some time gainfully employed as a pornographer's model), Bony assumed that certain other of his immediate wants would be similarly catered for by thus useful factotum, and this assumption was shortly proved to be perfectly correct. There was, as it turned out, a *real* Mr. Greaves, who was barely known by sight to the immediate neighbours (presumably since he availed himself of those same facilities rather infrequently) and who bore a sufficient physical resemblance to Bony Wright for this cunningly planned imposture to go, at least by those neighbours, undetected, since Bony's appearance occasioned them no surprise. The *real* Mr. Greaves was currently enjoying a well-paid holiday of indefinite duration somewhere in the South of France and would not, therefore, be spoiling matters with an ill-timed personal appearance. These and many other details had not been particularly difficult to arrange, but setting it all up had cost a lot of money; the gentlemen concerned looked on the expenditure as a profitable investment, but not in any sense a long-term one. That was why they, too, looked with disfavour on so much Fleet Street publicity. They had, as reasonable businessmen, to admit that it made of their prompt reimbursement a rather difficult matter.

The investment was not quite as secure as they had been led to suppose. Conceded that the Bond Street hit had been a fairly happy doddle, yielding tax-free benefits of around fifty thousand pounds, it was not the case (Bony explained, caressing an incipient moustache) that he had collected a half-share. He had split with a mere handful of spending money; the rest he had agreed to pick up once the loot was safely fenced. So now he had to find the money man and shake the stuff loose. It wouldn't, he thought, be too much of a problem.

The representative of the gentlemen concerned hinted that it had better not be—managing to convey this hint in such a way that the underlying threat was heavily veiled; Bony was not the sort of man you'd choose to threaten directly, least of all when sitting in an arm-chair opposite. It was simply that, as reasonable businessmen, his principals considered it necessary to impose a delivery date. In six weeks' time, they would expect to have recouped their expenses or to have written off the loss. For the first three weeks, Bony could enjoy Mrs. Greaves's hospitality and the protection of Mrs. Greaves's respectable suburban flat. From then on, he'd be on his own. Though if he needed any other kind of co-operation . . . ?

Bony was quite sure that he didn't. Because once anyone other than himself learned who else had been in on the doddle, it was obvious that someone other than himself would be running round fast to do the shaking. Bony, as has been said, indulged like all of us in constant self-deception, but that didn't mean he was anybody's fool. Mrs. Greaves, adopting in the early hours of the morning rather too intimate a line of questioning, had to retire to her respectable suburban bathroom to bathe a badly bruised cheekbone and a cut lip, and didn't make the same mistake again. Hers was not a brilliant academic intellect, but she was no fool, either.

Bony was doubly sensitive on this topic because he had reason to believe that things mightn't be quite easy as he'd pretended. The truth was that he had never bargained for the night watchman's dying in hospital; it was the sort of thing you always bargained for and yet didn't bargain for, so to speak. And since he hadn't bargained for it, then probably his trusted colleagues Tommy and Rusty hadn't bargained for it, either. One of them or maybe both of them had got cold feet. Bony hadn't just been caught; he'd been shopped. He had suspected this at the time of his arrest; the evidence emerging in his trial, considered in the subsequent cold light of a prison cell, had solidified his suspicion into certainty. One or both of them had grassed, had let out the word. Naturally, when under interrogation Bony hadn't returned the favour; with his share of the loot still under wraps, it wouldn't have been a bright thing to do. And later, though virtually certain that the skids had been slipped into place and a convenient method found of putting his half-share to other and better uses, he still hadn't coughed; instead, he had thought a lot. They hadn't been very edifying thoughts, but he'd derived a certain satisfaction from them. Though nothing, of course, to the satisfaction he'd derive from putting his ideas into practice.

Tommy and Rusty doubtless would have guessed what he had in mind. When they knew that he was looking for them, they'd probably dive into holes in the ground and shovel the earth back over themselves. And so, no, it wouldn't be so easy. He'd said nothing of this to his present patrons, because if they thought the enterprise was *too* difficult, they might decide to write off their losses ahead of time. Bony didn't want that to happen. And, in his view, the enterprise wasn't really too difficult. Not for a Bonaparte. He fancied his chances.

Within twenty days his moustache had grown to sufficient dimensions to warrant a trim, his sideburns were lowered to within three inches of his chin, his hair had lost the characteristic outline of the prison cut. Nothing alters the appearance so much as the presence or absence of hair; his face looked different, older, more careworn. He bought faintly tinted hornrimmed glasses and, for the first time, went out of the flat, wearing a well-pressed grey worsted suit and a blue silk tie. He began to institute inquiries. Not through the grapevine, of course; that would have been stupid. He engaged instead the services of a private detective agency, not to find Tommy but to find Tommy's missus. Rusty Keyes had no missus. He looked for Rusty himself.

Two days before his three-week period was up, he moved from the Greaveses' establishment to another small flat—not a bed-sitter —in the Earl's Court area. He also bought a secondhand car. You may think that to rent a flat or to buy a secondhand car you need documentation. You'd be surprised. The car was a D registration Mini-Cooper. The flat was at rather less than a mile's distance from the very much more expensive apartment where, according to the detective agency, Tommy's missus lived. Except that she didn't. Currently she was living with someone else. They gave a name and address. She went to her own apartment mostly afternoons, and not every afternoon at that. Bony let himself in one morning and had a long look round. It was a large apartment, quiet and peaceful. He didn't find anything of interest.

The following morning he located Rusty Keyes and, at Bony's pressing invitation, they went to the apartment together.

CHAPTER 2

But what had Tracy got to do with all this?

As yet, nothing.

That was what I meant when I said that you could regard Tracy and Bony Wright as being equally the victims of circumstance. At exactly that time when Bony was pushing back the lock of the apartment belonging nominally to his ex-partner's missus, circumstance, to Tracy, was taking tangible form, bowling down to Brighton on the A23 at an ultraconservative eighty miles an hour. Circumstance had the blue and shining shape of what might, by the insensitive, have been called a motorcar; circumstance and Bony's souped-up Mini could, that is to say, both be called cars, as shoughs, water rugs, and demiwolves are clept all by the name of dogs, but circumstance had an unquestionable air of choosing not to recognise any such relationship—of making pedigree a distinction of kind rather than of degree. Circumstance was a brand-new Lambo. To be more precise, a Lamborghini Espada GT, a shade under four feet high and pricing out at approximately two hundred pounds an inch. Tracy was expecting the arrival of circumstance that morning and took delivery of it punctually at 11 A.M.

He left it parked in the forecourt of the workshop, where passers-by could see it, and himself walked slowly round it several times. Circumstance wasn't *his*, of course. No such luck. He was there merely to take delivery and later in the day to hand it over to its owner; he didn't even know, as yet, who the owner was.

And being the workshop manager he would also, of course, be there to take the can back if anything subsequently went wrong with the thing. *Wrong?* . . . With a Lamborghini? . . . The idea was inconceivable. All the same, he'd run a check. Personally. Just the obvious things. Like making sure there was enough petrol in the tank to take the new owner more than five hundred yards. He was in his overalls and didn't have to change. One of the mechanics brought him out a very respectful mug of indifferent coffee. He put it on a spread newspaper on the concrete apron and let it cool there. From the centre of the opened page of newsprint, Bony Wright's face stared up at him; Tracy paid it no attention. For the next ninety minutes or so, Tracy was to be totally absorbed with circumstance. Tracy, like the journalists, the historians, and like everyone else, admired success; but being a simple man, the god had, for him, two names and two names only. Lamborghini and Ferrari. To these twin deities Tracy would at almost any time willingly prostrate himself, according to the modern usage—face upwards, with his back on a trolley and a set of spanners comfortably to hand. He was an easy fellow to keep happy. Twelve thousand pounds would do it, or a little more or less, if placed before him in the shape of complex and sophisticated machinery. Simple people have simple satisfactions.

Not many people treated Tracy very respectfully, but his staff did, especially his mechanics. This wasn't because he was the present manager of C. E. Tracy Motors, Ltd., Poulters Lane, Brighton, Sussex, but because he had once been a racing driver; not a top-liner, but a good one nonetheless. He had had the bad luck to coincide, in the middle '60s, with a round half-dozen of the finest ever —Clark, Graham Hill, Stewart, Suretes, Innes Ireland—and he hadn't managed, quite literally, to last the pace. Now, moving round the Lambo again to peer under the bonnet, he walked with a hint of a sidling motion, a barely discernible roll of the right hip. He wore his hair long, collar-length, in the current mode, a fashion he approved of since it hid completely the small metal plate that had been let into his skull just behind the right ear. The carve-up that would, but for his helmet, have splintered his head like an eggshell had also detached the retina of his right eye; no visible trace of that damage now remained, but three or four times a year—usually in the winter—the blinding headaches would return and with them, when he slept, the nightmares. You could say that he'd had bad luck in that respect, too, but that wasn't how he saw the matter himself. The way he saw it, the ones who'd had bad luck were all dead— with some of the finest ever among their number.

Against that kind of competition and before the shunt, he'd amassed over four years a grand total of eight World Championship points. That in itself was nothing great; Clark had knocked up seven Grand Prix wins in 1963 alone, the year Tracy had started. Some people had thought he'd been about to come good in '67, the year of the bad one; he might have and he mightn't have; now they'd never know. He'd been in the one race since that year, partnering Billy Winter at Le Mans in an Aston-Martin, but leaving the White House and with only a hundred and twenty on the clock he'd seen the road growing narrower and narrower in front of him, the car going faster and faster down the straight though the needle was hanging obstinately steady, and he'd backed off, and that had been that. Billy had never said a word. He hadn't had to. Now Tracy was thirty years old, an old, old man; he'd owned Tracy Motors, Ltd. for three years, but for the last two had been running the show for someone else. In his racing days he'd been fairly wealthy. Now he was broke. Still, better that than dead. *Much* better.

In his racing days, again, he'd been married. But his wife had gone off with someone called Tony Hay—another racing driver, as it happened. Tony wasn't as fast as Tracy, hadn't got as much money, and certainly wasn't better-looking, so it obviously was just that Anne liked him better. In other words, it was one of those personal things and nobody's fault. Tracy hadn't borne any grudges and hadn't worried about it at all; the bad one had come along five weeks later, but he didn't think Anne's leaving him had had anything much to do with it. His chief worry, in fact, when she'd come to see him in hospital had been that she'd think it the proper thing to put on the big reconciliation act, but she'd been much too sensible a girl for that. After that first time, she and Tony had always shown up at the hospital together and the three of them had had some good old laughs together. Then they hadn't come any more and he hadn't seen them since. He didn't know what they were doing now and he certainly didn't very much care.

He drank his coffee. The mug had left a damp brown ring on Bony Wright's face, but he didn't look at it; he'd read the paper already. He was looking at Deason. Deason was coming across from the office, moodily, his hands pushed deep into his pockets.

"Someone to see you," Deason said.

Deason was Tracy's foreman.

Tracy put down the mug and looked at his hands, which were oil-stained. "In the office?"

"Yep."

"Well, can't you handle him? Or is it a her?"

"It's a him all right."

"Ancient or modern?"

"Dunno. I mean, it's Mr. Greene."

"Mr. Greene? Why the hell didn't you say so?"

. . . knowing very well, really, why the hell he hadn't said so. Deason was a monosyllabic type, but he liked to make his little dramatic effects. "Mr. Greene to see you . . ." No. Too easy. Too simple. Tracy grabbed a wad of cotton waste and started wiping.

He found Mr. Greene standing in front of the office desk and staring at the July girl on the wall calendar, whose attire, or lack of it, was distinctively and appropriately seasonal; there wasn't, however, anything remotely lecherous about his gaze, which was merely speculative, as though he were undecided whether to sell her now or hang on till August. He looked at almost everything in this way, irrespective of whether the article under examination were his to sell or not; in the present case, his attitude was justifiable, since the calendar was—indirectly at least—his property, as was everything else on the premises. And it was probable that he had dropped in, as was sometimes his custom, simply to remind Tracy of the fact. "Ah, there you are, Mr. Greene," said Tracy breezily, closing the glass-fronted door carefully behind him. "Take a chair, why don't you?"

"Prefer to stand," Mr. Greene said. "Doctor's recommendation. Spend too much time sitting down in the ornery way of things."

Mr. Green rarely used the word "I" in conversation. He didn't need to. He could normally assume that what he and his listeners thought about any given topic would amount to very much the same thing and that pronouns could hence be considered linguistically redundant. He had, by the same token, the habit of omitting from his pronouncements such syllables as seemed to him mere superfluous adornment, which custom made him on occasion—as he might have said—somewhat incompressible. Tracy, who was fortunately familiar with the idiom, edged awkwardly past Mr. Greene's stillproferred back—the office was a very small one, providing in effect space only for his desk, his filing cabinet, his chair, a visitor's chair, with a small uncarpeted opening beside the latter where an unenterprising mouse might have practised high jumps—and seated himself, no less awkwardly, behind the desk; his stiff hip made it difficult for him, on these occasions, to display a well-tailored agility and grace. "Sorry about that. It's rather a small office."

"You're rather a big man," Mr. Greene said. "A small man might fit in a good deal better."

"Ergonomically, yes."

". . . Eh?"

Tracy decided to start again. "What can I do to help you, Mr. Greene?"

"To help me?" Mr. Greene thought about this for a moment in silence. "Well, you can't make money. That's for sure."

With this initial approach, too, Tracy was altogether familiar. "You know what I told you when you took over this show, Mr. Greene. I'm trying to run a prestige outfit. And it's really building up very nicely this summer. We had Sir Michael Alveston's Maserati in only last week. He sent it all the way down from Ascot."

"I know," Mr. Greene said. "I told him to."

"Ah. Well, then that Lambo out there. That's being delivered today."

"Tomorrow."

"Tomorrow? I was told—"

"Tomorrow. It's mine."

Tracy closed his eyes for a moment. "The name on the books is Pope. I wasn't told it was for you. In fact, when I took the order—"

"Didn't say it was for me. Said it was mine."

It was bad enough getting this sort of thing from Deason. Clearly, Tracy thought, it was going to be one of those difficult mornings. "I see," he said, warily and untruthfully. "It's some kind of an investment?" *Fiddle*, he would have said five years ago. But as manager of a prestige high-pressure business outfit, naturally one learns discretion.

"It's a present," Mr. Greene said, descending to particulars.

That made it almost certainly a fiddle, though an alternative possibility remained that might be thought a little more flattering. "I'm sure she'll be delighted with it, Mr. Greene."

"She'd better be," Mr. Greene said.

"It's not what I'd call a ladies' job, mind you, but it's very much more docile than most people think. It holds the road like glue, which is the important thing. So if she's even a halfway competent driver, she'll have no trouble at all."

"Supposed to be a good driver, yes. And if she isn't," Mr. Greene said, "she will be when you've finished with her."

There was another brief silence, during which Tracy wondered if it was worth while going on even *trying* to understand. Greene, like many another very rich man in advanced middle age, was reported once in a while to have his little feminine fancies, but it was also pretty freely recognised that elueting from him those little gifts and tokens of esteem that mark the progress of a ripening friendship was about as easy as taking Jack Brabham once he'd closed the gate. This production, like rabbit out of a hat, of an astronomically priced motorcar as memento of an affectionate liaison was so startlingly unprecedented as almost to bring on one of Tracy's intolerable migraines. While Tracy stared at him, the object of his bewilderment blinked once or twice very slowly, like a ruminating tortoise, but otherwise remained totally expressionless. He seemed now, indeed, to be thinking about something else, and—judging by his next remark—was.

"Take it you'd like to go on running things here for another year or so?"

"Why, yes. I think business is improving. But I can't guarantee much increase in the profits yet awhile."

"Profits, what profits? So far you've not even managed to break even. Still, that side of things doesn't much worry me. This is a prestige shop, we're agreed on that. Going to keep it open right enough. But do I keep you in charge of it?—*that's* the burning question."

"I don't know of anyone," Tracy said, "I could recommend to do the job better."

"That's as may be. You've been working hard, certainly. Maybe too hard. A holiday, now, might do you a world of good. Paid, of course." Tracy's air of puzzlement was now bordering on outright incredulity. "Then while you're enjoying a well-earned rest and relaxion, you can do me a little favour at the same time."

"What sort of a favour?"

"Oh, just a little . . . favour . . ." Now, and for the first time, Mr. Greene's manner became a trifle hesitant. "You know my daughter, don't you?"

"Your daughter?"

"Yes."

"Your daughter Bernadette?"

"Yes."

"Yes. Yes, I do. Yes."

Possibly aware that their dialogue was now somewhat lacking in sparkle, Mr. Greene transferred his attention once more to the unclad young lady on the wall calendar; whether he perceived any connection between her and the object of their present conversation it was, of course, impossible to say. "She's in London, y'know."

"Ah, I didn't know that, Mr. Greene."

"Well, she is. And that car's for her. It's a birthday present."

"Very nice, very nice."

"Like you to drive it up to town tomorrow. Deliver it to her."

Things were at last beginning to make something resembling sense, and Tracy's perplexity had given way, at least partly, to relief. "Oh, is *that* all?"

"Well, no. That's not all. No. Led to understand she's a fairly good driver, but she's never driven one of these high-power things before. So she's promised me to take a few lessons."

"Prudent," Tracy said. "And I'm to . . . ?"

"If it's not inconvenient."

Whether it's convenient or not, was what of course he meant. "No, sir, it's not inconvenient. I wouldn't say it was at all inconvenient." Therefore, you had to look on the bright side of things. "Your daughter's a very attractive girl, Mr. Greene."

"Not worried about that," Mr. Greene said. "You're not her type."

"Like, because I don't make a musical clinking noise whenever I sit down?"

"Because," Mr. Greene said coldly, "you're not her type. Forget it."

He was, Tracy reflected sadly, only too likely to be right.

"It's a very well-behaved car. The response is a little fierce until you get used to it, but she should get the hang of it in no time."

"Mebbe. Don't want her driving in London, though. In all that London traffic. Want you to get right out of town before you start the lessons. Right out into the country and make a long weekend of it. Bernadette knows where."

"Good. And am *I* allowed to?"

"Got a little place in South Wales. Doubt if the name'd mean much to you. But it should be quiet there."

Quieter than Piccadilly Circus, certainly. "And if I do this, you'll consider it a favour?"

"Certainly."

There had to be something . . . Clearly it was important from the outset to get this matter straight. "You want me," Tracy said slowly and distinctly, "to take out your attractive daughter for a long weekend in the country, and thereby I'll be doing you a favour? I don't want there to be any—"

"Surely I'm explaining myself with perfect clarity."

He seemed to be getting a little testy. "Yes, yes, I quite understand," Tracy said hurriedly. "Always glad to be of service to you, Mr. Greene."

"Good," Mr. Greene said with satisfaction, withdrawing finally his attention from the wall calendar and gazing instead at the litter of miscellaneous paperasserie on Tracy's desk. "Thought from the first that would be how you'd see it. And now if you'll just get out of those dirty overalls of yours, we can take a little stroll together just round the corner. You're going to need a gun."

Funny thing, Tracy thought, smiling to himself; I thought he said I was going to need a gun. It's odd how easily you can misunder . . . He *did* say I was going to need a gun. Good heavens. ". . . A gun? A gun? But that's ridiculous. We never use guns in the motor trade. I wouldn't need one even if we made a profit. I don't think I ever—"

"Just an itsy-bitsy little gun. It won't even be licensed."

"Oh," Tracy said. "Well, that's different."

"You must see how it is, Tracy. I'm a rich man, after all. And a rich man's daughter has to be adequately protected at all times. From kidnappers and such. It's common sense, really."

"But she's married, isn't she? What about her husband?"

"Oh, well, no," Mr. Greene said. "Don't shoot *him.*"

"I mean, why can't *he* do the protecting?"

"Who, Tommy Pope? You must be . . ." *Joking,* Mr. Greene had been going to say; but in the end, didn't. People didn't joke with Mr. Greene any more than they had with William Ewart Gladstone. "Understand they've just about packed it in, anyway. Not that that side of things is any of your business."

"Bodyguarding isn't my usual line of business, either."

"That's an overdramatic way of looking at it," Mr. Greene said. "Simple everyday precaution is what I'd call it."

He was, of course, in a position to call it anything he wanted without too much risk of starting a slanging match. Tracy couldn't see that it'd be worth his while to argue, though he was still a little puzzled as to why he'd been elected for the honour. "You've got people who're much better qualified, is all I'm saying."

"People? What people?"

"Frankie Main, for one. Starshine, for another."

Mr. Greene meditated for a few moments. "So you know that lot, do you?"

"I know *about* them. Who doesn't?"

"Believe," Mr. Greene said, "that oddly enough my daughter doesn't. And I prefer things to stay that way. It's true that on occasion one may need to employ some rather stronry people, an' when one does one's motives are almost always misunderstood. But there you are. Daresay Bernadette's got very few illusions about me these days, anyway. But those that she does have I'd like her to retain for as long as possible."

"They're probably not her sort, either."

"Who?"

"Frankie-boy. And Starshine."

"As to that, wouldn't be too sure. Haven't many illusions left about *her*, if it comes to that; not after Tommy Pope, I haven't."

It would be indiscreet, Tracy thought, to commiserate. He rose from his chair—since Mr. Greene was now showing certain signs of impatience—and reached across to wrestle the office door open. "I'll do my best not to disillusion her, sir. One way or the other."

"My dear chap," Mr. Greene said, "when all's said and done, you're a gentleman. Not like those other fearful fellers." He ruminated a little more, exercising meanwhile the more salient of his jaw muscles. "Besides, you know what would happen to you if by any chance—"

"I do indeed," Tracy said.

"Quite so. That's what I mean. A gentleman always understands these things."

CHAPTER 3

Tracy left the pistol and the box of ammunition on the night table while he finished his packing. He knew very little about pistols; he didn't even know the make or calibre of this one. The rounds in the box would fit, presumably, but he had no intention of ever loading it, let alone using it. Lying on the table, it didn't look particularly alarming or even out of the ordinary—nothing, certainly, to be worth making any kind of fuss about. Old man Greene had his eccentricities, and other people (and Tracy, specifically) just had to put up with them. Certainly, the Lambo in young Bernadette's hands was likely to be the hell of a lot more dangerous than the pistol would ever be in his. *That* was what he should worry about, if any point could be perceived in, at this stage, worrying about anything.

He paused with a cellophane-wrapped laundry-fresh shirt—deprived, doubtless by a special launderers' device, of several of its buttons—in his hands and looked out of the window. Home these days for Tracy was a large high-ceilinged bedroom, in Regency days perhaps elegantly proportioned, that had been partitioned off and variously mutilated to form an extremely small two-room flat and kitchenette, the chief advantage of which was that it made his office seem, in comparison, luxuriously spacious. Another advantage at one time had been the rental, which when he had first moved in had appeared pretty reasonable; it was now, however, at a price that he couldn't really afford. The flat was a lengthy three-iron shot from the forecourt of Tracy Motors and overlooked the Steyne, this second fact making of it a desirable property. One day, no doubt, someone would offer Tracy a substantial bribe to toddle on some place, so it didn't make good sense—in spite of the inflationary rental—to move out for nothing; that, at any rate, was how Tracy rationalised to himself his reluctance to leave, though his real motive was probably mere public school conservatism. Or in other words, laziness. He had travelled so much and so widely and sometimes so very fast in his days on the racing circuit that packing his suitcases had come to involve no sense of anticipation but to be simply and in itself part of his business and so of his way of life. He had no sense of anticipation now—

(but then neither, curiously enough, had Bony Wright when, some three weeks earlier, he had started down the moorland track leading to the crossroads where a car was waiting. Bony hadn't really escaped from prison until some hours after that, because escape is really a state of mind. Tracy had no idea at all of escape; why should he? He didn't even know that he was in prison.)

—though from his window he could see some of the other prisoners, just a very few of them, moving in slow chain-gang file up the Steyne in their gleaming wheeled cages, through the shadows of trees and under the arc lamps. Once in a while the file would break and one of them, or even a small group, would weave away, whining joyously, in a glorious fifty-yard dash to an open space at the corner by the traffic signals; then they would stop; then move forwards again, sedately, recaptured by the long unbroken yellow lines and by the other cars that moved in front of them, behind them, to either side. It wasn't freedom that was hoped for, that was symbolised by those occasional spurts and eddies in the traffic flow, but only the illusion of it; just how jealously that illusion was guarded you could tell by the sustained, frustrated Klaxon moan that arose whenever, for a few brief seconds, that illusion was threatened. Motorists, these prisoners called themselves. Tracy was, or had been, a motorist, too; but the idea that the long, perpetually unwinding spring of the Curva Grande at Monza, the spit and lurch of the grits against the nearside wheels, the Homeric surge of engine power as the swing of the bend at last catapults you into the long straight —the idea that such experiences had any connection with, or even perhaps contributed directly to, that rush-hour traffic jam down below was one that he found rather disturbing. Tracy, from his second-floor vantage point, could survey the scene that he had helped to create and think, as possibly does God on occasion, *No, this isn't what I meant. This isn't what I meant at all.*

He turned away and put the shirt into his suitcase. Tomorrow, he thought, I'll be taking Mr. Greene's Lambo up to London. Through that little lot. A war relic, that's what I really am. A shell-shock case. A world fit for Lambos to live in was what I've wanted. And this is what I've got.

Not that war is fun. Or freedom, either. It's not as simple as that. War is a means to an end. They strap you into a narrow space, so narrow you can hardly move your arms, in the middle of a light-weight metal container that will transport you and forty-odd gallons of explosive at speeds of anything up to two hundred miles an hour. You have to steer this projectile round an endless series of diabolical corners and keep on steering it faultlessly for three hours or more. Sometimes for very much more. And sometimes for less. What the container chiefly contains, apart from yourself, is high-octane fuel, and the fuel can do one of two things; it can feed the motor or it can go off, *bang*. Along with the fuel you're also carrying three or four gallons of oil. What happens to the oil is that it boils. When it boils a bit too hard, it squirts out into your lap. That's when not being able to move your legs is a bit of a nuisance. In spite of all this, the motor gets so hot anyway that it blisters your feet through the pedals, and when it gets too hot it seizes up or breaks down or bits start falling off it. This happens, naturally, to all the other cars as well. So you may encounter, for example, the rear part of a Matra-Ford exhaust tube that, bouncing off the road at something over a hundred miles an hour and spinning substantially faster, smashes your radiator, shatters your windscreen and finally impacts against your helmet; this was exactly what Tracy *had* encountered. Once. If his car had been six inches farther forward, he'd have had no face left; a yard farther back, and it would have missed him completely. Well, and so once had been enough. To make him what he was; a war relic . . .

Now he worked with rather different cars. Cars that had the speed and elegance and something of the excitement of those other hissing, spitting fuel-containers, but that provided comfort and civilised styling as well, cars that could cruise down the length of an Italian motorway or from Madrid to the French frontier in the space of a summer afternoon, smoothly, effortlessly, almost silently, with airflow conditioned to an ideal constant and with soft music playing through the stereo speakers, the Ferraris, the Corniches, the Maseratis, the Lambos . . . Nice cars, really. If you were lucky, you could get one for a birthday present. Just as if you were unlucky, you could get some part of a racing car all mixed up with your brains. You had to believe in luck. What else was there?

Money.

Well, yes. Running costs, insurance fees, depreciation—that side of things didn't bear thinking about. Not these days. Mr. Greene was of course a whole lot richer than Tracy had ever been. Mr. Greene was reputedly a millionaire. Well, you could buy the key all right, but not everyone could turn it. Tracy had never quite managed it. Maybe Mr. Greene couldn't, either. Escape is a state of mind, but then so is the other . . .

Freedom come, freedom go (Tracy sang to himself, left foot tapping against the footrest, right foot pressing lightly, caressingly, the pedal), *tells me yes and then she TELLS me no* (his flat blue eyes registering in terms of tenths of a second the fast-diminishing distance of a determinedly driven two-tone Morris Oxford, its check-capped inmate crouched at the wheel), *freedom moving along,* (wwwwwwhhhuppp, and the double carriageway veering left, wide open now in front of him) . . . *singing a song* . . . easing up a little now as Lambo approached the first of the Horsham roundabouts; he had taken the A24 from Worthing instead of driving straight up the A23, and the decision seemed to have been a good one. The traffic would be building up, naturally, from Dorking onwards, but he was having a reasonably fast run out of Sussex and he could detect no fault whatsoever in the smooth unlaboured murmur of the engine. He was getting a shade of understeer, perhaps, but nothing that an extra couple of pounds' pressure in the front tyres wouldn't correct. And it was a fine summer morning, the heat mounting under a few patches of towering white cumulus cloud over to the west, the sky elsewhere blue, the thick-leaved trees of a one-time forest casting deep shadows outside which on grass and road the sunlight glittered. Most of the main-road traffic was headed the other way, towards the coast, and it was dry enough for that flow of wheeled movement to have thrown up a thin haze of dust. He himself would be through Dorking by one o'clock, would have lunch at the White Horse near Box Hill, would drive on through Leatherhead and Epsom and would get to the West End of London some time around three. That, at least, was the programme. The address that Mr. Greene had given him was in a street he'd never heard of, but he had the London A–Z in the glove compartment, together with other necessary documents, and he'd check up on it after lunch, for which he rather fancied home-made pork pie with a green salad. There'd be no problem.

Or he wasn't expecting any.

In fact, though, things weren't quite so easy. The British have had a long history, as histories go, and live as a result in a state of semi-permanent linguistic confusion; Albemarle Street, wherein young Bernadette professedly had taken up her residence, turned out in the event to be a square, which Tracy duly drove past three times before realising it was the place he was looking for. In the middle of the square there was a rectangular strip of yellowing London grass, crisscrossed by asphalt pathways and enclosed by iron railings, while around its edges were ranked three-storey Georgian houses of varying degrees of dilapidation. Along the narrow pavements cars were parked bumper to bumper, leaving, however, an occasional gap, into one of which Tracy was able cautiously to reverse the Lambo. He had lost some twenty minutes in discovering Albemarle Street, but the time was still only eight minutes to three, so he was still well up to his self-appointed schedule. He could even have claimed to have got there early, if he'd been expected there at any particular time that afternoon. As far as he knew, he wasn't.

It was certainly a very quiet square. There were benches on the central grass strip where a few elderly people were sitting, possibly even sleeping; they obviously didn't contribute much to the general animation. There was a black dog of indeterminate race sprawled out on the pavement who, apart from an occasional twitch of the hind leg, didn't contribute much either. There was a man leaning heavily against the railings with the air of one who has established certain proprietorial rights; he, alone of the square's inhabitants, displayed an interest in Tracy's arrival, though this might have been because Tracy had parked the car no more than a couple of paces from his right foot. He went so far as to incline his head slightly, either the better to observe Lambo's distinguished profile or—just possibly—in salutation. Tracy thought it best to return this nod, though distantly, as was proper.

"Nice job," the man said.

Tracy moved his chin sideways in courteous disclaimer and walked across the road to where, beyond the far pavement, a half-dozen stone steps rose towards the front door of young Bernadette's apartment block. Her flat—he learned by perusing the resident board, just inside the door—was on the third floor front. There was no lift. Naturally not. He sighed and continued walking up the stairs, feeling now slightly disconcerted. A nice quiet square and a nice old house, not unlike the one where he lived at Brighton and really pretty much to his taste; but not, he'd have thought, to the taste of Mr. Greene's only daughter. He'd expected something a whole lot livelier than these surroundings.

The flat had a bell-push, so he pushed it. A buzzer hummed softly somewhere inside. He could hear it clearly because the door wasn't properly closed, but stood an inch or so ajar. No one answered, though. He pressed the bell again, to identical result.

Nobody home.

He strolled across to the window at the end of the landing and looked down on the square. It seemed he'd just have to wait. She was supposed to have been notified, no doubt by some anonymous henchman, of his arrival in town that afternoon; but then the only daughters of near-millionaires aren't as a rule punctilious about keeping appointments with visiting tradesmen, and she might well have remembered something more important she had to do, like looking in at her hairdresser's. It was even possible that she *was* at home, but was currently engaged in some form of activity which precluded her from answering the doorbell immediately, or indeed at all. The routine would be to wait a couple of minutes, then try again. Then, in all probability, to settle down for a very much longer wait.

Not here, of course. He'd join the jetsam set down there in the square. Its air of somnolence seemed to have deepened, if anything, since his arrival; he had a brief and somewhat fantastic vision of himself afloat in a kind of metropolitan Sargasso Sea, a sedate green-and-grey rectangle into which passers-by helplessly drifted and became, on those hard wooden benches, totally becalmed for the rest of the day. The dog, certainly, seemed to have escaped. But the dark-haired man was still there, leaning against the railings with his hands in his pockets and gazing moodily at the Lambo; he'd moved all of three yards in the last five minutes, carried, maybe, by some obscure crosscurrent that hadn't affected the seawood-encrusted veterans marooned in the park. They were all elderly, though. This fellow was young. Tracy felt a spasm of unreasonable irritation with him; he ought, at his age, to be usefully employed, hitting nails with a hammer or sticking bombs into suitcases or engaged in some similarly rewarding creative endeavour. Not just waiting around, doing nothing. Tracy, shaking his head disapprovingly, went back to Bernadette's flat. He rang the bell once again and, giving vent to his feeling, knocked on the door very sharply. Under the impact of his knuckles, it swung open a farther three or four inches.

". . . Mrs. Pope?"

Still no answer. But now he could hear, very faintly, a radio playing, or possibly a television set. One of those tediously recognisable tunes that one can nevertheless never put a name to, involving some fancy work by the fiddle section. The Merry Wives of . . . ? No. It wasn't that. And the hallway light was burning. No doubt it was the sort of hallway that would need a light burning even at three o'clock on a fine July afternoon, but . . . No. Not Gilbert and Sullivan, either. Pompety-*pom*-pom . . . Tracy pushed the door farther open and went in.

The hallway was very small indeed, with space for three dark-painted doors and a built-in cupboard and with, as he'd supposed, no window space at all. All three doors were closed, but the nearest opened easily enough when he turned the handle. It led into the sitting room, again as he'd supposed. The radio inside was playing quite loudly, except that it wasn't a radio but a record player with a separate speaker. A man in shirtsleeves lay on the floor directly beneath it, staring at a protruding length of cable.

"Sorry," Tracy said, for no very clear reason. He hadn't done anything lately he felt sorry about. The man on the floor quite rightly took no notice. "Is Mrs. Pope in?"

The man didn't say anything, didn't turn his head, didn't move at all. His grey pinstripe jacket lay crumpled on the floor beside him; there was something curiously crumpled about his own appearance, if it came to that. Tracy moved forwards, now with some caution. "Good God," Tracy said. The man made no reply to that, either.

A young man—somewhere around Tracy's own age—but a man who wasn't going to get any older. He had fair hair and staring blue eyes, and the skin of his face was oddly mottled. There was a screwdriver and a pair of pliers lying just clear of his half-clenched right hand. The loose length of cable ran between them, and at the end of it was a glint of naked copper wire. Tracy followed the cable back to its wall plug and disconnected it with a jerk. The record on the turntable continued to play.

All very odd. And rather nasty. It wasn't Tommy Pope, of course; Tracy knew Pope well enough, at least by sight. And it probably wasn't a professional repair man, either. Not many people die of electrocution these days, and very, very few of those who do are professionals. Besides, the dead man didn't seem to have a toolbag, or indeed any tools other than those on the floor. It wasn't easy to make out quite what had happened. The cable didn't run to the record player or to the speaker or to anything else; it was a loose live cable, that was all you could say about it. But since the record player was still working, the accident had to have happened very recently. In fact in the last ten minutes, because the record was only . . . Ah. Oh. The control switch was on automatic. So it could have been playing the same record over and over again. Tracy pushed the lever into the *Off* position; the arm withdrew, the music stopped, the turntable gradually slowed and halted. *Orchestral Selections*, the record label said, *from Gilbert and Sullivan*. Tracy sighed. It wasn't his day. That was obvious.

Pom pom pompity *pom* pom. *The Mikado,* of course. What else?

He oughtn't, maybe, to touch anything. He stooped and with one hesitant finger tested the dead man's cheek. It felt stiff and cold. Dead some time, then. That was rather a relief. He had had an unpleasant image at the back of his mind of this chap's being startled by the sound of the doorbell, jerking round his head, letting the cable slide through his fingers . . .

He straightened up, expelling rather more breath rather more sharply than he'd intended. He thought he'd do best to ring the police direct; there'd be no point at all in calling for a doctor or an ambulance. And then . . . But then, of course, the police . . .

He rubbed his chin, looking vaguely round the room without really seeing anything. Then he remembered what he was looking for and tried again. The telephone, he then saw, was over on a small table by the window. He walked over and looked at it and read the number on the dial. He didn't feel very well. He'd seen worse ones than this, naturally; once he'd helped to pull the corpse of a Belgian driver out of a blazing Porsche . . . The Belgian driver had been blazing, too, and he'd carried a big splinter of the steering column through his ribcage rather as a butterfly under glass carries a pin. That had been the high point of nastiness in Tracy's career, but thinking about it didn't make him feel any better. And then there'd been others almost as bad; some bad because they'd been friends of his, some just bad any way you looked at it. On the track, though, you expected that kind of thing. Here in a flat off a quiet London square it was altogether different; it took you by surprise. It confused you. He wasn't sure what to do. At least, he knew perfectly well what to do; but he had an obscure feeling that he oughtn't to do it without thinking first. And he was finding thinking difficult.

The point was, this wasn't Tommy Pope. That was for sure. And it wasn't an electrician; that seemed reasonably certain. But whoever he was, he was dead in Bernadette Pope's apartment. And that wasn't good. At least, the newspaper boys might like it; but Mr. Greene most certainly wouldn't. Bernadette could easily have been here when it happened. Perhaps she'd gone for help, to find a doctor or something. But no, that didn't make sense. Not with a telephone to hand. Perhaps she'd . . .

Struck by another nasty thought (if thought you could call it), Tracy went back to the hallway and tried the other two doors. One gave onto a double bedroom with bathroom, the other onto a kitchenette; all these rooms were empty, at least in the sense that there wasn't anybody else to be seen in them, alive or dead. Tracy hadn't really supposed that there would be, but he'd probably been wise to check. Standing once again by the telephone, he leafed through his pocket diary and found Mr. Greene's office number. He dialled it. He talked to a switchboard operator and then to a secretary and then to Mr. Greene's private secretary and then, after a short pause, to Mr. Greene himself.

Mr. Greene sounded even testier than usual.

"Told you to report back to me, yes, but didn't mean every five bloody minutes. You're in London, I take it?"

"Yes. I'm at the flat. But there's somebody here."

"What d'you mean, somebody here?"

"Other than Bernadette, I mean. I don't know where *she* is. This is a fair-haired bloke. About thirty. Not very tall, about . . . five foot eight or nine. At a guess. It's not Tommy Pope. I know Tommy Pope. This isn't him."

"Can't make out," Mr. Greene said rather slowly, "what the hell you think you're raving about."

"Well, this chap's dead," said Tracy, coming in desperation to the nub of the matter.

"Dead? But where? Where are you speaking from?"

"From the flat. In the flat. Right here on the floor. Him, I mean. Not me. I'm talking on the telephone."

"In Bernadette's flat? Where's Bernadette, then?"

Tracy closed his eyes. He had the impression that he'd already covered that one. "I don't know. Except she's not here. The door was open, you see, when I got here, and the radio was playing but it turned out to be a record player, and then when I looked inside there was this chap—"

"Look," Mr. Greene said. "All this has got nothing to do with me, has it? You've found a dead man in the place, isn't that the gist of it? Well then, ring a doctor. Or the police. Or the undertaker. Or Alcoholics Anonymous or whatever. But why tell *me?* I've got clients waiting to see me, I can't be forever answering the phone—"

"I was only thinking," Tracy said, "that it wouldn't look good in the papers. That was all."

"Papers? *What* papers?"

"I mean, it's Friday evening. It'd be just right for the Sundays."

"I see," Mr. Greene said. "I see." There was a short silence, broken only by rather repulsive sucking noises at the other end of the wire. ". . . Yes, that's good thinking, Tracy. You may have a point there. You've thought this thing through. This chap, I suppose he isn't *naked* or anything?"

"Oh no. He's in his shirtsleeves. But no, not naked, sir."

"Thank heaven for that. What does it look as though he died of, then? Heart attack, something like that?"

"He was trying to do some kind of electrical repair job. It looks as though he electrocuted himself."

"And there's something fishy?"

"Well . . . A bit odd, maybe."

"You're sure," Mr. Greene said, "you're in the right flat?"

"Quite sure."

"All right. You'd better wait there."

"What?"

"Wait there," Mr. Greene said. "Just make yourself at home. I'll have all this looked into. Right away."

The phone clicked dryly in Tracy's ear.

Make yourself at home. All very well. It wasn't so easy. A corpse on the carpet isn't conducive to a cosy atmosphere. But you can't always choose the company you keep; so better face up to it . . . Tracy put the receiver, which he'd been holding at his side for the last thirty seconds, back on its cradle and moved across for a longer, steadier look. The man's face seemed intangibly different from this angle; he was older, perhaps, than Tracy had first thought. The dark mottling on the face obscured the lighter shadows where skin wrinkles ran, but the wrinkles were there when you looked closely, at the corners of eyes and mouth and under the chin. The cheeks, too, were fleshy, just beginning to sag. Tracy stooped abruptly and picked up the dead man's discarded jacket.

There was a good-quality pigskin wallet in the inside pocket. The initials *R.K.* had been stamped on it in gold. Inside the wallet: three five-pound and six one-pound notes; a driving license; a woman's photograph, so rubbed and creased that the outlines of her face were barely discernible; a Clubman's Club membership card; the guarantee ticket for a Longines wristwatch; a thin silver ball pen, affixed to the wallet through a loop in the leather; that was all. It certainly wasn't the wallet of an inveterate hoarder. It was the wallet (according to the driving license) of Robert R. Keyes, Paddick Lane, Islington. Tracy replaced the wallet and tossed the jacket onto the nearest chair. As he did so, the telephone rang.

". . . Tracy?"

It was Mr. Greene again. "Speaking."

"Ah. Good. We've got the matter in hand. Someone'll be along very shortly."

"Yes," Tracy said. "But—"

"You haven't rung anyone else, have you?"

"No, I've been waiting here. Like you said."

"Good. Go on doing that. You had the right idea. Don't ring the police now, not on any account."

"This man," Tracy said. "His name's Keyes."

"Keyes, eh? Splendid. Splendid."

Mr. Greene rang off, without having explained what he thought was splendid and leaving Tracy with his mouth open. Tracy sighed and went to sit down on the chair where he'd just thrown Keyes's jacket and wondered what he ought to do next.

The sitting room was a reasonably comfortable place in which to wait, but there wasn't much else that you could say for it. Most of the furniture was old and obviously rented along with the flat and the room had therefore an oddly impersonal air, rather like that of a family hotel. The bedroom, too, now that he thought about it; you might have expected the bedroom to be a bit more feminine. But no, it hadn't struck him that way. The bed, indeed, had had that intangible look of not having been lately slept in at all, a sort of reproachful expression; there'd been no perfume, no scent, nothing like that. No perfume in here, either. No flowers. No television set, even. Fairly comfortable, yes; but homey it wasn't.

So what exactly had Robert R. Keyes been trying to repair?

Not the gas fire, obviously. Not the TV; there wasn't one. Not the record player or the speaker; they'd been working all right. There was just the plugged-in cable with the naked end, the pliers, the screwdriver. And, of course, the corpse. Blackened face, burn marks on right hand and forearm, other small contusions on his neck, just beneath the ears; where, if you looked closely, the fair hair was very slightly charred. There had to be an explanation. But the only one that Tracy could think of he didn't like at all.

123830   WRIGHT, Albert a/k/a "Bony"

Identifying data: 29 year old u/m male, parents believed deceased.

Past medical history: No previous illnesses of note.

Personal history: Illegitimate child brought up by mother in working-class district of London (East End). School records n/a; we have, however, reports of temper tantrums and of occasional aggressive behaviour towards other children and his teachers. A previous prognosis associates these outbursts with the witnessing of violent quarrels between his mother and various male "relatives," also with the infliction of physical punishment (by his mother) for minor misdemeanours, such as rising too late.

In spite of above-average intelligence and exceptional skills of orientation, he left school (at age of 14) with no qualifications and was thereafter briefly employed as an assistant mechanic in a number of local garages. He has considerable mechanical aptitude, but was invariably dismissed for unpunctuality at work and/or insubordination. He tried, though without success, to become a professional racing driver; these attempts seem to have been his induction to a life of crime, in that he was subsequently "engaged" to drive the getaway car in a series of armed robberies, February–November 1965. His mother died, of bronchial pneumonia, that same year.

Though he undertakes desultory sexual relationships, he has a marked dislike for women in general, as for games and sports of all kinds (except motor racing, which he does not regard as such). He has no hobbies and no known friends, other than professional associates.

Psychiatric examination

Patient usually sits quietly, smiling slightly as if amused at private thoughts, with hands held stiffly in his lap, fingers flexed and thumbs extended. This pose is characteristic. Lips are occasionally protruded (schnauzkrampf grimace) or slightly pursed. Speech is clear and often considered, though with frequent verbigeration and lack of circumstantiality. He is correctly oriented, however, recalling seven digits forwards and in reverse with ease.

Psychological examination

No organic factors have been revealed and intelligence is classified as Bright Normal. Reaction times, however, are exceptionally fast. He seems rarely to experience doubt or indecisiveness. Responses to the similarities subtest indicate a tendency to infantilism in his thinking.

Physical examination

EEG reveals unusually high incidence of cerebral dysrhythmia. Reflex and sensory changes are normal and there are no visual field defects or signs of optic atrophy. All physical and laboratory studies were within normal limits.

Referential diagnosis

Schizophrenic, with marked paranoid symptoms, fitting none of the classic categories.

Statistical diagnosis

Major reaction type, chronic undifferentiated.

Prognosis

Unfavourable. Further consultations are recommended.

CHAPTER 4

That was what the psychiatrist's report had said; no one had taken much notice of it, because no one takes much notice of psychiatrist's reports in H.M. Prisons, and no further consultations had in fact been arranged. Even if they had, the psychiatrist might not have discovered that his jargon could be simply related to a complete, though elementary, philosophy, because in psychiatry, as in everything else, a great deal depends on your point of view. The psychiatrist thought that he himself was sane and that Bony was an affective schizoid sociopath. Bony thought that he himself was perfectly normal and that the psychiatrist was a bearded weirdie who couldn't have told him breakfast time from Thursday. We needn't argue as to which of the two was right; it was certainly the psychiatrist, not Bony, who wrote the report, but that proves nothing either way. As we've said, no one took any notice of it. And no one cared very much what Bony thought, either.

About Bony Wright's philosophy. It had at least the considerable merit that—like that of Descartes or of Harold Macmillan—it could be conveniently summarised in a single easily memorable phrase. The phrase was not, of course, of his own invention, but was one that since his childhood he had made peculiarly his own. He had been caught, a few weeks before his ninth birthday, pinching fruit from a neighbouring greengrocer's shop and had been punished, on the spot, by the irate shopowner: *"Well,"* small Bony had unctuously thought, strolling a few days later past the grocer's stone-shattered plate-glass window, *"he arst for it,"* and had derived a thrill of virtuous pleasure from the reflection. It was an admirable phrase indeed, accounting, like any true philosophic talisman, for both cause and effect. In the years that followed, many other people were to ask for it and, in most cases, later to get it; Bony's philosophy, in other words, was to prove itself pragmatically justified. And if it might be held, by the modern positivist, to reveal a taint of unfashionable subjectivism, the same could be said of the Cartesian *cogito* or the Macmillanian *numquam tam bonum;* it was not, in any case, an accusation to which one whose chosen hero was Napoleon could well give particular importance.

It may be that Bony's mother, an exceptionally bad-tempered and slovenly tart, had something—as the psychiatrist had thought —to do with it. But when, shortly after Bony had left school, she found herself—as a consequence of a vigorous and unexpected push —lying at the bottom of a wooden staircase with a bruised arm and two broken ribs, Bony had no difficulty in relating this experience to its philosophical context; she, perhaps more than anyone, had arst for it. Most children learn to objectify the world as they grow older, but Bony increasingly had learnt to subjectify; by the time he was twenty, people and objects alike were real to him only insofar as they impinged on his own existence and, to a greater or lesser degree, threatened it. Everything not inimical and therefore not real was, simply, Bony.

> I, this incessant snow,
>   This northern sky;
> Soldiers, this solitude
>   Through which we go
>   Is I . . .

It wasn't so much that he had no moral scruples. He had. And he was, as the psychiatrist had insisted, perfectly well orientated. He knew—for example—that he had killed a man some hours ago; specifically, one Robert Keyes. And he knew that it was wrong to kill other people. But then this was, or had been, Robert Keyes, and that made all the difference. Keyes had been a real object, something that had offered opposition; *ergo,* not part of Bony Wright. In other words, Keyes had arst for it. And that was all that needed to be said.

Towards the other occupants of this London square on this sunny summer's afternoon Bony felt no animosity whatever; he felt genially disposed, indeed, towards all and sundry—even towards the snooty Lord-Pomfret-of-Puke bugger with adenoids like Julie Andrews's who'd parked his posh new Batmobile on Bony's big toe, or near as sod it. A man with Bony's philosophy, after all, doesn't feel envy or jealousy as more objectively minded people do—least of all for mere material possessions. Having a Cambridge degree, a luxury yacht, or a Lamborghini—that sort of thing didn't arouse Bony's resentment in the slightest. He wouldn't have minded—or not so much—if his share in the loot from the Bond Street grab had come to less than he'd expected; doing him out of twopence that was legitimately his was another matter. That was asking for it. You could say that his *amour propre* was involved, except that for an *amour* to be really *propre* there must presumably be some other kind of *amour* with which one's *amour propre* can be contrasted; in Bony's case, as we have seen, this wasn't so. His was an ego pure and undiluted—ego as Absolute—and he was therefore happy now in a broad and general and widely tolerant way, as one may be happy who recognises that God's will and one's own have been comfortably reconciled in every particular and to whom no other state of affairs is properly conceivable.

Of course he had been waiting in this sunny London square for over six hours now, but this didn't worry him in the slightest. There was nothing else he specially wanted to do. He could survey here, as well as anywhere, this remarkable world which the abrupt departure of Robert R. Keyes had unquestionably rendered a better, much happier, and far more beautiful place. Sooner or later, Tommy's missus would show. Sooner or later Tommy's missus was going to find Robert R. Keyes stretched out peacefully on her drawing-room carpet. Then, in Bony's view (and Bony, though no psychiatrist, was not without a smattering of practical psychology), then would be a very good time for a very patient man to drop in and ask a few questions; nothing lowers the resistance to interrogation like finding a corpse on the carpet. Bony didn't know Tommy's missus and therefore didn't dislike her—not personally, anyway. He'd make that clear, gentleman-like, at the outset. Only the refusal to answer his questions—he'd explain—would be construed as *asking for it*. That, as she'd be able to see for herself, was what Robert R. Keyes had been so misguided as to attempt. As for the rest of the things she might be frightened of—rape, robbery, arson, pillage—nothing could be further from his mind. He wanted the griff, that was all. Inside information. Honestly and sincerely Bony hoped that Tommy's missus wouldn't be difficult. It'd be a shame if she was.

All he wanted to know was where Tommy was hiding. That wasn't much to ask for, now was it? Keyes would have coughed all right, but Keyes hadn't known; of that, Bony had before the end become convinced. There was always the chance, it had to be admitted, that Tommy's missus wouldn't know, either; and if she didn't, that'd be a shame, too. Because Bony, naturally, would need to be convinced. There'd be no need, strictly speaking, for him to kill her, just in making sure; but Bony was aware, in that respect, of something in himself that in a lesser man might have been considered a weakness. He just had to be thorough. Like old Napoleon. That geezer at the jeweller's shop . . . What had been his comic name? . . . Redpole, something like that. He'd never really meant to kill Redpole. He'd just had to be thorough, that was all; to make a certainty doubly sure. It made sense, when you thought about it, and you certainly couldn't feel sorry for the stupid sod. It wasn't as though you'd made any kind of a *mistake*. Because Redpole, when all was said and done, had arst for it.

Tracy, confirmed objectivist, lacked as a matter of course Bony Wright's extraordinary gift of patience. Not that he couldn't display it, when his was the active role—his the hand on the spanner, the foot on the pedal, the ear to the labouring clamour of the faulty engine. But the passive role, that was different; that was something that he'd never enjoyed. And sitting in a room alongside a deader, waiting for someone to *do* something . . . How passive can you get?

He had even, through some effort of the will, stopped thinking about his present situation. The trouble wasn't, as at first he'd thought, that it was totally new to him—though this was true. The trouble was just the opposite. It was really a cliché situation, wearisomely familiar, encountered (even though he wasn't an avid reader) in he didn't know how many books of exciting intrigue, culminating the week's episode in he couldn't imagine how many spine-chilling television thrillers. So that once the initial shock had worn off, he'd found it difficult to respond to the situation other than in cliché terms; that had to be the only explanation for the absurd compulsion he'd felt to search for "clues," to establish the dead man's identity, to pursue the observed facts to a completely preposterous conclusion. It was all too schoolboyish for words. I mean, what *am* I? he thought . . . *Imaginative* or something?

Sound thinking, Mr. Greene had said. Well, praise was always welcome. But the truth of the matter was that he'd thought too much, instead of doing the obvious thing. He hadn't really expected Mr. Greene to react as he had. He'd only intended . . . Intended what . . . ? Well, to give the old boy warning, he supposed, an hour or two in which to use his undoubted influence with the fuzz and the newspaper magnates and all that mob, time in which to squash the story. But *what* story . . . ? Tracy clicked his tongue. Only a fervid imagination dictated that there should be a story at all. WEST END PLAYBOY MAKES CONNECTION IN HEIRESS' LOVE NEST, DIES OF SHOCK was one thing, certainly; FATAL MISTAKE BY AMATEUR ELECTRICIAN was quite another. Keyes didn't look very much like an electrician, amateur or otherwise, but then he sure as hell didn't look like a West End playboy, either. He looked, if anything, like the one-time undermanager of a small suburban supermarket.

Or, no. He didn't. No.

He looked dead.

Tracy decided he'd better look at something else. He picked up the newspaper that lay folded on the table to his right and shook it out; HEIRESS' LOVE NEST, indeed. That was reading a whole lot too much into a double bed that hadn't even by the look of it been slept in. And besides, she was married, wasn't she . . . ? Well, then. A double bed's what you'd expect. Still, some of these rags would say anything. Look at this, for instance. POLICE CLASH WITH PICKET LINE, SEVEN INJURED. We know what *that* means. Four leg abrasions, one barked elbow, some twit with a nosebleed and his wife who's fainted at the sight of him. It all helps, though, to keep the cops busy and to prevent them from molesting motorists. BOND STREET KILLER BREAKS CORDON, yes, well, they *must* have been on the run. He turned to the back page, scanned the First Division football results; Leeds United 7, West Ham 0 . . . They seemed familiar. And anyway, damn it, today was Friday. He turned irritably to the front page again and looked at the dateline. The bloody thing was nearly a fortnight old, just as he'd suspected. So what was that? Another clue? Did that mean Bernadette hadn't been here for almost a *fortnight?* Or did it just mean that this was one paper she hadn't bothered or had forgotten to throw away?

There he went *again*. Clues. He had to be bonkers.

He refolded the paper, threw it back onto the table. The upper half of a blown-up photograph of someone's face stared up at him accusingly. He stared back at it. The face seemed familiar, just as the football results had been; but in a different way. Someone he'd seen on television? . . . Nose, eyes, high sloping forehead, yes, someone he'd . . . Above the face, the words BOND STREET BREAKS, the full headline masked by the fold in the paper as the face itself was masked; something about an escaped criminal . . . Tracy picked up the paper, opened it again. It was odd. The man hadn't got a moustache. Why no moustache?

More to the point, why had he *expected* a moustache?

It was puzzling. And at the back of Tracy's mind, something to do with a coffee ring . . . No, it wasn't that . . .

Tracy got up from the armchair and went quickly over to the window. All was very much as it had been before, except for the laundry van now double-parked directly outside the block. But the young man with the big moustache wasn't leaning on the railings any longer; he had gone. Something had been added to the scene, something extracted; that was life. Ebb and flow, ebb and flow. The young man's departure was perhaps to have been expected; even among the stolid fraternity of inveterate railing-leaners, few are static-minded enough to remain in the same place for over ninety minutes when no positive entertainment is being offered, such as the excavation of a hole in the ground. Anyway, the bloke wasn't there. Tracy surveyed the square absently, the pathways, the benches, the ragged-leaved trees . . .

Someone rang the doorbell.

He went to answer it.

What, meanwhile, of Mr. Greene?—to whom, after all, as yet we've been offered no formal introduction? Very well, then. Meet Mr. Greene. He is, as we've probably gathered, a rich man—richer in fact than many people, including his own accountants, suppose. He owns a number of South Coast garages and a chain of filling stations and a small but highly competitive car-hire service, together with a travel agency and most of a motel near Barcelona. He has also interests in property and in insurance broking. He is on the directorial board of eleven London-based companies and of a Costa Brava estate agency, and he is the principal shareholder of three of these companies—Lewis's, who run a chain of jewellers' stores; Carr's, the paper manufacturers; and Hewitt Donaldson's, a factory producing inoffensive plastic toys—rifles, tommy guns, and such —for sale to small children in Northern Ireland. He was at one time a well-known figure in the motor-racing world, recognised at all the major European circuits and to some extent a patron of the sport; Tracy wasn't the only former racing driver working for him now. Racing motorists, even when they've lost their nerve, possess a certain snob appeal that can be capitalised on, and Mr. Greene was very good at that sort of thing. Most people thought him very good at most sorts of thing that had to do with making money; they certainly thought of him as being successful.

In fact, he was successful at some things and not at others. Of his lack of success in the matrimonial field he was only too acutely aware, though privately he considered himself unlucky rather than innately ill-adapted to the marital role. From the first of these three unfortunate alliances, however, had sprung the further problem of Bernadette; here again, it wasn't so much that he thought himself an unsuccessful father as that he considered her an unsuccessful daughter. The annoying fact was that he did need Bernadette very much more than she needed him; he would never have admitted this in so many words, but this was what he meant when he said—as on occasion he did—that he loved his daughter. It wasn't that he used a different form of phrase to mask an unpalatable truth; this, to Mr. Greene, was what "loving someone" meant. He didn't love anything or anybody else. His position precluded it.

He most certainly didn't love his son-in-law.

And it was, in fact, of Tommy Pope that he was at that moment thinking, his elbows resting on the polished leather of his desk blotter, his hands supporting his incipient double chin, his face— though he was alone in the office—betraying, as usual, no emotion at all. He was thinking about Tommy Pope and—like Tracy—waiting. Waiting for the telephone to ring.

That was all.

The man with the moustache came in, stepping lightly, delicately, not moving his eyes for a moment from Tracy's face.

"Mr. Greene sent me round," he said.

It wasn't, of course, the same man. The man who had been leaning on the railings was taller, thinner, indefinably more chipped about the edges. There wasn't really very much resemblance. "Yes," Tracy said. "I was expecting someone."

"Well, there you are. I *am* someone." He moved—still lightly, delicately—across the hallway and pushed open the door of the sitting room; he knew, as was obvious, his way around the place. "Lewis is the name. Leo Lewis. So where's the stiff?"

Whereth the thtiff, he had nearly—but not quite—said; there was a lisp there that had been carefully eradicated. He went on into the sitting room without waiting for an answer; stood for a few moments staring with sad brown eyes at Robert R. Keyes's mortal remains. Here, clearly, was an experienced operator in the Philip Marlowe country; he had precisely the right casual air of untroubled nonchalance and didn't seem to have learnt it, either, from watching late-night television. He was a Jew all right, but not the downtrodden-refugee type; he was post-war Jew, public-school Jew, Nine Days' War miracle-boy, smoothly tanned from his last business flip to Tel Aviv, impeccably tailored, totally unflappable; an impressive figure altogether. Tracy was, despite himself, impressed. "My name's Tracy," he said, endeavouring to recover his own aplomb.

"I know. Mr. Greene told me. I wonder, though"—swinging thoughtfully round on one highly polished heel—"how you managed to get into the place? Did he give you a key?"

"No. The door was open. Or sort of ajar. Nobody answered when I called, but I could hear music coming from inside—"

"So you thought you'd investigate."

"That's right. Well, and there this chap was. Lying on the carpet."

"I didn't suppose he was bowling off-breaks at the kitchen sink. Must have given you a bit of a turn, though?—I shouldn't wonder?"

"A bit of a surprise, yes."

The surprises, it appeared, were to continue. Something bumped loudly against the door and two men in white coats stepped briskly in, carrying between them a very large wicker laundry basket. Lewis stepped back as they approached the corpse with business-like celerity; one of them stooped to the corpse's shoulders, the other to the corpse's heels. They lifted the corpse competently, unhurriedly, and placed it inside the laundry basket. One of them closed the lid, the other strapped it down. Then they picked up the basket and departed whence they had come. "Good God," Tracy said.

"All a part of our Keep-Britain-Tidy campaign. Our posters are everywhere."

"But a *laundry* basket?"

"Oh, I know, I know. It's been done before. But so what, if it's simple and effective? It's a good job, as things've turned out, that you *did* look in, old sport. Otherwise our little Bernadette would have had a nasty scare. Delicately nurtured girl an' all that—not used to having stray bodies cluttering up the flat. We're just saving her distress, that's the way to look at it."

Tracy had the impression that he wasn't thinking overmuch about what he was saying; but if his mind was elsewhere, that was understandable. Nothing else seemed to be, though. ". . . Look, I'm sorry. I'm a little confused. You *know* Bernadette, do you?"

"Indeed I do. And of course you're confused, it's my fault for not having introduced myself properly. Leo Lewis, né Lewisohn. Ring any bells . . . ? No? Ah, well. My father's in the jewellery business. He and Mr. Greene, they're what you might call associates. That's how it is."

"I didn't know Mr. Greene was in the jewellery business."

"He's got his finger in all sorts of pies."

As though to provide unostentatious proof of his *bona fides*, Lewis produced a very flat gold cigarette case, initialled *L.L.* in black enamel, and took a cigarette from it; offering the case, as an afterthought, to Tracy. "Thank you," Tracy said. Balkan Sobranies, naturally. "The thing is, I really came around to deliver a car."

Lewis nodded, as though giving this statement sober consideration. "To Bernadette."

"To Bernadette, yes. You wouldn't know where she is, by any chance?"

"She's in my flat, as a matter of fact. Little place off Castelnau." Lewis replaced the cigarette case and took, this time from his inside jacket pocket, a no less resplendent morocco leather wallet; he flipped it open and extracted, with the dexterity of long practice, a card. *Here you are. Quieter than Chelsea, y'know, and really not too far removed from where, as we used to say, it's at. Just ring that number and ask for Lulu.*

"Lulu?"

"A joke," Lewis explained.

"I see. A joke. Yes. Well, when should I ring?"

"Say, in an hour's time."

"I was thinking," Tracy said a little wistfully, like some one of the minor characters in *Winnie-the-Pooh*, "that if I were to give *you* the car keys and if you were to give them to *her*, she could pick up the car—"

Lewis shook his head. He stopped lighting his cigarette in order to do so. He didn't like the idea. "No, that wouldn't do, old sport, really it wouldn't. You've got to take the lady to Wales, or that's what Mr. Greene tells me. Can't go round changing her plans like that. It's not gallant, not gallant at all."

"He said something about our going to Wales, yes. He didn't say anything about bodies popping up all over the place. Or about their being carried off in laundry baskets. It makes me see things in a different light."

"I can't think why. You hadn't anything to do with this chappie's sudden demise, had you?"

"No, of course not. But what about Bernadette?"

"Oh no. Good heavens, no." Lewis seemed horrified. "You mustn't think that, not for a moment. She doesn't know anything at all about this, er . . . unfortunate business. And it's much better that she shouldn't. That's Mr. Greene's view, perhaps I should add —not just mine. I thought he'd made all that clear to you."

"No, he didn't. I mean, this *is* her flat."

"She hasn't been here for the last ten days, though. Only off and on."

"Then why did Mr. Greene send me here?"

"Because he didn't know that she's been these last ten days in *my* flat. That's why."

Tracy was getting a headache. "It all sounds damned complicated."

"You'll bear in mind, though, that you're not to mention anything about . . . ?" Lewis gestured towards the oddly naked-looking strip of carpet to his right, a flake of ash dropping onto it from his cigarette. "When you *do* get to see her?"

"I suppose it all has something to do with her being allowed to retain her illusions."

"Now *that* had a bit of a barb in it, didn't it? Is there an unsuspected streak of cynicism in your nature . . . ? You surprise me."

"Well, I still think—"

"Ah, believe me." Lewis gave a graceful and unmistakably Levantine shrug, raising his hand with the same movement to take Tracy gently by the elbow. "There's no percentage in it."

"In what?"

"In thinking. Not for poor sods like you and me, that is. We're cogs in the wheel, Tracy, mere cogs in the wheel, as Bertrand Russell so memorably puts it. Walk down with me?"

"All right," Tracy said.

Lewis unhurriedly collected Keyes's jacket from the chair and the pliers and screwdriver from the floor; pulled out the wall plug and rolled up the cable neatly; then took Tracy again by the arm and accompanied him down the stairs, his fingers exerting upon Tracy's elbow-joint a constant friendly, almost protective pressure. "It's a funny old business, of course. But there's no need for you to worry. Forget the whole damn thing, is what *I* should do."

"I'll try," Tracy said.

"That's it. You try. But while the memory, so to speak, is green —you won't have noticed anyone round here? Hanging about?"

"Hanging *about*?"

"Yes. Maybe when you arrived . . . ? Down in the square?"

"There were quite a few people sitting around on those benches. I didn't notice anyone in particular. Why do you ask?"

"I just wondered if you'd noticed anyone," Lewis said; and Tracy nodded, as if satisfied with the answer. He blinked a little also, since they had just emerged from the hallway into the sharp evening light. The laundry van, he saw, stood no longer at the foot of the steps, but a slim, grey-suited executive type with a neatly furled umbrella stood at the door, lost, as it seemed, in meditation. He looked up, however, as Tracy and Lewis came out and in a low, strangely cavernous voice, spoke. "Nothing, Mr. Lewis," he said. And then strolled off along the pavement, swinging his umbrella.

"What did he—"

"Oh, that was Jackson. My assistant. Is that the car?"

"That's it. Over there."

Lewis stopped, surveying Lambo's squat outline with a proprietorial air. "That's a Lamborghini."

"Yes," Tracy said. He knew it was.

"Nice car. My word, yes. Yes, she'll like that."

"I hope so," Tracy said. "I'll ring that number you gave me, then." Looking at his wristwatch. "At six o'clock?"

"You do that small thing."

"What happens if nobody answers?"

Lewis chuckled quietly, as at some private joke.

"Somebody'll answer. You couldn't get *that* unlucky."

"You wouldn't think so, no. But the way things are going," Tracy said, "I wouldn't care to bet on it."

CHAPTER 5

. . . And either way I hope to God (he thought, extended once more comfortably beneath Lambo's padded steering wheel and trickling gently northeastwards through the flow of London traffic) that I've heard the last of *that* little caper . . .

He almost wished (being at heart a conservative, when not an outright reactionary) that he'd followed his original impulse to call in the police. Why hadn't he . . . ? Oh, just *because.* Because the police meant trouble, questions, interviews, papers to be painfully filled in and signed in triplicate. Because over the last few years his innate respect for the law and its long, if somewhat palsied, arm had become corroded through constant contact with pilferers, skinners, fiddlers, con boys, and all those odd byproducts of the car trade whose unwritten codes were vastly different from those the police officially administered. Because some cops were bent and others weren't and you couldn't tell which was which. Because, if he faced the facts, he was a lazy bastard who'd run away from any problem, if given the opportunity. Especially from Robert R. Keyes, whose death was none of his business.

Because of all these *becauses,* he hadn't, as he knew, come out of the affair particularly well. He wasn't at all pleased with himself. He couldn't help but compare his own uncertain ditherings with Lewis's masterful handling of the situation; he'd been driven—metaphorically speaking—off the track. Tracy didn't like that. It rankled. That was why he was now going to call Kevin O'Brien.

If Tracy's relations with the police were these days both tenuous and dubious, his acquaintanceship—as an ex-racing motorist—with the gentlemen of the fourth estate was much more extensive and cordial. It was true that at the time of his final bunt-up Kevin O'Brien, then as now the sports editor of one of the livelier evening newssheets, had offered him a very substantial sum for the publication rights of his racing memoirs and had later withdrawn the offer for no stated reason and virtually without notice, but Tracy knew that the negation of unwritten obligations constituted the lifeblood of the journalistic profession and bore, therefore, no rancour. He felt, however, that O'Brien owed him a favour and that this might be a suitable time for O'Brien to acknowledge the fact. Here, of course, he might have been, in his innocence, oversanguine; but since all that he required, in this case, was an introduction to a knowledgeable colleague whom O'Brien particularly detested (though to few indeed of his intimates would this qualification not have applied), O'Brien—exuding synthetic Irish bonhomie down an unsympathetic telephone line—felt able to oblige. Dinky Fox was the man for the job. Dinky Fox was the lad with the winners. Dinky Fox would know the answers to Tracy's questions before they were out of his mouth (begob). And as to where Dinky Fox was to be found, why, nothing was easier, boyo. Tracy, as a result of this brief friendly interchange, sought the multistorey car park off Warwick Lane and made his way thence to an expresso coffee bar situated in the Street of Adventure (itself, entirely); the great Dinky Fox himself, identifiable as a small sharp-chinned gentleman with a receding hairline and a sports coat of astounding hairiness, was indeed therein, peering lugubriously into an empty coffee cup and a brown-stained saucer half filled with cigarette stubs. If he was, as O'Brien claimed, the nation's outstanding crime reporter, he didn't look it.

He was, however, talkative enough.

"Bony Wright? . . . Oh, we got our stringers out sure enough. But all we've really had to go on are guesses, and it's my belief that Scotland Yard are no better off. *I'd* say somewhere right here in the smoke, but I could be wrong. He can *think*, can Bony. He's one of the few who can think and people don't realise that. They imagine because he's a nutter he can't be intelligent. Well, he is. And if they don't get him in the next few weeks, my bet is they'll never catch the sod at all."

"What did he do?" Tracy asked.

"*Do?* Broke out of Strangeways. Don't you read the papers?"

"I meant, in the first place? What was he sent there for?"

"Oh, he hit Lewis's place in Bond Street. Jewellers an' goldsmiths, branches all over—you probably know the name. Bond Street's the central store, though. Neat job, as far as it went. But he coshed a night watchman a bloody sight too hard and they had him for murder. Came before Mr. Justice Cornwell, old Frosty-Face himself. Hadn't a hope. Took a lifer."

"What did the others get?"

"They didn't pull in the other feller."

"Isn't that a bit odd?"

"Wouldn't say that. It often happens."

"Well, what put them on to *him?*"

"They acted," Fox said, "on information received. Someone grassed on him, in other words. As to who and how, me old darling, I wouldn't like to say. The Yard don't care for it, you know, when you try to push too hard in that direction. Never come between a copper and his pigeon. Don't learn that the hard way—just take it from me."

Splintered wooden boxes and packing cases stood along the wall of a deserted warehouse. One box, freshly boarded and nailed, had been pushed back into a recess a little apart from the others, beside an empty laundry basket. In the warehouse it was warm, dry, and almost silent, except for the soft chutter of a barge moving slowly up the nearby river and the sound of a motor van, nearer still at hand, starting wheezily up and driving away.

"And who was the other bloke? On the job with him?"

"Not knowing, can't say."

"He couldn't have done it by himself?"

"Who, Bony? Lord, no. Not in a hundred years. The safe was blown, for a start—a neat job, like I said. Well, that takes an expert. Bony's a first-rate snatch driver and a nasty little sod to get round if it comes to a carve-up, and he's got some brains, too, like I told you. But blowing safes . . . ? Never. He hasn't the know-how."

"But then," Tracy said, "I suppose these days you've got top-class safe-blowers holding up the walls on every other street corner in town. All this redundancy. It's the highly skilled professionals who suffer the most."

Fox wagged a finger at him, rebuking this flippancy; then extended the other fingers and thumb of his right hand and waved them before Tracy's nose, as though inviting him to have a sniff. "That's how it is, me love. Fingers of one hand—four or five—*that's* how many are operating in London. Maybe as many again out in the provinces, and every man jack of 'em in solid demand. I tell you, if I had a son and heir—which thank the Lord I ain't, sir—I'd have had him booked as a peterman from the day of his birth. Oh, you have to put 'em down for Wandsworth these days the way you used to have to for Eton—years in advance. That's where you get the best training. In stir. These Army-trained boys, they're just bloody amateurs. It's the coming profession, no doubt about it, safe-cracking. That and accountancy, which comes to pretty much the same thing, mind you, under another guise."

"It's the present generation, though, we're talking about."

"Eh?"

"I mean, if there's no more than four or five of them in London—"

"The good ones, that is. The experts."

"But you said *this* job was done by an expert."

"It looked that way, yes."

"So which one was it? If you had to make a guess?"

Outside, the hub of the nation was closing down for the week-end, the shops, offices, stores quickly emptying. Four trim little Aldwych numbers came into the coffee-bar, chattering in high anticipatory voices and displaying between them something like eleven yards of leg; Fox watched them sliding their four tautly gift-wrapped behinds into place on the high stools at the service counter, moaning softly under his breath. Tracy had wondered, earlier, what one of the country's most distinguished journalists would find of interest in a small Fleet Street coffee-bar between five and six on a Friday evening. Now he knew. Soon there'd probably be further arrivals. Just as he was wondering if he'd irremediably lost his host's attention for the rest of the interview, the other said in a hoarse and tremulous rasp:

"Rustic knees."

This was not how Tracy himself would have described them. He turned to check. As he did so, however, Fox cleared his throat and tried again. "Keys, I mean. Rusty keys."

"I'm not with you," Tracy said. This was probably the latest in-jargon around the discos, though the use of it was rather surprising in one who insisted on referring to the fuzz as "the Yard." It was better, though, to admit to ignorance than to be led into further inevitable obfuscation. "Keys? Why keys?"

"That's his *name*," Fox said plaintively. "That's who I'd guess it to be. Rusty Keyes. A good worker, and he hasn't made a hit in a good long while—that I know about."

"Oh, Keyes, *Keyes*. And they call him Rusty?"

"I never heard him called anything else. In fact I doubt if any-one knows his real name, 'cept maybe his mother."

"Robert," Tracy said.

"Robert, is it . . . ? I believe you're right." Fox turned his head with a slow, undulatory motion to stare at Tracy, his eyes going briefly out of focus as a new, and clearly unexpected, train of thought struggled to oust from his brain the prevailing retinal image of agreeably arranged and enticing nineteen-year-old bums. A small vein bulged in his forehead, indicating the intense mental effort this required. "Well, now. Yes, I believe you're right. And does that mean that *you* can tell *me* something?"

"Not really. It's all a bit confusing. About how much jewellery did they get away with? I mean, how much was it worth?"

"Insurance claim, around sixty thousand. Probable true value about fifty. Not jewellery, though. It was gold, mostly."

"*Gold?*"

"For ring setting and such. Jewellers' findings, they call it. It seems they kept most of the company stock there for distribution. It's easy stuff to handle, you know, if you can get hold of it, and a pretty fat profit if you can sell abroad. Especially in the East."

"That'd take some time, though. And Bony hasn't been abroad, has he?"

"No. They reckoned they got him in stir before he could shift it."

"So Keyes might never in fact have got his share."

"They don't usually work for a cut, those boys. Flat payment, that's Rusty's usual line. And he wouldn't normally go in for less than ten. Of course, if by any chance he *didn't* get paid off . . . it's like I told you earlier. Someone grassed on Bony and it could have been Rusty. How did *you* bump into him, if I may make so bold as to inquire?"

"I never met him," Tracy said, with strict adherence to the truth.

"So what's your interest?" All kinds of people, as Fox knew well, are interested in crime and in criminals; indeed, some few years previously he had been granted the *entrée* to that esoteric and ex-clusive section of London society with which normally only the gossip-columnists deal entirely on the strength of his casual ac-quaintanceship with a then-fashionable child-murderer and a gang of teen-age rapists. But the Truman Capote syndromes were now, and unhappily for him, right out of vogue—otherwise he'd be pick-ing it up in Cheyne Walk, now wouldn't he? instead of running the dreary old office girl's beat in his own home patch—and Tracy seemed to him, in any case, much too uninterestingly normal to have that kind of a *refined* taste in criminology. "Not bounty-hunting, are you?—by any chance? I certainly hope not."

"Bounty-hunting?" Tracy, yet again at a loss.

". . . After the reward?"

"I didn't even know there *was* a reward."

"Ah, be your age, old dear. There's always a reward. And I'll tell you this, that none of the pros are interested—not remotely, even. Bony Wright's not a boy to tangle with, oh, dear me, no, he's a right savage little bugger. About as nasty as they come."

"So I've reason to believe," Tracy said. He pushed back his chair. "I have to make a phone call now. But thanks for your time. And the information."

He held out his hand; Fox paused in the act of shaking it. "Reason? What reason?"

Tracy stretched out the fingers of Fox's hand, doubled one of them back. Glancing back from the coffee-bar door, he saw Fox still staring mutely down at the three remaining fingers, puzzled. One shouldn't—Tracy thought—give way to these generous impulses, but Fox had certainly done his best to be helpful and the problem might divert his mind from its present unhealthy channels; though that seemed a pretty forlorn hope, from where he was sitting. It must be terrible, Tracy reflected with the cheerful intolerance of youth, to be fifty years old and still on the feel. In the phone box on the Blackfriars corner, he took Lewis's card from his pocket with a sigh and dialled the number. The phone rang three, four, five times, then someone picked up the receiver at the other end and a woman's voice said:

"Yes, who is it?"

"My name's Tracy."

"Yes, Mr. Tracy?"

"It's about the car. That *is* Mrs. Pope speaking?"

"It is. And you'd better bring it round. You've got the address?"

"In Baronsmead Road, yes. I'll bring it right away."

The telephone clicked in his ear; Bernadette seemed to have her father's habit of closing telephone conversations without any form of verbal dismissal. Tracy looked up, as he left the callbox, towards St. Paul's, its rooftops darkening now against the egg-blue sky. It was a nice, warm, sunny summer's evening.

CHAPTER 6

"So just be friendly," Lewis said. "That's all."

"I don't like being friendly. I'm not the friendly sort."

"Reasonably polite maybe would do."

"Oh, I'll be polite, why shouldn't I be polite? After all those long years of expensive training? It's just such a bloody drag, that's all."

"It's only the one weekend. It'll soon be over."

"In Wales? Look, the weekends last for a *fortnight* in Wales. I've been there. I know."

"A nice car, though." Lewis, still gently persuasive. "A Lamborghini."

"That's the trouble with Dad, though. Why for once in his life can't he give me something without any strings attached? Just out of the goodness of his heart?"

Lewis stifled the reply that rose instantaneously to his lips and said, instead:

"Oh, he's fond of you, Bernie. In his way."

"In his *devious* way."

"Devious? He's not all that devious. You should take a run at *my* old Yiddisher momma, you want to know what devious is. No, he's fond of you all right."

"*She* isn't. She doesn't like me a bit."

". . . Parents." He moved away from the window, giving the edge of the gaily coloured flowered curtain a valedictory tweak. "Yes, they're a pain, but what can you do?"

"There has to be *something*."

"You don't crowd 'em is what. That's the thing with parents. You don't crowd 'em. Right?"

He picked up two of the four packed suitcases that stood in the corner of the room beside the door, carried them through into the hallway. Then turned, put one of them down and raised two fingers into the air. "Peace," Bernadette said. She watched the door close thoughtfully, filing her nails.

Bernadette didn't look anything like her father. She was small, for a start, and red-haired, with huge eyes, wide cheekbones and an unusually tiny chin; these last three features gave her face a peculiar triangularity, both in full view and in profile. From some angles she was pretty and from some she wasn't. When Tracy arrived they went for a long walk, just the two of them, right round the Lambo. She didn't seem very pleased. She seemed, if anything, dismayed.

"I thought it was a *small* car."

"Fifteen six and a half inches. I wouldn't call it a small car, no."

"I'd call it a bloody tank, mate. Where's the engine?"

"Eh?"

"You know—the engine, the motor, the works. What makes the wheels go round."

"Oh. You mean the engine. Yes. There. See . . . ? Under the bonnet."

"What I thought. Someone told me it was at the back."

"Ah," Tracy said. "You're thinking of the 400S. The Miura. A different model. No, this is the Espada. You'll find it a lot more convenient than the Miura. Much more luggage room. And then again—"

"Damn the man," Bernadette said. "Why does he have to get *everything* wrong?"

The allusion, Tracy guessed, was to Mr. Greene and not to himself. All the same, he found it a little dispiriting. "I'll never be able to drive *this*," Bernadette said, giving one of the tyres a moody kick. "And I don't like the colour."

"Drive it?" Tracy cried, summoning up his faded resources of professional optimism. "It'll sit up and beg for you. I mean, the steering lock goes on forever. And the road-holding's quite exceptional. It's a very safe car, *very* safe."

"What'll it do?"

"How fast, you mean? Oh, it moves. It moves."

"Gets me there and takes me back?"

"Well, a bit more than that. If I were to give it a bit of a tweak for you, get the pressures exactly right and so forth, you could probably push it along at say a hundred and seventy. Or thereabouts. Or not far short."

"*That's* more like it. I like driving fast."

"I was af . . . Well, in that case, this is the car for you."

"Let's go up," Bernadette said, "and have a drink."

The flat was cool and quiet and well lit and ostentatiously modern, quite different from the one in Albemarle Street. Yet, somehow, also impersonal. There was a Ladderax cocktail cabinet and Swedish steel trays and rows of bottles with brightly coloured labels and neatly stacked chunky glasses. "Whisky and ginger?" "Yes, fine," Tracy said. He sat down in a squashy green chair which tilted to his weight like a hammock, then proved much more comfortable than he'd expected. "I've seen you before somewhere," Bernadette said, sitting or—more exactly—reclining in a similar chair directly opposite him. "I'm sure of it."

"I run a garage place just off the Steyne," Tracy said. "Mr. Pope used to bring in the Alvis once in a while. Perhaps it was there."

"Oh yes."

It didn't sound as though she now remembered any particular occasion and it certainly didn't sound as though she thought it mattered either way. And it probably didn't. Tracy eyed her surreptitiously over his glass of whisky, wondering what to say next, if anything. He couldn't help feeling that Dinky Fox would have disapproved of Bernadette intensely, swathed as she was from neck to ankles in what looked remarkably like a Persian rug with long fringes and the odd dangling tassel; there was so little to suggest the presence beneath this monstrosity of your actual female body that the small head poking out of the top of it appeared a complete incongruity. It could as easily have been that of a penguin or of a dancing doll. ". . . Does Mr. Pope still run the Alvis?"

"I've no idea," Bernadette said coldly.

Tracy sipped more whisky and tried again.

"I'm sorry I'm a little late with the car. But this isn't the address your father gave me."

"I've sort of moved. He doesn't know."

"Luckily Mr. Lewis came along, or I mightn't have found you."

"Oh, he just went round to pick something up."

"Yes," Tracy said. "I saw him do it."

"I got fed up with that damned place. So I moved out. I tend to do things like that, on the spur of the moment."

"You'll be staying here now, will you? Permanently?"

"I don't see," Bernadette said, even more snootily than before, "that *that's* any business of yours."

"No, no. Of course not. I'm sorry. I was only thinking that you might like me to arrange something about garaging the car. I mean, being in the trade myself, I could probably get you some kind of special rates . . ."

"I don't usually have to concern myself about getting special rates."

"No. I suppose not. No."

She wasn't the easiest girl in the world to talk to, Tracy thought. She seemed ready to take offence at almost anything. And he was getting the least bit flustered. But—

"Well," she said, seeming to have relented slightly. "It was a kindly thought. But we'll be leaving for Wales tomorrow, anyway."

"Oh yes. So we will."

"I thought we could start about seven. Get away before the Saturday rush."

"Jolly good, righty ho," Tracy said, feeling, in the face of this new amiability, more and more like something out of P. G. Wodehouse. "I'll try and find a hotel and I'll let you know—"

"You can stay here."

"Jolly g . . . *Here*?"

"There's a spare room."

"Oh," Tracy said. "That's very kind of you."

"It is, isn't it? And in return you can take me out to dinner. I usually get peckish, around this hour."

This was also rather embarrassing, since Tracy's total immediate financial assets, now reposing in his trousers pocket, amounted to just over eleven pounds. At the sort of restaurants that young Bernadette would frequent as a matter of course, that would barely suffice to see them past the prawn cocktails. "I'd like that very much, Mrs. Pope. The only thing is, your father didn't make any arrangement with me that would cover, er . . . incidental expenses."

Bernadette stared at him. "You one of those *mean* bastards? Or just broke?"

"I'm certainly broke by Mr. Greene's standards."

"And by yours?"

"Well, yes. By those, too."

"Never mind. It happens to us all."

She opened the enormous crocodile handbag that lay in unoccupied territory somewhere on the western boundaries of the hammock-thing she was sitting on and took from the bag a large, unaddressed brown paper envelope. This she handed to Tracy. "For me?" Tracy asked. He tore open the envelope and a thick wad of ten-pound notes, held together with a rubber band, fell heavily into his lap. "God, wealth . . . ! Beyond the dreams of avarice!"

"Things seem to be looking up," Bernadette said.

"At least we can start off tomorrow with a full tank."

"And tonight with a dinner."

"*And* tonight with a dinner," Tracy agreed. There appeared to be fifty ten-pound notes in the wad, making, if his mathematics were not at fault, a sum of five hundred pounds in all. "But who's this from, or shouldn't I ask?"

"My great friend Mr. Lewis," Bernadette said, "gave it to me to give to you."

"Any message?"

"You've got the message."

"Yes," Tracy said. "I think I have, at that."

The dining-place they eventually favoured with their custom was small and, Tracy imagined, select and almost incredibly noisy, with a five-piece West Indian band who sang cacophonously amplified ditties about the futilities of war and of European colonialism while the clientele tucked into the smoked salmon and asparagus shoots and other forms of capitalist-bourgeois nosh, conversing with their partners the while in farmyard like screams and bellows. The walls were painted green and blue in wavy streaks and there was next to no light to see them by. This worried Bernadette not at all; her attention throughout the meal was concentrated exclusively on the four full courses she felt herself competent to deal with. She certainly had, for a small girl, a quite remarkable appetite. Her teeth, Tracy had observed, were small, white, and jagged, like a sheepdog's, a resemblance enhanced by the sharp, snapping motion with which she engulfed objects even as unrecalcitrant as spoonfuls of onion soup. The Persian rug, however, had been earlier abandoned; "I'm going to change," she said, "but you needn't bother"—returning some twenty minutes later transmogrified by a miniskirt and a cashmere blouse into a stupefyingly stimulating bit of crumpet; Tracy wasn't sure that his jaw hadn't fallen open. She hadn't put on any make-up and her skin, after a cold shower, had had a peculiar pale translucency, like honey in the sunlight. "Hey."

"Yes?" Tracy said, putting down his wineglass.

"You're not very conversational, are you?"

"No," Tracy said. "But I have a rich internal life." He patted his pocket, where the folded banknotes rustled reassuringly.

"All you do is *sit* there. Still, I don't mind. People talk too much, in my circle."

"What *is* your circle, Mrs. Pope?"

"I don't know, really. I seem to have known them all a hell of a long time, is the only thing."

Tracy replenished her wineglass and then his own. This brought them to the end of a very nice bottle of plum-colour plonk, Mouton-Chanel '69 or some such tipple, so he was now, at least, fortified against any further disaster. "Maybe I qualify for membership, then. You'd have been about seventeen when I first saw you."

"At your garage? I don't think so."

"No, I didn't have a garage then. It was at Brighton races. You were there with your father."

"I must have impressed you favourably, since you remember it."

"I won a lot of money that day. I backed an outsider."

"What was its name?"

"Beautiful Dreamer."

"So you back winners, do you? I'm impressed."

Again, she didn't sound it. She sounded bored to tears. Tracy knew, of course, that his company as an escort invariably aroused his lady companions to agonised extremes of total indifference, so there was nothing at all unusual about this and he felt no embarrassment or discomfort. There was a sense, he knew, in which it wasn't personal. The trouble was his unfortunate physical appearance. If you discounted the facial scars, which expert surgery had in any case rendered pretty well invisible, he was an extremely good-looking man in the traditional Anglo-Saxon mould, with a regular profile, firm chin and a pleasant quick shy smile of the kind that in the heyday of Gregory Peck could have been seen emerging from the darker corners of every other film set with the regularity of a nervous tic. Sadly for Tracy, however, that golden age was more than ten years past; girls nowadays, he had learnt from experience, didn't care to be seen out with anyone who didn't have bow legs and a face pitted with smallpox scars, or at the very least seamed with wrinkles like a gipsy guitarist's, while the ideal physique of the contemporary dream-lover had to conform not so much to Tarzan's as to that of Tarzan's chimpanzee. There were times when Tracy regretted this change in fashion, times when he didn't, and times like now when he'd taken in a skinful and didn't give much of a damn either way.

". . . But then I suppose you've won a few yourself, if it comes to that."

"Horse races?"

"Cars, I meant."

"Oh yes. A long while back. But I was never very good."

"Why not?"

"I don't know. I suppose I chickened out a bit too often."

"You were afraid of getting killed?"

"Well, in the end, yes. Though everybody is. But yes, perhaps me more than most. Anyway," Tracy said, aware of impending incoherence, "I packed it in."

"Life's not worth all that much, is it?"

"Life's not worth anything at all. It's what we use to tell what all the other things are worth."

"I never thought about it from that point of view," Bernadette said. Frowning, she did so; and came, in the end, to a decision. "It doesn't make sense."

"No, it doesn't. That's why I packed it in."

"I didn't mean motor-racing. I meant what you said before."

"Before what?" Tracy sighed. "You're confusing me."

"I'm sorry."

"That's all right."

"What's your name?"

"My *name* . . . ? Tracy."

"Yes, but your other name. Your friends don't call you Tracy, do they?"

"Yes. Everybody does."

"*Everybody?*"

"Yes. Even my mother used to. Except at school for a while they used to call me Dick."

"Oh, so your name's Dick?"

"No."

"I don't get it."

"There used to be a detective, you see, in a strip cartoon." Tracy sighed again, more windily than before. "But that was even longer ago than the other thing."

"Look, you do *have* a Christian name?"

"Oh, yes. Two."

"But they're unbearably horrible? Is that it?"

"That's it exactly."

"They can't be worse than mine."

"They are. Much worse. Cuthbert Delamere."

"Christ," Bernadette said. "Boy, you have problems."

"Not really. People just call me Tracy. That's all."

"They *are* worse than mine."

"Yep."

"I *hate* Bernadette, all the same. People always making cracks about me and the Virgin Mary."

"Quite quite."

"Then I have to go and marry someone called Pope."

"Ha-ha, yes."

"Innit bloody ridiculous? Just as bad, in a way. Just as bad. Cuthbert what-you-said, that's at least *aristocratic*. You ought to be blue-blooded as all get-out, with that kind of a handle."

"Not really. Just an old West Country family, that's all. But my father was a great one for all the dynastic stuff. He landed me with the old patronymics and then kicked the bucket a year later. A dirty trick, any way you look at it." And why, he thought, the hell was he talking all this cobblers? He had to be drunk. He'd better order coffee. Black coffee. For both of them.

"But your mother calls you Tracy."

"Yes. Well, she called my father that, too. Like in the nineteenth century."

"Hey, that's *cool*," Bernadette said. "I rather believe I'd like your mother."

"She's dead, too."

"Mine's alive. But I haven't seen her in years. Not that I care. She's a bitch."

Tracy beckoned the waiter and ordered the coffee.

"Now that I think of it," he said, "your friend Lewis."

"What about him?"

"He calls me 'old sport.'"

"Oh, he calls everyone that. Even me, sometimes. He's got a fixation, you see, on the Great Gatsby."

"The great what?"

"He copies somebody in a book," Bernadette kindly explained. "Those square things in the libraries?"

"That's right."

Quite unexpectedly, she gave an explosive little giggle, mostly through her nose. "Comedian," she said. But not, as it seemed, in reproof. Tracy smiled back at her, thinking: This is odd. I'm quite enjoying myself . . .

"By the way," he said.

"What?"

". . . Happy Birthday."

". . . Good Lord. So it is. I'd forgotten."

CHAPTER 7

The Lambo nosed quietly in to the side of the road, its dimmed headlights touching for a second the pavement and the low stone wall beyond before flickering out. Bony Wright watched them swing the doors open and, one after the other, descend; first the tall fair-haired geezer, sliding easily from the driver's seat in spite of his length of leg, and then on the other side the red-haired bird, Tommy's missus, moving rather more awkwardly and showing, though regrettably briefly, about as much as you'd hope to see any-

where outside of one of them educational films. The time, by his
wristwatch; 12:25 A.M. He watched them cross the road, side by
side and without speaking, and go together into the block of flats
directly opposite. If he felt any surprise, his face didn't reveal it. He
knew who the first-floor flat belonged to. Mr. Leopold Lewis. He
knew that because he'd followed Leo here from Albemarle Street;
and he knew that Mrs. Pope was living here with Leo because the
Carney Detective Agency had told him so. But now it seemed that
Lewis had hopped it and here, in his place, was this other twit with
the Lamborghini, nice goings on, Bony didn't think. Still, his face
showed no surprise and very possibly he didn't feel any. Bony's was
in no way a speculative intelligence.

When they had disappeared from view, he lit a Gold Leaf cigarette and switched on the car radio. The usual *Night Ride* from
Radio One. He didn't go for pop music or for music of any kind,
but while it was playing he wouldn't drop off to sleep. He would
wait, he had decided, another hour. If the tall bloke came out again,
then maybe there'd still be time to pay a little call and ask some
questions; it would have been much better, of course, to have
caught her in Albemarle Street, but that little plan hadn't worked
out and Bony wasn't one to cry over spilt milk. He kept on trying.

He wasn't very hopeful, though. Before he'd gone across the road,
the tall bloke had opened the boot of the Lambo and had taken out
a suitcase. It looked like he'd be staying. Bony wasn't optimistic,
but he wasn't pessimistic, either. He was going to wait and see.
That was all.

The suitcase, open, was now in fact on the bed in the spare bedroom. Tracy was on the bed, too. He had taken out his wash things
and shaving tackle and had placed them on the night table; now,
sitting with his knees together, he was recounting the money in the
brown paper envelope. When he had finished doing this (there
were still forty-nine ten-pound notes there; the restaurant hadn't
been as expensive as he'd feared), he threw the envelope into the
suitcase, where it fell, with a comfortable flop, on top of the blued-
steel barrel of the pistol. Tracy's pistol.

It still seemed a little ludicrous, that pistol, but not quite as amus-
ingly so as before. You don't, after all, get paid five hundred nicker
for taking a girl—even Bernadette Pope—out to dinner, or even on
a weekend jaunt to Wales. Tracy knew what you get paid five hundred nicker for. You get paid five hundred nicker for keeping your
trap shut. And people who get paid for keeping their mouths shut
don't find pistols very funny, as a rule, because there are other and

better ways of keeping people's mouths shut and pistols constitute
an unpleasant reminder of the fact. Not everyone is tough enough
to resort to the alternative method. But Mr. Greene was. Mr. Greene
was tough enough for anything. Tracy was free from doubts on that
score.

In an odd way, he had earned the money through carrying that
pistol. Because if he hadn't had that pistol in his suitcase, maybe
he'd have called in the police right away. And maybe not. Well,
would he or wouldn't he have . . . ? It was hard to say. He didn't
think that at the time he'd consciously remembered the pistol; but
the memory must have been there at the back of his mind, an in-
hibiting factor. When you're reporting the sudden death of a stranger in another stranger's flat (which you had no real business to have
entered anyway) it doesn't look at all good if the police find an
unlicenced pistol in your suitcase. *And* ammunition. It leads to
trouble. And that was a word which Tracy didn't like. Police trouble,
especially.

He didn't think of himself as being in any way better or worse
than the average big-town repair-shop operator with a high-class
and therefore impatient clientele. All the same, there were the nicks
and the tricks. There were spare parts that he'd found in too much
of a hurry, invoices that hadn't corresponded to the true secondhand sales price, depreciation vouchers that didn't reflect the true
condition of the car—all the minor paraphernalia required by cus-
tomers who wage a constant war of prestige against their business
competitors and of attrition against the Inland Revenue. You supplied the parts and the papers because if you didn't they'd get them
someplace else and you'd lose a client; but not, of course, in any
hope that if anything went wrong the people you helped would
give you any support, let alone protection. The one thing Tracy
therefore wanted of the police was—except for the inevitable routine calls—to be left alone by them. Some few could maybe, in a
real emergency, be bribed, but Tracy didn't know which of them,
and payola would have been a further strain on an already rocky
economic base. To stay in business as Mr. Greene's manager, Tracy
had to keep his nose clean; he had no choice. He knew it. And he
knew it wasn't easy.

He picked up his sponge bag, wrapped a towel around his neck
and went off in search of the bathroom, wandering by accident, in
his abstracted mood, back into the sitting room instead. The corner
light had been left on there; he was crossing the room to switch
it out when he saw that Bernadette was in the room, standing by

the window in a blue nylon housecoat. The curtains were drawn and the window, he saw, was open. But then it was a hot night.

"I thought you'd gone to bed," Tracy said. "Sorry."

She turned her head when he spoke and he realised that until then she hadn't been aware of his presence, either. She had a glass of something in her hand. Probably whisky.

"It's damned hot."

"Yes. What sort of a place is it we're going to?"

"In Wales . . . ? Well, it's a house. I don't know how else you'd describe it."

"It may be cooler there."

"It should be. It's right by the sea."

"Ah," Tracy said. "Good night."

CHAPTER 8

Next morning there was a fresh southwest breeze and the sky was almost clear of clouds. Lambo gambolled, dolphin-like, through the thick and glittering shoals of traffic nuzzling round the columns of the Hammersmith flyover, took an unneeded tow from a BEA bus on the fast lane of the M4 approach road and a little later burst finally and happily out into the deep main channel of the motorway. Bernadette, with a sigh of anticipation, moved up into fifth gear; the speedo needle steadied at seventy-five while that of the rpm indicator continued to do its duty in an unconcerned sort of way, though clearly wondering why, as yet, it bothered. This wasn't even a decent cruising speed; they ordered these things better, its hauteur implied, on the dear old *autostrada*. The deep racing-engine snarl of the exhaust pipes was muted, within the car, to a soft near-musical hum, blending with, rather than competing against, the massed chords emanating from the twin speakers of the stereo radio, currently embarked on a rousing exposition of Beethoven's Sixth; an appropriate enough choice, Tracy decided. They were driving westwards, into the country, and into the gathering heat of the day.

"D'you want the air conditioning on?"

Bernadette shook her head. She didn't seem to be in a conversational mood this morning. Tracy wasn't, either, if it came to that; it had been a hot night, he hadn't slept particularly well and he wasn't feeling on top of his intellectual form. Also, he'd nicked his chin shaving. This didn't stop him feeling relatively cheerful. They were off now, after all, to Wales. Well, London was London and odd things could happen there and often did; but nothing much could happen, surely, in Wales . . . ? An easy and comfortable morning's run was what he was looking forward to, turning off the motorway, say, around Marlborough to give Bernadette a chance to practise on the country roads before crossing the Severn Bridge. Then Cardiff, he supposed, and on towards Swansea . . .

"Will there be many people?"

"Where?"

"At this place we're going. Has it got a *name*, by the way?"

"Of course it's got a name. Y Bannau."

"How was that?"

"Y Bannau. It's Welsh. Means, the beacon."

"Ah. The beacon. I see."

"I'm told Tommy ought to be there. I don't know who else."

"What, Tommy your husband?"

"Yes, Tommy my husband. Why the show of surprise?"

"I thought you were separated."

"Separated . . . ? No. Just separate."

"Sorry. I was going by something your father said. But I probably misunderstood him."

"Don't ever go by anything my father says. Nothing he tells you'll be quite the truth. Anything he gives you'll have strings tied to it." She glanced briefly at the rear-view mirror, reached up a hand to make a minute adjustment. "You may not see them. But they're there."

The scream of jet motors was now audible above the violins as a Trident climbed the sky ahead of them, a cigarette trail of grey smoke drifting down from its sleek dark fuselage. They were coming up to the airport. "You sound rather bitter," Tracy said.

"Do I?"

"You don't get rich, giving something for nothing."

"He's rich, all right," Bernadette said.

"The trouble with being rich, you make enemies."

"I suppose so. I don't quite know what you're getting at."

Tracy wasn't sure, either. "It was just a remark."

"*I'm* not an enemy of his, I promise you."

"No. That's what I meant. You know how to deal with enemies, or you do if you're Mr. Greene. You've got so many. Daughters have to be something else again, especially if you've only got one. Tricky, sort of."

"Look," Bernadette said. "What do *you* know about it?"

"Next to nothing, really."

"You haven't got a daughter, have you?"
"Oh no. Nothing like that."
"Well, then," Bernadette said.

CHAPTER 9

Ignorant, naturally, of being the subject of this verbal interchange, Mr. Greene, at that moment as for some three hours past, had been seated at his desk in his office. In this there was nothing to be accounted unusual, since he was accustomed to spend from nine to fourteen hours each day (except Sundays) in precisely this manner. It might perhaps have been thought a little odd that the room in which he spent so much of his time should bear so few traces of its owner's admittedly forceful personality; Mr. Greene, however, disliked the outward appurtenances of business tycoonery and had gone to some pains to make his office resemble, as far as possible, that of some moderately fubsy provincial solicitor—this even to the extent of installing, behind his desk, a complete set of Law Reports bound in brown leather and kept, through subscription, punctiliously up to date. Mr. Greene himself had never enjoyed the undoubted benefits of a legal training and never opened any of these substantial volumes from one year's end to the other, this for the excellent reason that, had he done so, he would most certainly have failed to make head or tail of the delightfully tortuous complexities detailed therein. They gave him, nevertheless, a comfortable feeling of having all the majesty of British law, if not precisely at his beck and call, at least within easy reach; since few systems have been more carefully designed to protect the criminally inclined, this feeling is more prevalent among members of the general public than is often supposed. For the rest, his office contained very little that was not thirty years old and could not, indeed, be certificated to that effect; this was true even of the three telephones that stood on the desk, one of which was at that moment ringing. The office walls were oak-panelled and on them were hung a number of original hunting prints; the windows moved erratically up and down (and sometimes to and fro) on well-worn runners and were insufficiently screened by heavy grey curtains of some indeterminately chintzy material; the large brass ashtray on the corner table had every appearance of having been filched from the Great Western Railway some time in the early 1930s. If such an office was itself incongruous on the top floor of a twelve-storey block built largely of metal, concrete, plate glass and plastic in the year 1969, Mr. Greene was unconcerned; the idea had, in any case, probably never occurred to him. He was not, in some respects, an imaginative man. Though in others, yes.

The telephone was being obstinate. Mr. Greene glared at it petulantly. Decisions, decisions. All right. He had decided. He picked it up.

Mr. Lewis (his secretary said), the *young* Mr. Lewis was calling from London. Mr. Greene would . . . ? Yes. On the private line . . . ? Naturally.

"Hullo," the *young* Mr. Lewis said. "Have I Mr. Greene?"

This wasn't a form of address of which Mr. Greene approved. An American innovation, no doubt. "Speaking."

"They've left."

"Splendid, excellent," Mr. Greene said, though appearing outwardly unmoved by this intelligence.

"I take it everything's in order at the other end? They'll be arriving midafternoon, or so I should think—allowing them a fairly lengthy stop for lunch, which Bernie's pretty well certain to insist upon. There's nothing in the AA reports to suggest otherwise. No holiday holdups, nothing like that."

"Pope's there all right," Mr. Greene said, "if that's what you mean."

"No, I was wondering more . . . who you'd got in."

"Starshine. And a couple of friends."

"Starshine's usually reliable."

"I'd hardly employ him if he wasn't. Any sign as yet of that other, er . . . gentleman?"

"Well." Lewis seemed hesitant. "You know about—"

"Any *further* sign of him, should perhaps have said."

"Yes. Well, no. Not really. There's word that he's bought himself some transportation. A Mini-Cooper, blue, I believe. And of course he's an expert driver. The trouble is, of course, that with a Lamborghini—"

"The driver has express instructions not to hurry," Mr. Greene said. "And anyhow, Bernadette will be driving some part of the way. Maybe most of it. That's supposed to be the object of the excursion, so far as Tracy's concerned."

"Quite so. It should be plain sailing, then. I mean, he shouldn't miss a brand-new Lamborghini, should he? And if he loses them, well, our friend's clearly a persistent sort of cove. He'll manage to—"

"Don't want an analysis of his character, thank you very much," Mr. Greene said with asperity. "Don't want to know a thing about him, in point of fact. Want him looked after. That's all."

It was stupid of him, he knew, to allow himself to be irritated by the peculiar blend of patronage and sycophancy he detected in Lewis's tone; that was the way all young men of executive promise spoke to their seniors nowadays and he should long since have grown accustomed to it. Lewis, though, was something of a special case. Mr. Greene was perfectly aware of what had to be the relations those days between Lewis and Bernadotte, but this, too, was something he chose not to know about. He had, as it were, extended in that direction a special grace. And Lewis, he felt, should possess sufficient of his race's notorious psychological subtlety to know when Greene wished that grace to be extended in other directions—this, without being told. Sometimes, though, Mr. Greene wondered if Lewis possessed any subtlety at all. Strange, if he didn't; his father had that quality in abundance. But then, young Mr. Lewis was still exactly that. Young . . .

"Tracy, now. What's your opinion?"

"He seems intelligent," Lewis said. "Of course he has to know there's something wrong."

"What, in someone dying of an electric shock? Nothing much wrong in that, is there?"

"There is in being carted off in a laundry basket afterwards."

"*Spahhhhh*," Mr. Greene said. It was a moment or two before he continued. ". . . You didn't let him *see* that, did you?"

"I thought it best, yes. Now he must at least know there's something to keep quiet *about*. Otherwise, of course, he might have—"

"How much?"

"Five hundred."

"Um. And *will* he keep quiet?"

"I think so. He has to be intelligent enough for that, too."

"Yes. It's a pity he walked in on it, but it can't be helped." Possibly, Mr. Greene thought, he had misjudged Lewis. Tracy had been handled, when you considered the matter, very sensibly. And subtly, too. He leaned back in his chair, gazing through the window at blue sky, flecked far to the south with high streaks of cirrus. "Better see that he gets sent back here as soon as he's got to Wales. Tonight, if possible. If not, tomorrow morning. I'll inform Starshine to that effect."

"Try not to worry, Mr. Greene. Everything's going very much to plan."

Again that infuriating suggestion of the omnisapient young doctor in the television series, reassuring the nervous patient before the op. "Got other things than *this* to worry about," Mr. Greene said, essaying a bluff joviality. "This is *your* show, as far as your father and I are concerned. And we've every confidence in you, every . . . How is he, by the way?"

"Just been chatting him up on the blower," young Lewis said. "He's not worried, either—or so he tells me. Though if I were him, I can't help feeling I would be. A teeny bit."

He rang off. Mr. Greene replaced the receiver and went on gazing out of the window at blue sky, at flecks of cirrus, an uninterrupted view from a two-hundred-foot high vantage point raised above the Brighton Front. Just below the windowsill would be the sea, the white foam of the wave caps near at hand and the long green-blue bulge of the horizon. Beyond the horizon, France. He hoped, though, that it wouldn't come to that.

If it did, he wouldn't be altogether unprepared. He had a lot to lose, certainly, but it wasn't as though he'd spent the last five years angling for a peerage, like old man Lewis. He'd never had aspirations in that direction. So that if it did . . . Ah, but so much better if it didn't. He had to admit it, if only to himself—he was worried. Not all *that* worried, mind.

Just a teeny bit . . .

And England seemed a good place to Tracy, too, that morning. Lambo was humming now down the motorway north of Newbury, south of Oxford; no longer a fish but a great bird skimming the rolling surface of the outstretched downs. There was a dry radiance in the air, the earth was unfolding itself to the gathering heat as the smooth ribbon of the road unwound beneath the spinning tyres, and again the shadows under the trees were becoming dark and deep. At just under a hundred miles an hour Lambo held the road to perfection, and there was not the slightest fault in the modulated purr of the engine that Tracy could detect. He couldn't help feeling along with Candide (with whose character, after all, his own had certain affinities) that, at any rate while this state of affairs lasted, all was certainly for the best in the best of all possible worlds. And, since in such a situation much satisfaction can be derived from reflecting on the portion of others less fortunately placed:

"They'll be having a right old snarl-up in London round about now," he remarked.

"You don't like London?"

"No."

"Nor do I."

"Then why," Tracy said, "live there?"

"I don't know. You have to live somewhere."

She'd be a middling-to-good driver before long, Tracy had decided. She was calm and neat and competent in her movements and she wasn't, like too many women drivers, ever obviously distracted by her own thoughts. Moreover she gave the instrument-board a glance every five minutes or so; Tracy couldn't remember having seen a woman driver do that before. "Yes, but if you don't like—"

"There are people, aren't there? It's like I was telling you last night. There are people you know, and you just have to stay in the circle. Or what is there . . . ? Besides, where else would I live? Bloody Glasgow?"

"You could live anywhere you wanted, surely. If you're separate like you say."

A valley, opening to the right. A wood. A narrow road. A moss-roofed farmhouse, a five-barred gate, a lolloping black dog. Gone in a flash.

"You know Leo?"

A little girl's question. A disguised assertion. She seemed to be waiting for an answer, all the same. "I've met him, I think," Tracy said guardedly.

"They'd like me to marry him. My father would. His parents, maybe. Though what the hell that'd solve, I can't imagine."

"How can . . . ? You're married already."

"Yes. That's part of the deal."

"What deal?"

"The string I told you about. That's tied onto this car and I don't know what else besides. I'm supposed to see Tommy down in Wales and talk about a divorce."

"I see," Tracy said. He often said this when he really didn't. Like now, for instance.

"*Arrange* a divorce, in fact."

"But that's not what *you* want?" He had to feel his way here, cautiously.

"I'm buggered if I can see," Bernadette said, "what difference it makes to anyone either way. It's all so damned stupid."

"It's an outworn institution?"

"Marriage? Well, of course it is."

"But unless people got married, they couldn't have divorces."

Sharp as a nail this morning, was Professor Tracy.

"People ought to be free, that's all. To do what they like."

"But you *are* free. Or so you say."

"No, I'm not. That's the whole point. Women never are."

"I don't think it's all that different for men."

"Pah," Bernadette said conclusively.

Tracy looked through the slanted windscreen at the hills ahead, at the dusty flicker of the road, at the West of England drawing steadily nearer. They'd been driving now for almost an hour. He'd had a cup of coffee before they'd started, but now he was feeling like some breakfast.

"What does Tommy Pope do these days?"

"What d'you mean, *do?*"

"For a living?"

"Who, Tommy? You don't imagine he *works,* do you? Never in his life."

"I always thought he managed pretty nicely."

"So he does, one way or another. Snapping up unconsidered trifles —like myself, for instance. Suppose he agrees to a divorce . . . which he probably won't . . . but *if* he does, you can bet your boots he'll do well on the deal. Oh, it'll cost, all right. *That's* how he keeps managing to scrape by."

"You mean you'll have to pay him something?"

"I mean," Bernadette said, "it'll be for a financial consideration. *I* shan't pay him, no. *I* don't want a divorce. I couldn't care less. That's what darling daddy wants. So darling daddy can bloody well pay for it, and I only hope it's through the bloody nose."

The truth was, Tracy decided, that once you had got used to Bernadette's uninhibited mode of expression it was not without a certain charm. It was rather like having a particularly cuddlesome teddy bear spit, without any great show of animosity, into your eye; a harmless and perfectly comprehensible reaction which you felt you'd like to see repeated before your friends, especially if the winsome beastie could be persuaded to spit in *their* eye, instead.

"*You've* never been married, have you, Tracy?"

"I was once. But not to any great effect."

"Broken up?"

"Yep."

"Offhand I can't think of any marriage that hasn't. Among the people I know, anyway. There's some that keep trying . . . but it's the whole damned system that's wrong. Anyone can see that. Goes to prove my point."

Tracy, whose mind once more was turned towards eggs and bacon rather than upon these subtler matters of the spirit, said nothing; and Bernadette drove for the next few minutes with an unnecessarily tight-lipped concentration. The radio went on playing until, rather abruptly, she flicked it off.

"All the same," she then said, "you're a funny chap, Tracy."

CHAPTER 10

They breakfasted, eventually, in a large and shiny transport caff beyond the Marlborough turnoff; the choice was Bernadette's, not Tracy's (who would have preferred the Polly or the Allesbury Arms). Most of the lorry-drivers on the Bristol run had eaten and gone, but the Taunton-bound crowd were still in lethargic conference over their massive cups of char and a score or so of the black-leather-jacket brigade were more noisily in evidence; this very much to Tracy's surprise, since the bovver boys down Brighton way never showed so much as a whiskery sideboard until well after the lunch break. The plum-colour stretch pants that Bernadette was currently affecting created not so much a stir in their wake as an intense and heavy-breathing silence; Tracy had the feeling that they were being pursued down the length of the cafeteria by a spotlight. They carried their heavily loaded trays over to a vacant cubicle, Bernadette's hip movement being observed the while by an appreciative and indeed fascinated audience, and there, so to speak, concluded the act. "Oh. We forgot the sugar."

"I'll get it," Tracy said hurriedly.

The interest of the public, thus aroused, wasn't immediately withdrawn and Bony Wright, entering some five minutes later, hadn't any difficulty in spotting them at once. Bernadette was, after all, the only woman in the place. He could sit at a corner table, discreetly in the shadows, dispose of a dollop of scrambled eggs and keep a watchful eye on her without exciting any attention at all; that was what all the other gaffers were keeping on her, too. Not that he didn't resent the fact, vaguely. He didn't care to be associated, even in so loose a way, with those other long-haired yobbos. Scum, was what they were. Filthy minds, they had. His own motives for watching the little scrubber were of the purest.

He wasn't concerned in the slightest with whether she would or wouldn't, or did or didn't, or how often. He already knew that she would and did. He wasn't concerned, even with where she was going or why. If he kept on following her, he'd find out where; and that was just what he was going to do. Maybe she was running away and maybe she wasn't. Maybe she knew what had happened in her flat yesterday and maybe she didn't. He'd find out soon enough. He'd know because she'd tell him. Until she did, there wasn't any point in making guesses. Bony's, as has been said, was an unspeculative mentality; and single-minded. Frighteningly so.

Oddly, though, he *did* feel a certain faint curiosity about the fair-haired geezer. Not as to his identity, which didn't matter, nor even as to the relations prevailing between him and the girl, which as they'd spent the night together were pretty obvious. The thing that he wanted to assess was the extent of the opposition that Chummy might put up to his plans for an intimate interview with the bint. Bony's intuition was definite that here he had an archetypal muggins, of the kind that imagines any woman he may happen to be accompanying to constitute his personal property and responsibility. This attitude Bony, of course, found incomprehensible; he knew very well, nevertheless, that such muddy-minded individuals, when held up at gunpoint, would part with their wallets, their watches, their chequebooks and whatever and do it with a patronising smile, yet if you laid no more than an exploratory hand on one of their droopy little foxes in their presence, they would leap on you with vim and dash and nearly bite through your ankle. Naturally there could be no accounting for such behaviour; they got brought up that way and that was all there was to it. You just allowed for it, if you had any sense. It was a pity, though, that people were educated so stupid.

CHAPTER 11

The Devizes Road was naturally trickier than the motorway, but not really difficult; the country was open enough for Bony to be able to tail the Lambo from well back without any great risk of losing it, and the road wiggled about enough to hold the girl's pace down to a moderate fifty. Coming up to the Avebury roundabout, however, he found the motorbike wolfpack from the Marlborough caff snarling half-a-dozen strong at his heels before streaking past him, one by one, blue smoke puffing from their exhaust pipes. His thoughts, again, were uncharitable. But it was, of course, the Lambo they were after; closing up, each in turn, to play tag with its minimal slipstream before pulling out to scream contemptuously past.

At the roundabout they were circling, waiting, the sun gleaming on their shiny helmets and metal studs, and when Lambo swung left they peeled off in neat formation to follow in a loud-buzzing chain, dancing bees in pursuit of a fleeing queen. At least, Bony thought, they'd serve to distract attention from his own unassuming presence. He eased his foot a little on the pedal, dropping a little farther back.

Unfortunately, though not altogether surprisingly, the queen didn't seem to fancy being thus made the object of attention. Scuttling comfortably round a corner that preceded a lengthy straight, Bony discovered, something to his alarm, the ton up boys a half mile ahead of him and going like smoke, with Lambo virtually out of sight in the middle distance. Obviously she'd given it a bit of a squirt. Bony clicked his tongue in annoyance and pushed the pedal down to the floorboards again.

Tracy wasn't too happy about this development, either.

"This is a bit juvenile, isn't it?"

"We'll have those nits buzzing us all morning if we don't shake 'em off. Like, to hell with *that*."

"Sure you've got the feel of her?"

A silly question, he knew. She'd got the feel, all right. Coming out of that slow corner the rpm needle had jumped to the 6000 mark and the searing acceleration, coming when he hadn't really expected it, had pulled his heavily laden stomach nearly through his backbone. The full power surge of a racing engine can be as intoxicating as the lurch and dive of the Big Dipper; she'd never felt it before. But now she had and liked it. The corner at the end of the straight was coming up at them as though seen through a zoom lens; sharpish, left-handed, shadowed by a clump of trees. She touched the brake, once; then again; swung the wheel; loose gravel on the outer verge spat and sang as the offside rear wheel rocketed it upwards. Tracy sighed, though not without sympathy. He knew how it was.

"Not quite right?"

"Wrong line," Tracy said.

"Wrong line?"

"These tyres give you a lot of grip. And the car's so low the wind pressure won't hold you out. So you go exactly where you steer, not somewhere else. It takes a bit of getting used to."

"I'll try again," Bernadette said.

The next curve was more gradual and she didn't use the brakes at all. But the line this time was perfect. "How was that, then?"

"Very nice," Tracy said.

They reached Devizes in just under ten minutes. They lost the motorcyclists there and, but for an edge-of-town traffic light, would probably have lost Bony as well. He took the corner just in time to catch a quick glimpse of Lambo's unmistakable rear elevation shooting off down the A361 at an unabated velocity; lucky, that. But she'd taken him by surprise back there and he'd had a job getting past those bloody yobbos. It wouldn't happen again. At Trowbridge he was tucked in nicely a couple of cars behind them; at Frome he was tailing them from a couple of hundred yards back. You got rusty in prison, maybe, but not *that* rusty.

She was still fairly blinding along, though. There ought to be a law. And her cornering was pretty erratic. Tracy, who thought so too, was making helpful suggestions from time to time, but these weren't being well received. "What the hell d'you mean, I'm riding the clutch? You might at least talk English while you're about it."

"You see, when you change down for the corners—"

"When I *what?* I don't know what you're talking about."

Baring, as she spoke, her sharp little teeth. She reminded Tracy this morning not so much of a teddy bear as of a poodle. Poodles are among the most intelligent of dogs and thus find themselves frequently frustrated by the invincible stupidity of their owners; they then become aggressive and snappish. And Tracy wasn't much of a poodle-trainer. "I think the trouble is it *feels* like low-gear steering, even up in fourth, so you're leaving the change late and then you're grabbing for it, you see, like pressing your drive in golf, which makes you keep your foot down—"

That was when they nearly had a little accident. Though it wasn't, to be fair, entirely Bernadette's fault. The man was carrying a cardboard box tucked into one hip, rucking up his jacket to one side, and Lambo passed so close to him that Tracy's clearest impression was of the metal gleam of his belt buckle; he never saw the man's face. Stepping out from behind parked vans (or London roulette) is a common enough diversion, but one that never fails to take effect on the nerves of oncoming drivers. "Bloody twit," Bernadette said.

"That's the trouble with a quiet motor. I don't think he heard—"

"Not him. You."

"*Me?*"

"How can I concentrate on my driving when you're talking all the time? And I can't understand a word you're saying? Shut up for a bit, why don't you?"

Tracy, who had been about to comment on the desirability of looking *under* parked vehicles when approaching them, decided to make the point at a later stage. Clearly, his admonitions were getting on her nerves. "Sorry," he said. "This driving instruction lark, it wasn't my idea."

"Not your idea, no. But maybe your mistake."

She pulled the car in at the end of the queue waiting for a traffic light, slammed the gear crossly into neutral. "Where is this place?"

"This is Shepton Mallett."

"And where do we go from here?"

"Straight on. I thought we might join the A38 and run up to Bristol. Give you a little practice in city traffic. Then the motorway straight through to the bridge. That's if you "

"Right," Bernadette said, rolling the car forwards again with much too discernible a jerk.

Beyond the town, the beginnings of the Mendips. Hedges, trees, pubs with white plaster façades, all flashing by; Bernadette was driving fast again, or at least, as fast as she could. It wasn't a fast road; narrow, dipping, curving. Perhaps, Tracy thought, he should have directed her south to Glastombury and across the long flats of the Vale of Avalon. But then she'd probably have gone faster still. "Look," he said. "You drive all right. In fact, you drive pretty well. You don't have to try and *prove* anything."

"What's the matter? Getting nervous?"

She glanced sideways at him, giving the pedal a farther scornful half inch of pressure. At which precise moment, a farm tractor came blundering noisily out of a side turning directly in front of them; Bernadette span the wheel and, trying to straighten out, overcompensated; toed the brake and, changing her mind, used the pedal instead, getting just sufficient bite fron the rear tyres to pull herself out of the impending skid and to swerve back left across the face of an approaching lorry, which roared past with a bleating hoot of protest. "Nervous? Me? Old Iceman Tracy, they used to call me."

"You said you got frightened."

"Only at high speeds."

"Ah," Bernadette said, tightening her lips again. "That's all right, then."

A half mile or so of uphill curve, then a sudden dip that came at them from the right; a high hedge, a wide green field and, on the horizon, the uplifted warning finger of Glastonbury Tor. Now—as sooner or later had certainly to happen—she did the wrong thing, braking hard instead of changing down, and the consequent sideslip brought the wheels up against the bumpy grass verge. Tracy saw, with the absolute clarity of vision one achieves on these unpleasant occasions, the white walls of a large house at the bottom of the dip, the slates of its roof flecked with leaf-shadow from the tall ever-greens that grew beside it, a green-painted garden gate and a trellis-work from which there hung a rather fine show of climbing roses. He saw also, though less clearly, something white and vaguely rec-tangular much nearer to hand, something that swept towards him and then disappeared, with a sharp splintering sound and a jar, under Lambo's low-slung bonnet. The car shuddered and started to roll, steadied itself as though preparing for a leap, shook to another impact, slowed, stopped, stalled. Tracy unclipped his safety belt, leaned across to switch off the ignition; Bernadette, he saw, had remained motionless, staring in front of her, hands still gripping the steering wheel like Mr. Toad. She seemed to be all right, though. ". . . You okay?"

"Yes. What . . . ?"

"We had a bit of a shunt," Tracy said. "Nothing of importance."

There wasn't any smell of petrol. His head seemed to be ringing from the clapper-bell effect of those blows on the chassis, but he thought he'd be all right if he stood up. He got out of the car and found that yes, he was. Just about. He walked effortfully round to the front to inspect the damage. The nearside wheels were high up on a grassy bank from which, for some twenty yards back, the underchassis had ploughed a shallow furrow of turf. He stooped to peer under the radiator, noting out of the corner of his eye, as he did so, the passing of a blue Mini-Cooper, travelling very fast in-deed; the driver probably hadn't noticed anything wrong at all, since at that speed Lambo might well have appeared to be merely pulled in on the verge. Between the front axle and the ground was jammed that white metallic rectangle he had glimpsed before they'd overrun it; stooping farther, he was able without great difficulty to free it. It was now a hideously battered irregular triangle on which, however, the message, SEE THE LIONS OF LONGLEAT, could still be deciphered. The suggestion hardly seemed a practicable one.

Bernadette, too, had clambered down and was now standing be-side him. "Are *you* all right?"

"Yes, I'm fine."

"You're bleeding, though."

"Where?"

"Forehead."

Tracy took out his handkerchief and investigated. There was a cut there all right. "How big is it?"

"Not very big. An inch, maybe. But it's coming up, rather."

"I expect I'll survive. Let's have another look at the car."

As far as he could tell Lambo, too, had come off fairly lightly. The exhaust tubes would have gone, as had to be expected, and the front wheel was buckled. "The wheel's a write-off. That doesn't much matter, but the transmission's probably taken a knock as well."

"We can't go on?"

Tracy continued his investigations. Bernadette sat down on the bank and lit a cigarette. Five minutes later, Tracy came to sit down beside her and said:

"No."

"All right," Bernadette said. "I'll walk down and see if that house has got a telephone."

CHAPTER 12

Fortunately it had: enabling her to arrange matters (with not altogether unexpected efficiency) to such effect that a taxi had arrived within twenty minutes to transport her into town and to a comfortable hotel, while within the space of a farther fifty minutes a breakdown van had appeared to give Lambo, and incidentally Tracy, a tow to the nearest repair shop. It hadn't been in any way an uncomfortable wait, sitting coatless on the bank enjoying the sunshine. He didn't suppose that Mr. Greene would be any too pleased about this little incident, but things could certainly have been a great deal worse. His head now was certainly tender, but the fresh air had cleared up his initial giddiness and sitting—still coatless—beside the driver of the breakdown van, he felt in a mood for a little conversation.

"Good food at the hotel, is there?"

"What hotel's that?"

"White Stag, I think she said."

"Arrrr," said the driver.

And after a while,

"Drefful quiet place, the White Stag."

"Oh yes?"

"Does a nice trade with them unnymoon couples."

"The lady," Tracy said, "isn't my wife. No."

"Arrrr," said the driver.

And after a while,

"Reckon not many of them are, at that. But they're very unnerstanding, at the White Stag."

"They won't understand *that* one," Tracy said. "I'll be damned if I do. By the way, what's the food like?"

It wasn't idle curiosity. He was feeling peckish.

"The *food?*"

"Yes."

"Food at White Stag?"

"Yes."

"Not many as goes there for the *food*," the driver said, glancing sideways at Tracy with some contempt. "Nobbut they'd run you up a steak an' chips, if that was what you fancied."

"Arrrr," Tracy said.

The manager of the repair shop proved to be a little less rustic in his mode of intercourse and was most co-operative; Tracy left him, after some ten minutes or so of technical chitchat, walking round and round Lambo and rubbing his hands together in glee, rather as a heart surgeon might circumambulate a prospective transplant. The White Stag proved to be a mere five minutes' stroll up the main street; the reception clerk had been apprised of Tracy's imminent arrival and Tracy was therefore able, with a minimum of further delay, to scrub his oil-stained hands in a private bathroom, to bathe his wound and finally to change his shirt, onto the front of which substantial quantities of blood appeared to have leaked. Thus refurbished he made his way downstairs to the hotel dining room, where he found Bernadette duly embarked on the fish course. "I waited for you," she said, "as long as I could." It was typical, Tracy thought, not only of her but of her sex in general that she should contrive somehow to make of this remark an accusation.

"Well," he said, sitting down at the table opposite her where a place, he was glad to notice, had already been laid for him. "Things could be worse."

"Indeed they could. The *sole bonne femme's* not bad at all."

"With the car, I meant. They'll be sending the spares we need down from Bristol. Should be here by five, with any luck."

"Not till five? Won't the mechanics be knocking off then?"

"Yes, but that's all right. The manager'll let me have the keys to the shop, if he can't stay on to lend a hand himself. I'd want to do the fitting myself, anyway."

"How long will it take you?"

"Three hours or so. We should be off again by eight."

The driver of the breakdown van hadn't misled him; the White Stag most certainly seemed to be quiet. Apart from two middle-aged men in dark suits at the window table, he and Bernadette had the dining room to themselves. "But it's only just on one o'clock now. What the hell," Bernadette complained, "can I do for seven hours in a dump like this?"

"Take a walk. See the sights. Inspect the cathedral." Tracy, sensing the approach of a waitress, was himself avidly inspecting the menu card. "There's a fourteenth-century clock there, I believe. All very historical. I'll take the brown Windsor, please, and the sole thingummyjig. With boiled potatoes."

"Cathedrals," Bernadette said, "don't turn me on. And I'm not much thrilled by twentieth-century clocks, much less fourteenth-century ones. All they do is tell the bloody time, and who wants to know that?"

"You have a point there," Tracy admitted.

Later, and blissfully replete (for the driver had been wrong about the food), he stood with his elbows on the long stone wall at the end of the cathedral cloisters and with his jacket slung loosely over one shoulder, since it was hotter now even than the day before, cool only in the shadows of the cloisters themselves, and the wall where he stood, dry and gritty to the touch, lay, on the contrary, open to the full heavy beat of the afternoon sun. He was thinking that Bernadette was right about clocks. Clocks had maybe been a mistake. You couldn't or *he* couldn't, offhand, think of an invention which, while changing nothing, had more obviously and drastically changed absolutely everything. And what was wrong, after all, with the old-fashioned sundial? He was feeling rather like a sundial himself. He felt, that is to say, in a vaguely benedictory, pipe-smoking, post-prandial mood, like a Buchan clubman or some minor prewar creation of Dornford Yates (into whose more Ruritanian masterpieces Bernadette, however, seated now on the wall to his left with the air of one who wishes to be instead wedged into a crevice between the stones and converted, by some amiable magician, into a stick of dynamite, could admittedly only with difficulty have found a place). No, Bernadette certainly wasn't 1920s. And certainly not the Middle Ages, either. Jeffery Farnol was, if anyone, the man for her. She'd have been pretty much at home on the High Toby; Redhaired Polly, the highwayman's moll. She'd made a neat enough job of Lambo, anyway. All that was lacking, clearly, was the resident sadist; to have some sparky blade glim her a crafty crack in the old gobstopper would clearly do her nothing but a world of good. But that, as Tracy recognised, was sheer wishful thinking. Or escapism, as nowadays you had to call it.

Not that there was anything wrong—or at least, unusual—about escapism. The lawns behind him were seething with sweating tourists, all gazing preoccupiedly at the scenery and all thinking, privately and wishfully, how delightful the place would probably be without all these bloody day trippers getting in the way. What you want of a cathedral close on a summer afternoon is a certain historical glamour and the evocation of a cheap nostalgia, but the proper reactions are hard to achieve when the place resembles Margate sands on a bank holiday. Escapes, as from Colditz, have to be planned. You can't all do it at once.

He wondered if that was how he'd got off on the wrong foot with Bernadette, and had ended up on the wrong foot with Anne. They were girls, after all. Not cathedrals. You take your hat off in both cases, but there the resemblance ends. Maybe politeness is like marriage; an outworn institution. Bernadette would probably turn out to be tractable enough, if you didn't start off imagining that you were a poor but gallant musketeer curvetting about on your high-powered warhorse and that she were Ninon de l'Enclos (who, come to think of it, had probably employed a vocabulary every bit as uninhibited as Bernadette's). She might even be positively amenable if you (and this means *you*, Tracy) were to turn round suddenly (yes, right now) and paste her in the eye, *POW*, just like that. And *there* was a beautiful thought. The humble, unassuming Cuthbert Delamere translated in a moment into SUPER-TRACY . . . fierce as a tiger . . . fast as a panther . . . the only thing you can hear at sixty miles an hour is his wristwatch . . . A lightning turn, and *POW!* and "Thatsha way," you'd say, "itsh gotta be, baby." That's what'd turn her on, if cathedrals wouldn't . . .

"What the hell are you *grinning* to yourself about?"

"Who? What? Me? Oh, nothing." Tracy was startled. "I was practically asleep."

"Pah," Bernadette said predictably. Whatever the object of Tracy's thoughts, her tone implied, they could hardly be of interest sufficient to warrant any further enquiry. "Let's walk."

"Where to?"

"How would I know, dammit? Anywhere. I'm not going to spend all afternoon stuck here on my ass, I'll tell you that."

"Oh," Tracy said. "Righty-ho."

He followed her meekly (as befitted the ineffectual Wooster character to which he had unfortunately reverted) down the path that flanked the nearby moat. In the moat, there was water; also reeds, ducks, and a great deal of mud. The ducks seemed to have been incommoded by a large and gaily coloured plastic ball that had been tossed into the water some time previously; they were gathered round it, hissing at it nervously. Damn fool birds, Tracy thought uncharitably. They're not supposed to do that. They're supposed to dabble, adding thus to the serenity of the atmosphere. Instead of scuttering up and down like a lot of neurotic charwomen. What, he couldn't help asking himself, were things coming to in our quiet country towns when even the bloody ducks behave as though they've been caught in the middle of an urban freeway right on the rush hour? Maybe, of course, they were *French* ducks. Imported. You couldn't tell nowadays, with the Common Market. But you naturally felt that a decent respectable English duck would have a bit more . . . well . . . *savoir faire* . . .

"There used," he said sadly, "to be swans here."

"Well, there aren't any now."

"No. At least, I don't see any."

"Probably," Bernadette said, "the water's polluted."

"Nothing more likely."

They walked on. Perhaps the ducks, Tracy thought, had all gone quackers. This was a joke. Tracy hardly ever invented jokes. When he did, he found them extremely amusing. This one he found amusing, but not amusing enough to be tried out on Bernadette. Instead:

"They rang a bell," he remarked.

"*What?*"

"Over there somewhere. There was a bellrope. Every morning the swans'd come along and pull it. Then the porter or whoever it was'd give them their breakfast."

"Sagacious creatures," Bernadette said.

"Yes."

"Where in the world did you pick up *that* yarn?"

"It's true," Tracy said. "My mother told me about it. It was a long time ago, of course. When she was a girl."

"D'you come from this part of England, then?"

"More or less, yes. Farther west, though. We lived over in the Quantocks."

"Where are they? *What* are they? Sounds like something in a science fiction serial."

"Quantock theory, yes. Holes in space. That's just about what they are. No, they're just a lot of hillocks, north of Taunton."

"So you're a local yokel."

"That I be," Tracy said. "Gurt Tracy Ridd they call me. Strong i' the yarrum, weak i' the yead."

"I'll go along with that," Bernadette said acidly.

The idea of biffing her smartly in the left eye presented itself again to Tracy, and even more vividly than before. He could see that this was going to become one of those recurrent ideas, a sort of Wagnerian leitmotif underlying all his conscious thoughts. Then from somewhere within or beyond the cathedral there sounded four noisy, clattering bongs on a bell that had to have been made of rusty tin. That fourteenth-century clock was maybe doing its stuff. It sure as hell wouldn't be the swans. They—sagacious creatures—had already left. "Let's get out of here," Bernadette said, uncannily echoing his thoughts. "Let's go back and have a real nice rustic farmhouse tea. That may bring out some more of these fascinating childhood reminiscences."

Tracy privately promised himself that it wouldn't.

But they did nevertheless have tea and buttered toast and scones with cream and strawberry jam, and this in a small, dark, low-raftered room whose panelled-glass windows overlooked the lawns over which they had recently been walking, and where in the dimness it was surprisingly cool; the change of temperature made Tracy aware of how extremely hot it had been outside and compelled him to attribute to the heat much of his own uncharacteristic petulance. In the tearoom, his normal equanimity of mind was quickly restored. Certainly it was full of rather loud-voiced people, all eating buttered toast and scones and jam, to which comestibles they would be, Tracy supposed, in all probability no more addicted than he was —which was to say, not at all. You simply ate this highly indigestible stuff in the spirit with which what's-his-name climbed Everest, because it was there. A pretty inept procedure, when you thought about it. All the same . . .

"All the same," Bernadette said, snapping ravenously at a scone and squirting cream inelegantly over her small, pointed chin, "you have to see what I mean. One couldn't live in a place like this. Die, yes, possibly. But live here, no."

"I can quite see that this isn't where it's at."

Bernadette sighed. "People don't say that any more."

"You mean the *in* people?"

"I mean people, dammit, p double e p, *people*. I wouldn't mind it so much if you were just a dreary straightforward old square. But you're not. You're far worse. You're a *creep*."

"I don't know what that means," Tracy said, aware that, whatever it meant, this was almost certainly the sort of thing that a creep would say. His attitude was fast becoming fatalistic.

"Yes, you do."

"I don't. Really."

"All right, then. For your information, a creep is someone . . ."

She stopped short, glaring at him. Then, while continuing to glare, she put a hand the fingers of which were liberally besmeared with melted butter on Tracy's wrist and squeezed it gently, staining his shirt cuff rather badly.

"The weird thing is," she said, "I've quite enjoyed this afternoon. I have to admit it."

"You've *enjoyed* it? Why?"

"I don't know. Or yes, I do. I usually have a lot of things to worry about, and this afternoon I haven't. Haven't worried, that is. It must be that."

Tracy, while reflecting that now he'd have to change his shirt yet again, realised with something of a shock that this was true of himself also. Not at any time since Bernadette had shunted the Lambo had he given a moment's thought to his various financial problems, to Mr. Greene, to young Leo Lewis or even to the unfortunate Rusty Keyes and the curious circumstances of his demise. He, too, had spent a singularly carefree afternoon, without being fully conscious of the fact. For some peculiar reason he felt a shade of embarrassment at this discovery; looking away from Bernadette and out of the window, he saw, in the shade of an oak tree near the wall and leaning against the trunk in what seemed to be a strangely familiar posture, a man in a dark blue suit, white shirt and dark tie —a rather formal attire, one might have thought, for such a hot day. He was reading, or appeared to be reading, a newspaper, but at the moment when Tracy had looked up his face had been turned directly towards the window and Tracy had had an impression—no more—of a heavy moustache. It might have been a trick of the light, a shadow thrown by his nose, but Tracy didn't think so.

As he watched, the man folded his newspaper and began to walk away down the path towards the cathedral, unhurriedly but looking neither left nor right. Almost at once a group of sightseers— middle-aged women, mostly, in rather regrettable Op Art cotton dresses—drifted across the lawn to hide the retreating figure from view. Tracy tried to pin down in his memory the essential characteristics of Bony Wright's way of walking; in no way particularly distinctive, there had nevertheless been something semi-military about it, a high-shouldered regularity of pace, a certain inflexibility,

a certain fixity of purpose. Tracy thought that he'd remember it if
he ever saw it again.

"I haven't any worries, really," he said. "But I enjoyed it, too."

"Did you? Why?"

"I like fine weather," Tracy said.

CHAPTER 13

By seven o'clock the air was discernibly cooler. Bernadette, wearing a blue Pringle cardigan as a concession to the westerly breeze,
descended the hotel steps and started to walk down the main street.
She walked quickly, as was her usual custom. Her long and unquestionably elegant legs carried her rhythmically past the wide plate-
glass window of an antique shop full of Georgian furniture,
Victorian knickknackery and things that had vaguely to do with
horses, past a tall house of Cotswold stone with brass solicitors'
plates screwed onto the door, past the local Woolworth's, past a
radio and television store, past another plate-glass window behind
which stood a marble slab, empty, and a printed sign that said,
WILFRED STEBBINS, PORK AND FAMILY BUTCHER; then
there were various other shops, various other signs, a side turning
and another notice, placed this time fairly high up on the wall.
MENDIP MOTORS, it said, and in smaller letters, STAFF EN-
TRANCE. There was a door directly beneath it and a white arrow
pointing downwards, in case you hadn't got the message. Bernadette, who with all her faults wasn't slow on the uptake, tried the
handle and found that the door was unlocked, just as Tracy had
promised. You could say one thing for Tracy. He seemed to be reliable. She went in, closing the door behind her.

Inside there was a dark and gloomy passageway with peeling
plaster walls, onto which had been pinned charts showing the more
indecent parts of motorcars' anatomies. At the end of the passageway there was another door. This gave onto a small and equally
dark and gloomy knacker's yard, if you can imagine a knacker's
yard with a ceiling to it and with an infinitesimally tiny light bulb
dangling on a frayed length of flex from the middle of it. Bits of dis-
membered machinery lay all about; there was a powerful and per-
vading smell of motor oil mingled with rotten cabbage. Yet another
door admitted her to a vast, echoing cavern where the gloom was
positively Stygian; all around her loomed the mysterious shapes of
fossilised Fords and Morrises, like mammoths in ice, while a hol-

low, hammering boom sounding somewhere in the distance ac-
centuated the general eerie resemblance of the place to the Hall
of the Mountain King. Bernadette paused, aghast; the idea that men
should willingly spend a large part of their working lives in such
surroundings was one that took a little getting used to. Besides, she
wasn't quite sure now what direction to take; the hammering was
perfectly audible—in fact, it was deafening—but it was a hammering
of a generalised nature, emanating, as it seemed, from some source
deep underground rather than from any localisable position within
the cavern. It was, as she listened, supplemented by another weird
and sinister sound; a soft, bubbling hiss, as of marsh gas escaping
from a carboniferous swamp or as, perhaps, of Alph, the sacred
river, vanishing down some subterranean plughole. Bernadette's
sharply analytical ear, however, was able within a very few moments to recognise the true source of this Grimesby-Roylottish
effect; someone, she decided, was whistling. Someone who wasn't
a very good whistler. She was even able, a few seconds later, to
guess what the tune was supposed to be. It was *Beautiful Dreamer*.

Edging to and fro, first right and then left, in the end she perceived at some ten yards' distance from her a single bright glow of
light at ground level, illuminating the nether organs of a car which
—though it was hard to be sure—looked very much like Lambo. She
approached cautiously. Yes. It was Lambo all right. And in the blur
of light the silhouette of a man's head, of Tracy's head, was visible.
He was still making those peculiar noises. She sat down on a pile
of used tyres and watched him for several minutes; the
dismembered-head illusion she found alarming and enjoyable. Of
course he was standing in one of those pit things you put the car
over when you want to engage it in intercourse, but it all looked
very Grand Guignol. Just the head craning upwards, and an un-
attached hand moving about on the floor like in that Buñuel film.
What was it groping for . . . ? Ah yes. A spanner. She felt a peculiar urge to giggle, but repressed it sternly. She didn't want to spoil
the fun.

Tracy went on making funny noises and poking about. Twisting
this, screwing up that. Eventually, though, he broke off whistling
in order to say:

"Ow."

Sucking his finger, he suddenly caught sight of Bernadette and
remained peering out at her, owlishly, from under the car. "What
are *you* doing there?"

"Just watching."

"Watching what?" A shade grumpy, he seemed. But then he'd just caught his knuckles quite a bang.

"Watching you. Working."

"Yeah," Tracy said. "Fascinating, innit?"

"You seemed to be so happy," Bernadette said. "I didn't want to disturb you."

Tracy grunted unintelligibly, picked up the spanner and returned to the attack. Bernadette got up and came closer to the pit. "What's the weather like down there?"

"Warm and cosy." With his attention focussed on the recalcitrant nut, he was nonetheless conscious of Bernadette's interminable legs moving with considerable caution down the iron ladderway. ". . . And dirty and oily. Watch out for your dress."

She gave no sign of heeding this injunction. Standing beside him, rather close beside him, she squinted up at Lambo respectfully. "Gorn. All those tubes and wires and things. I'd no idea they were there. But then I've never been in one of these holes before."

"Don't worry," Tracy said. "You'll end up in one. We all will."

"You *are* grumpy."

"Not really. You're right. I like messing about with cars."

"I know."

She was standing, he thought, really very close to him indeed. Of necessity, of course. So as not to dirty her dress on the walls of the pit.

"A fine," Bernadette said, "and private place."

"But none, I think, do there embrace." He wasn't sure if he was following the quotation or pursuing his own line of thought. ". . . What're you looking so surprised about? Just because I like to mess about with motors doesn't mean I've never read Milton."

"It's Marvell, actually."

"Or whoever."

Happy, he thought; that wasn't the right word. Contentment, that was better. What he really got from mucking around with machinery was satisfaction; satisfaction is what you get when you've settled for what's within your reach. Happiness, though—that has to be something else again. He wasn't sure that he knew very much about happiness.

"I quite like poetry," Bernadette said chattily. "When it's *about* something. Like death, for instance."

"I did that one at school."

"Yes, so did I. More than once. That's because I went to quite a lot of schools. I kept running away."

"I wouldn't have had the nerve."

"I went to eight schools altogether. Hated the lot. They didn't give a damn, you know, my parents didn't. They just wanted me comfortably out the way. But they kept on trying—I'll say *that* for them."

Tracy picked up an adjustable wrench, span the screw thoughtfully with the ball of his thumb. "What didn't you like about those schools, though? Didn't you get a chance to do any embracing on your own account?"

"Christ, no. That came *much* later. That's why these foul places are so expensive, they're all running private police forces on the side. Lot of hard-eyed bitches prowling around to stop you having it off with the undergardeners. They drive you up the wall, they honestly do."

"Boys' schools," Tracy said, "aren't much better."

"Of course they are. Tommy shoots his mouth off all the time about when he was at Eton. Hell, I wouldn't have minded Eton."

"You'd have been very popular there. Maybe not with *all* the boys, from what one hears. But certainly with some."

"Oh, *that*. Well, we had that, too. I had a South American after me for two whole bloody terms—the Brazil Nut, we called her. She was really something. In the end I had to stick her head in a fire bucket. *That* did the trick."

"Dangerous," Tracy said. "You might have drowned her."

"Oh, there wasn't any water in the bucket. Only sand."

Reflecting sadly on the carefree, uncomplicated childhood supposed to be the unique prerogative of the British upper classes, Tracy turned away from her and resumed his interrogation of Lambo's entrails. "This is going to take me a little longer than I thought."

"What're you doing, exactly?"

"I'm just decarbonising this 'ere conglomerate, miss."

"Well, how *much* longer?"

"Till nine o'clock, maybe. I thought the chap who runs this shop'd be here to help me, but he had to shoot off somewhere at short notice. It's a hell of a note, running a repair shop." Tracy shook his head sadly. *He* knew.

Bernadette watched him for a minute or two in silence. Then:
". . . Are you angry about it?"

"About what?"

"My hurting your car."

"You can't hurt cars. They don't have any feelings. And anyway it's not my car, it's yours."

"*You* have feelings, though."

"Well, of course I do. I'm a man."

"Lots of people aren't."

"Aren't what?"

"Men."

"I know. Some of them are women. I learnt about *that* at school, too."

"I mean some people don't. Don't have feelings. Some men don't. Like my father. *He* doesn't."

"He must have. Everybody has. Maybe he just tries to hide them."

"No," Bernadette said. "He really hasn't any feelings, that I or anyone else can determine. He gives me a car . . . right . . . but it doesn't mean a bloody thing to him. So it doesn't mean anything to me, either. But I didn't mean to hurt *your* feelings, really I didn't."

"That's all right," Tracy said. What *is* this? he thought. An apology? From *Bernadette?*

"You're not angry, then?"

"No. Not in the least. Just busy, that's all."

"Okay," Bernadette said. "I'll leave you to get on with it."

CHAPTER 14

Young Mr. Lewis was also a man of feeling. What he was feeling, and expressing, was chiefly concern.

"They started off before me. A good three hours before me. I don't understand it at all."

To the west, one of those spectacular South Wales sunsets, with the last light burning pyre-like between tangled blankets of black and purple clouds, sharply silhouetting the jumbled tors of the Ogmore hills; Leo eyed it with no great show of appreciation. No water-colourist, he. Most of his attention was directed—and had been for the last half hour—at the narrow road that skirted the darkening moor and terminated beside the piled-stone wall, no more than three feet high, that marked, rather than protected, the outer edges of the forecourt of what had once been a stoutly built farmhouse, though a full century of change, of dereliction and renovation, had ravaged and altered its external and internal form until its original sparse economy of structure had become all but totally lost; in architectural oddities, however, Leo wasn't interested either. He was only interested in the road insofar as it provided a means of ingress to fresh arrivals—to two fresh arrivals, in particular. But on that road there were no signs of movement, none at all.

"I mean, twelve hours from London? It's ridiculous."

His own car was parked in the forecourt; it had been there since four o'clock that afternoon. Beside it was the imposing bulk of Tommy Pope's battleship-grey Bentley. The Bentley had been there a great deal longer.

"Maybe," Pope said, "you ought to give the old man a ring."

"I don't want to worry him unless it's necessary. And he's worried enough already—after yesterday's fun and games."

"Great mistake, worrying. Gets you nowhere. Take things as they come, that's my motto." Pope was obstreperously cheerful, a state of mind to which the half-empty bottle of Gordon's standing on the oak sideboard had doubtless made effective contribution. He couldn't—Leo thought with irritation—have fairly been described as drunk, but he wasn't completely sober, either. When was he ever completely sober, though? . . . That'd be the day. "So you're not worried? You certainly had *me* fooled."

"Worrying about other people is what I meant. The other thing, well . . . I wouldn't say I was *worried* about it. An inadequate term, what? Shakin' in me shoes—*that's* more like it. Well, wouldn't you be?"

Pope's fearfully, fearfully British pose was one that Leo found unsympathetic. It went well enough, of course, with his innocuous —not to say vacuous—personal appearance, with the sleeked-back straw-coloured hair and the bristly straw-coloured moustache, with the pale inquiring blue eyes and with the rustic ruddiness of his complexion; but nothing was more probable than that this disarming Ouida-Guardsman effect was itself the product of careful calculation and preparation, a deliberate attempt at camouflage like that of the predatory wasp that presents the outward guise of an inoffensive beetle. And his air of fearfully, fearfully British modesty was similarly designed to deceive the unwary; the British have grown so used to being disbelieved that they can reveal the truth about themselves with every confidence that no one will take them seriously, and later, squatting on the prostrate bodies of their wriggling victims, can preen themselves on the sturdy moral uprightness with which they have behaved throughout. No doubt imperial diplomacy had been sustained by this elementary form of bluff for the past three hundred years, but nobody was taken in by it these days and least of all the Jews, who'd become experts at the trick themselves. So he, Leo Lewis, should be so bamboozled? Ha! Not a chance, old sport.

"Scared? Maybe I would be. He made a real neat job of Rusty Keyes. So he's in business all right—if anyone was ever in any doubt about it."

Bony Wright, though, come to think of it, must have been taken in by it. And Wright didn't seem to be a fool.

"Let's hope," Tommy said, "he hasn't made a real neat job of our little Bernie, too. Bearing in mind that you're the one who organised this whole jolly lark. It wouldn't look good, Leo boy, it really wouldn't."

"God, no. It can't be *that*."

"Oh, I don't suppose so for a moment. Just my little joke."

"That *can't* have happened."

"She's been travelling in broad daylight," Tommy said, "up to now. So she'd be safe enough. Or at least, you'd think so. But then he fixed poor old Rusty in broad daylight, too, didn't he? I must say I'm sorry to hear about Rusty." He took a valedictory swig of gin-and-lime. "He wasn't what you'd call—"

"I wish you'd shut up," Leo said vehemently.

"Eh? Just tryin' to be helpful. I mean, there again, she's got someone with her—wasn't that what you said?"

"Someone the old man picked up. Of course it had to be somebody Wright wouldn't know—that was the trouble."

"Hefty sort of a chap?"

"Moderately so. But I doubt if he'd—"

"Young, I imagine?"

"Thirtyish."

"Well, there you are. *That's* what's happened. You know Bernie. She's just gone and seized the chance for one of her lightnin' seductions, that's all it is. She'll be at her old Manon Lescaut act again. No cause for alarm there, don't you know. Absolutely not."

Leo gazed out at the darkening scenery in deepening despondency. This suggestion was, of course, ridiculous. All the same, the road outside was as empty as before. He, personally, had no use for the large areas of nothingness into which, in the gathering twilight, the road disappeared; they gave him merely an alarming sense of being a long way from home. That wasn't surprising; he got agoraphobia in Battersea Gardens. He liked houses, people, shops, cinemas, lampposts, the *civilised* things of life. Here nothing seemed to move at all, except for the odd group of bored and moth-eaten sheep. No, there was no point in waiting around. He'd get back to Cardiff.

"All this fuss about Bernie," Tommy said plaintively. "But what about *me?*"

"You've got Starshine and his lot, haven't you? Who else should I bring in? The Coldstream Guards?"

"Fat lot of good Starshine'll be, if Bony doesn't even show up."

"He'll show up all right. You'll see."

"Not unless Bernie does. And you can't even be sure he's following her. It's all a pretty cock-brained scheme, if you ask me."

"You agreed to it, soldier."

"Yes, I did, but it's all *taking* so long."

With that last, Leo had to agree. He turned away from the window, cracking his finger joints irresolutely. "I'll run back into Cardiff and take a look round. There's just a chance they've stopped off there for dinner. Give me a ring at the Angel if there's any news."

"That where you're staying?"

"Yes."

"In amongst the fleshpots. Lucky sod," Tommy said. "I'm about fed up with this dump, if you want to know the truth. Stuck out the other end of nowhere. I'll be getting the creeping willies if this goes on much longer."

"A pint of bitter, please," Tracy said.

He looked dishevelled. Bernadette, seated at the bar counter, was bathed, changed and neat as a new pin.

"It's fixed?"

"Fixed," Tracy said. "As good as new."

It was twenty minutes to nine, by the clock on the wall above the barman's head. It was a very old clock, but it gave the right time.

"You'd better take a bath, when you've drunk your beer. Then we'll have some dinner. I'm starving."

"But aren't you in a hurry to push on?"

"No," Bernadette said. "I'm not. I've already booked our rooms. We're staying the night."

"Here?"

"Yes, why not? It's clean and comfortable. And you must be feeling tired."

"I've felt tireder," Tracy said, sinking the better part of his tankard with no discernible effort. "Of course, if I'd known there wasn't any rush, I'd have . . ." He shook his head bemusedly. "Well, I'll go and put the car away again."

"Have the cases brought in," Bernadette said, "while you're about it."

CHAPTER 15

Three o'clock in the morning. And Bernadette, asleep.

Or was she . . . ?

She thought about it for a little while and decided that no, she wasn't. She listened, meanwhile, her head lifted fractionally from the pillow, for any repetition of the sound that had woken her up. A bump in the passage outside? Or a rap on the door . . . ? She switched on the bedside lamp and looked towards the door, in time to see the heavy wrought-iron handle move through a quarter circle, then turn back again. She swung her feet out of bed, reaching for her dressing gown.

"Tracy?"

No answer. She went over to the door.

"Tracy? Is that you?"

"Yes," Tracy said, from outside. "Open up."

"I'll certainly do no such thing. What do you want?"

He said something else, but she couldn't catch the words, except for one that might have been "important." She bit her lower lip thoughtfully. "All right. Wait a moment. I'll just slip something on."

She went quickly back to the telephone on her night table.

The phone buzzed quietly in Tracy's room. In the darkness, a thump, a rattle, a muffled imprecation. He found the lamp switch, turned the light on, reached for the telephone.

"Yes?"

"Tracy?"

"Urghhhh."

"I *thought* so. Listen. Someone's trying to get into my room."

Tracy battled for a second or so with his yawn and successfully conquered it. "Must be a mistake. Someone got the wrong room number."

"No, it isn't. He's pretending to be you. I said, 'Is that you, Tracy?' and he said, 'Yes,' but he didn't sound like you, and he can't be you because you're there and he's . . . What should I do?"

It all sounded devilish complicated. "Hang on. What room are you in? I'll come round and have a look."

"Five four, fifty-four. Be *quick*."

Tracy put on his dressing gown and slippers. With one hand on the door latch, he hesitated; he'd just thought of the pistol. Well, that was what it was *for*, wasn't it? Of course he'd look a bit of a fool if it turned out to be . . . But yes. He'd better take it. He opened his suitcase and grabbed the pistol, then, clutching it nervously in his right hand, proceeded through his door and down the corridor at a pace as fast as was consonant with dignity and a rather floppy pair of bedroom slippers. His own room number was forty-eight; fifty-four would be round the corner, then the first door on the right. He stopped cautiously at the corner, peered round it . . .

There *was* someone there.

The very dim light burning in the passageway made it difficult to make out much of his appearance; he was, moreover, crouched beside the door of Bernadette's room as though listening or, possibly, fiddling with the lock. He seemed, in any case, to be concentrating deeply on whatever it was he was doing; he gave no sign of being aware of Tracy's circumspect approach, though, moving slowly over a fairly deep-pile carpet, the floppy slippers made, it was true, no noise. Tracy was able thus to attain a position almost directly behind the man's right shoulder and to pause there, wondering what to do next; the conversational opening appropriate to this occasion was one that, think as hard as he might, evaded him. "Excuse me" seemed a little overformal. "Hey!" on the other hand was overabrupt. In the end, he reached forwards and tapped the proferred shoulder firmly and, as he hoped, with authority.

The man thereupon turned, rapidly yet seemingly unhurriedly, straightening as he turned to something approaching Tracy's own height; Tracy saw again, and recognised at once, the heavy black moustache, the curved nose, the incurious light blue eyes that registered, as they rose towards his face, the pistol he still held in his right hand but did so without any apparent emotional reaction. The next moment, Tracy was chiefly aware of a sudden and unbelievably violent pain stabbing mercilessly at his groin; he doubled up with a loud burp of anguish, falling back against the wall of the passageway that held him up when, without its support, he would almost certainly have collapsed to the floor. He was also aware, though very much more vaguely, that his assailant was advancing upon him with confidence and brio, with the obvious intention of administering some kind of *coup de grâce*—most probably of a drastic and humiliating variety.

His failure immediately to bring about this desirable end had to be attributable to the fact that Tracy, more than most men of his age, was thoroughly familiar with pain; there are few things that human beings can do to you that compare to the excruciating agonies that can be inflicted by a racing car, and of not a few of these agonies Tracy had direct experience. He was able, as a result, to dismiss the head-spinning cramps that were driving like swords through his abdomen for just sufficient time to aim, at the right moment, not so much a punch as a desperate straight-arm push at his opponent; hardly a damaging blow but one that, taking Bony Wright completely by surprise, knocked him off balance and sent him staggering back to cannon awkwardly off the opposite wall. Tracy saw his teeth gleam briefly under the dark shadow of the moustache, not in a rictus of pain but in a grin of half-admiring acknowledgement; then saw, further, Wright slip one hand into his coat pocket and bring it out again holding something that at first was black and then, amazingly, alive with a cold metallic lustre. The sharp click that the switchknife blade made in springing forwards was, Tracy thought, the most frightening sound he had ever heard in his life.

At that moment, however, and as though by miraculous intervention, the door before him jerked abruptly open and he overbalanced rather than jumped through it, throwing out a hand as he went to slam it shut again. "Lock it," he said, in a weirdly gritty voice not recognisable as his own, *"Lock it"* . . . and, curled up on his hands and knees on an unending arid desert of blue carpet, heard the lock snap back into place. There was silence. The pain churned his stomach up into a cheesy, sticky morass and then, gradually, began to ebb away. He raised his head a little.

Bernadette. ". . . You all right? What happened?"

"That sod out there. He kicked me in the groin."

She moved away. There was a trickle of running water. Then the pressure of a cold, damp towel being applied (he was rather relieved to note) to his forehead. "Dashed ungentlemanly of him, hey what?"

"I'll ungentleman him all right if I get my hands on him again. Grinning little idiot. He had a knife."

"A knife? . . . Well, but you've got a gun."

"A gun?" He looked down. It was true. There it was, in his hand. He had a gun. "God," Tracy said, "I gotta *gun*." He lurched to his feet and over to the door, unlocked it, threw it open and stepped out into the corridor, gun held low at belt level and angled at that position from which, as he knew from study of spaghetti westerns, one can shoot a round half dozen baddies stone dead without moving the gun barrel more than three quarters of an inch out of its original alignment. Unfortunately, a serious shortage of baddies had now set in. The corridor was empty.

Tracy peered to his left, peered to his right; then hobbled quickly round the corner into the adjacent passageway and, loosening the waistband of his dressing gown, feverishly began to massage that part of his anatomy to which, in the excitement of the moment, he had not hesitated to allude but which motives of delicacy had prevented him from overhauling in Bernadette's presence. The assuaging effect of this treatment was immediate and, he found, immensely satisfying; throwing back his head towards the ceiling, he emitted several long, low, bovine moos of content. He was disconcerted to discover, however, on lowering his head once more, that his movements had in the interim become a subject for speculation on the part of a very small, bald, bespectacled gentleman who, clad in purple pyjamas, regarded him intently from the half-open door of a neighbouring bedroom, though with interest rather than with alarm or horror; there might—for all Tracy knew—be a special category of pervert that at three o'clock in the morning indulges in unspeakable practices in the deserted corridors of respectable English hotels, and it was possible that the bespectacled gentleman was in fact a collector and annotator of such harmless whimsies—a Jewish-American satirical novelist, conceivably—but Tracy felt, with proper British reticence, reluctant to figure, even as the result of a misapprehension, in any such a hypothetical casebook; smiling winsomely, therefore, he drew his dressing gown once more about his person and beat a retreat. Bernadette was waiting anxiously, not to say impatiently, at the door of her room; he pushed past her and, panting, subsided into the only reasonably substantial armchair provided there by an economy-conscious management. It was a hard and unyielding armchair but that, in the circumstances, was all to the good. He endeavoured to continue the treatment he had found so effective through a series of surreptitious undulations and wriggles, like those of an exceptionally nice-minded worm impaled on a fishhook.

"Well?"

"No. No good. He got away."

"Look," Bernadette said. "Scratch if you want to. Don't mind *me*."

"It's okay. Maybe tomorrow I can get them seen to. Or anyway, counted. But I'm all right for now."

"You certainly look a bit pale and worn."

"So would you, if . . . You've got no idea what it feels like."

"No," Bernadette said. "And in the natural order of things I don't suppose I ever shall. But it's all very odd, isn't it? I mean, I've had this sort of thing happen before in hotels . . . but they've always tended to rely on friendly persuasion. Maybe you gave me chap a bit of a fright."

"Yes, I had the feeling the whole thing would probably turn out to be my fault. You say it's happened *before?*"

"Well . . . Only once before. To be honest."

"And what happened then?"

"Oh, it was years ago, I'd've been about nineteen . . . Just the same thing, really. Some strange man knocked at the door and asked me to let him in."

"Good God." Tracy was aghast at this revelation of the caddishness and depravity of his own sex—always assuming that it still *was* his own sex. "And did you?"

"Why, *Mister* Tracy . . . ! I did not. Though I'll admit to having felt a certain curiosity as to what he looked like."

"You didn't know?"

"No, how *could* I have known . . . ? Without opening the door? I expect that's what they rely on, these chaps. Sheer feminine curiosity. By the way," Bernadette said, "what did *this* one look like?"

"Great huge towering red-eyed bloke. Something on the general lines of Johnny Weissmuller, but a great deal bigger and more powerfully built."

"A good job you were able to scare him off."

"Yes, wasn't it?"

"Especially if he really did have a knife. Or did you make that up, too?"

"He had a knife all right."

She thought about this for a while, seeming to find the idea somewhat disturbing. Doubtless switch-knives weren't standard equipment among those who thus sought access to her charms; Tracy, personally, wouldn't have cared to risk breaking into her bedroom armed with any instrument of intimidation less formidable than a Thompson submachine gun, but then a casual nocturnal prowler couldn't be supposed to have Tracy's intimate, if recently acquired, knowledge of Bernadette's explosive temperament at close quarters. "And if it comes to that," she said, "how do *you* come in on the deal with all this Wild Bill Hickok stuff? You don't usually carry those things around in your dressing-gown pocket, do you? I wouldn't have thought you were the type."

Tracy looked down at the pistol, the butt of which was indeed coyly protruding from the deep muted-orange folds of his Paisley pattern. "That was Mr. Greene's idea, really."

"*Dad's* idea? A *gun?*"

"He seemed to think that something like this might happen."

"I don't believe it. How could Dad know anything about it? It doesn't make any kind of sense."

This indeed was very much Tracy's opinion, and always had been. "He thought someone might try to kidnap you. I didn't think he was serious about it, but I couldn't see any harm in humouring him —so to speak."

"To *kidnap* me?"

"Yes."

"Tommy'd never do a thing like that. What would be the point of it?"

"He didn't say it was Tommy."

"But he must have *meant* Tommy. Who else?"

Tracy made a helpless gesture. The pain had now largely withdrawn, leaving in him a dull, watery ache and a sense of inordinate tiredness. "I couldn't say. But he must be someone who knows you —that chap outside. Or who knows *us*. How could he have known my name, otherwise?"

"Did he know your name?"

"*You* said he did."

"I never."

"You said he was pretending to be me."

"Oh yes. But it wasn't quite like that. I heard this sort of tapping noise at the door, you see, it wasn't exactly a knock, and I saw the door handle turning, so I said, 'Is that you, Tracy?' and the man said, 'Yes,' and I said, 'What do you want?' and he said—"

"You told me all that," Tracy said. "But what made you think it was me in the first place? What would I be doing, I mean, trying to get into your bedroom at three in the morning?"

"What, indeed," Bernadette said expressionlessly.

The question might, as Tracy now realised, be taken to have been something less than gallant. "Not that I wouldn't, or rather, not that you're not . . ."

"Whoever it was," Bernadette said, cutting across this dithering, "the excitement's over. It may have been just a sneak thief, I suppose."

No. It had been Bony Wright. Tracy hadn't been completely sure before of the correctness of his identification; he was quite sure now.

It had been Bony outside Bernadette's flat, Bony walking in the cathedral grounds, and now Bony seeking entry to Bernadette's bedroom. It was probably better, though, that Bernadette shouldn't know that; even a girl of her sanguine disposition might legitimately be alarmed at the knowledge that her footsteps were being dogged —as the saying has it—by a condemned murderer and prison escapee who seemed only too anxious to grab at any chance of presuming on a nonexistent acquaintance. But *was* it a nonexistent acquaintance? Could she conceivably *know* Bony Wright? That, of course, was what Tracy wanted to ask her; what he couldn't think of, in his present state of physical and mental desuetude, was a way of framing the question that wouldn't awake in Bernadette the most active of suspicions.

"I think he said something about a man called Keyes."

"Who did?"

"Mr. Greene. Your father. Do you know anybody name of Keyes?"

"I thought as much. It *is* something to do with Tommy."

"Why with Tommy?"

"Because he has a friend called Keyes. Or used to have. Yes, with some odd sort of a nickname . . ."

"Rusty?"

"That was it. Rusty Keyes. Oh, he has some peculiar chums, has dear old Tommy. I remember Rusty Keyes quite well. Not quite our class, darling, no . . . but not without appeal."

"Wright?"

"Ready when you are."

"I mean, have you met anyone *called* Wright?"

"Everyone's met somebody called Wright. There was a music teacher at one of my schools—"

"This would be a friend of Keyes's. Or known to him, anyway."

"And hence another friend of Tommy's?"

"Well, that's what I was wondering." Tracy shook his head, smothering another yawn. "It doesn't matter. I'd better be toddling along."

"Be sure to lock the door after you."

"How can I . . . ?" Tracy shook his head again, rather more slowly. "You'd better do just that, all the same. I don't suppose your visitor'll come back, but I can't be sure he won't. In fact I'm not sure about *anything*."

"Good night," Bernadette said.

She did, in fact, lock the door behind him; and then, before returning to bed, sat at the dressing table to view herself for a few moments in the tilted mirror. The gown she'd pulled on so hurriedly wasn't a warm and comfy wrap-around affair, like Tracy's; so far from wrapping round her, it didn't even meet in the middle, and a generally diaphanous effect had in any case been aimed at (and substantially achieved) by the kindly manufacturer. That being the case, Tracy, she thought, had remained rather noticeably unaffected. Doubtless, though, there had been what a lawyer would call extenuating circumstances. The dressing gown, she finally decided, hadn't really had a fair test.

She got back into bed and turned off the light.

Tracy, dozing quietly and peaceably in the cockpit seat, woke abruptly to the music of stuttering Spandaus; whirling his Camel round in a blinding bank, he plummeted down into the centre of the German formation, which scattered to right and left like leaves in the wind. Singling out his prey, he closed in on it rapidly, watched it veer helplessly into his levelled sights. His machine guns spoke. "Watch out," they said unexpectedly in a high-pitched staccato, "for the Hun in the sun . . . Hun-inna-sun . . . Hun-inna-sun . . ." He was still staring at them dazedly when the sinister Fokker triplane of the Red Baron disintegrated before him and cartwheeled crazily earthwards, pluming flame and greasy black smoke. "Damn good show, Tracy," the C.O. said, emerging craftily from behind a wing-strut; his voice and features bore a distinct resemblance to those of Mr. Greene. "Have to put you up for another gong." "Pretty much of a piece of cake, sir." "Keep it up, my boy, bag a few more of the bastards, *that's* the spirit." The radio meanwhile continued to entone in the background a disorganised and dispirited bulletin in which reports of gang rapes, bank robberies and prison breaks alternated with hair-raising accounts of bomber raids from which all our aircraft had returned missing, this while clutching hands lifted Tracy (Wing-Commander "Killer" Tracy, DFC) and carried him shoulder-high down the long runway at a pace that grew more and more vertiginous. "She was only the Air Vice-Marshal's daughter," the news announcer said in Tracy's ear, "but," (in a conspiratorial whisper) *"she know how to make an Immelmann turn . . ."* The scream of burning tyres drowning his voice, the Curva Grande coming up, Tracy fighting it, frantically spinning the wheel, he too screaming into the vast sonic reverberations of Air Vice-Marshal Greene's cavernous yawn, "Good show, aw good show, jolly good showwwwwwww . . ."

He woke up. *Really* woke up. He found he was sweating.
That had been a damned odd dream.

The fact of the matter was that he was more than a little confused. Not at the general haphazardness and violence of recent
events; that perplexed him, certainly, but didn't *confuse* him. No,
what was confusing him had to be Bernadette. He couldn't remember having ever, in so short a space of time, been brought so forcibly
and intimately into contact with a specifically feminine mentality—
an altogether (he thought) extraordinary phenomenon. His wife
had been a woman, too—well, of course—but altogether different;
looking back on it, he wasn't sure that he'd ever been aware of
Anne's mentality at all. Of course she'd *had* one. Obviously. You
could say that in leaving him, she'd proved it. On the other hand,
even in doing that she hadn't *surprised* him. Bernadette was surprising him all the time. It wouldn't be right, or fair, to say that he'd
always thought of Anne just as a body; there *were* girls he'd thought
of that way, yes, but not Anne. He'd married her, after all. But then
it wouldn't be right, either, to say that he was thinking of Bernadette
just as a mentality. Most emphatically, he was not. It was confusing,
right enough.

Besides, when you thought about it more closely, it wasn't really
Bernadette who was surprising him; it was he who was surprising
himself. But *because* of Bernadette. Take last night, for instance.
Rushing back out of the bedroom to have another whang at Bony
Wright—that had been completely *mad*, however you looked at it.
He'd had a gun; so what? He didn't really know how to use
the thing. The other fellow had had a knife, and could probably
skin a pea with it at twenty paces. The odds had been all one way.
Yet there he'd gone, barging out through the door like Errol crazy
Flynn, how stupid could you *get*? And *why* had he done it? He'd
been angry, certainly, as well as terribly, terribly hurt; but anger,
like pain, was something that he knew all about. You're angry all
the time on the circuit, or damned nearly, but you keep your cool
with it or else you don't finish. Last night he shouldn't have finished,
he hadn't deserved to; he should have been run off the track. What's
more, he'd known it at the time. So why, why, why?

Oh, he knew why all right. But it didn't add up. What, in the last
resort, did he care what Bernadette thought of him? People just
don't come out of these situations very well in real life, however
they behave on the telly. He was just an ex-racing driver with the
accent pretty heavily on the *ex;* he wasn't Cassius Clay. And even

as a driver, he was a self-admitted coward. So what the hell . . . ?

Yes. What the hell.

This morning, unpredictably again, Bernadette was being good as gold. Lambo was running as smoothly as ever and she was driving, it had to be admitted, pretty well; almost faultlessly, in fact. There were heavy pillars of cumulus in front of them to the west, but the Somerset hills were bright with sunshine and the radio was playing, with total appropriateness, some piano concerto or suchlike foolery by W. A. Mozart, deceased. Tracy couldn't, all the same, recapture his euphoric mood of the previous morning. It was all very well saying to himself, *What the hell.* The unpalatable fact remained.

He was confused.

By way of compensation, perhaps, he was keeping himself geographically well orientated—even more so than usual—keeping conscious check on the signposts and mileages drifting back in Lambo's unhurried wake; Chewton Mendip and Midsomer Norton, the long tree-lined straights of the Roman road, then the steep, winding descent into Bath and the usual midmorning flurry of traffic lights, of lorries grinding past the tall buildings of Cotswold stone; and underneath this vigilance, underneath his thoughts and preoccupations, a growing sense of an indefinable familiarity, a feeling that didn't emerge to full awareness until, with Bath behind them, they were bowling up the twisting hill with the deep valleys opening up to their left and bringing him, extended to the sunlight, a small, unexpected shock of surprise. Because it was true; this was the West Country. Hills and moors and lanes and hedges, dips and sudden vistas, always with the damp warmth of the Atlantic breezes in the air. Tracy hadn't driven this way in he couldn't remember how many years, but it was as though each eastwards-slanting tree they now passed, each five-barred gate, each narrow dock-fringed sideroad was known to him. Because this was Somerset, his home county. He'd left it and now he was back. The trees, the gates, the roads weren't the ones that he'd climbed and swung on and walked down twenty years ago, twenty miles and more farther west, yet they were exactly the same. *He* was different. Not just older, but different. Hence he felt this strange, very gentle sadness, like a faint, disturbing ache in the mind. The names on the signposts didn't help at all; SWAINSWICK, COLD ASHTON, MARSHFIELD, DYRHAM PARK . . .

"What do we do when we get to Bristol?"

"We don't. We've gone the other way. We'll be back on the motorway in five minutes."

"Are we still in Somerset?"

Well, no. They weren't, come to think of it. Which went to show how silly the whole thing was. "We're about five miles into Gloucestershire."

Bernadette clicked her tongue. "Don't you *ever* need a map?"

"Sometimes," Tracy said.

The names on the signposts didn't mean anything very much to Bony Wright, travelling unostentatiously a thousand yards or so behind them; he'd never been through this area before and wouldn't much care if he never did again. The wide swathe of the M4 stretching downhill and away to the west came to him as pretty much of a welcome sight; tracking Lambo on the motorway was far easier a task than snooping discreetly after it through an endless succession of curves and hills and valleys and busy crossroads, and this morning he, like Tracy, had a vague preoccupation at the back of his mind . . . Not one that disturbed in any way his relentless concentration on the job in hand, but simply a problem that, from time to time in moments of relative relaxation, he allowed himself to consider, this being, in his experience, the best way to handle problems that seemed to arise from some temporary malfunction of his normally excellent memory. He knew now—had learnt last night—that the name of the man in the car in front was Tracy. And somewhere, some time ago, he had seen this Tracy before.

Even the best-regulated of memories can play peculiar tricks. The face of the man he'd seen in Albemarle Street had been, as he'd have sworn, quite unfamiliar; yet now that a name could be put to it, a certain contact had been made in his brain and a little warning bell was silently ringing. As yet it was only a contact, not a connection—that was the trouble. It was odd, but something that could with profit be thought about; it wasn't idle speculation, it was something he'd forgotten. Something that had slipped his mind. Like the name of that geezer who'd copped out; Foreman? Redman? What was it . . . ? That didn't matter, though. Remembering who Tracy was; that just possibly did.

There was fairly heavy traffic on the motorway. He moved out into the fast lane, closing the distance between the Mini and leisurely Lambo to five hundred yards, then returned to the slow lane, screened from his quarry by a round half-dozen cars and a couple of vans. From the slow lane, he could keep an eye on the turn-offs. He didn't think it'd be Bristol, though, or they'd hardly have come up through Bath. It looked to him very like the Severn Bridge. Tracy, now. Tracy. Who the *hell* was Tracy . . . ?

CHAPTER 16

There was a dip and then a rise and then, through a gap in the encroaching hills, a glimpse of the sea, with the coastal slopes visible on the far side of the estuary and with grey and white towers of cloud piled up beyond them. There was a signpost of weather-beaten wood that said, Y BANNAU, and a narrow one-track road winding westwards across the moor with another sign that said, PRIVATE, and in the distance, on the flank of a slope thrust out like a finger towards the sea itself, there was a grey stone house. A cottage, also of grey stone, stood in a walled garden on the far side of the road and marking the junction. These were the only buildings in sight, unless you counted the broken walls of a ruined barn that interrupted the otherwise perfectly blank monotony of the long matching slope that rolled, like an enormous wave, towards them from the east. Lambo, stopped at the side of the road, hummed quietly to itself in neutral gear, awaiting its owner's next behest. "Well," its owner said, "there it is."

"Ah."

"Looks damned desolate, I expect you're thinking. And appearances don't deceive."

"Uh-huh."

He seemed a little inattentive, Bernadette thought; as though his mind were elsewhere. Then, following Tracy's gaze towards the front lawn of the cottage, she saw, at some fifty paces' distance and extended on a brightly coloured armchair, a very apparent reason for this lack of alertness. "I'm glad," she said, engaging first gear and laudably contriving to do so smoothly, "you can find *some* sort of distraction in these primitive surroundings. But do you think perhaps we might now continue?"

"Okay," Tracy said. "Perhaps when we get there your husband can lend me a good pair of field glasses."

"I'm quite sure he can," Bernadette said acidly. "He'll probably give you an introduction, if that's what you want. He's a friendly fellow, is our Peeping Thomas. Likes to get on well with the neighbours."

The blonde didn't turn her head as Lambo purred past, but remained gazing up at the sky through huge blue-tinted sunglasses. Or, possibly, continued to sleep. "Wasn't there a song," Tracy said, "about a polka-dot bikini? I seem to remember—"

"If so, it'd be *well* before my time."

"Ah," Tracy said; and became thoughtful.

Lambo moved slowly, cautiously, down the narrow driveway, bringing the bleak façade of the grey house steadily nearer. It certainly was remarkably isolated, standing like a solitary cliff against which the long swell of the moor silently lapped; the driveway was flanked to either side by low walls of undressed granite, one of which swung across and rose in height to cut off, rather than to shelter, the northern side of the building, leaving as the only apparent means of access a heavy wrought-iron gate that stood open, unattended. Beyond the gate was a cobbled yard where, as Tracy now saw, a car was already parked in the lee of a squat outbuilding—probably the former stable. The place looked rather like a farmhouse, but of course you knew that it wasn't. There was no farm smell. There was no smell at all. Only that of the moorland, rising on a hot dry southwest breeze, and a faint tang of ozone and of diesel oil coming in from the sea. Once the moor had maybe provided grazing ground for sheep; the grass there was short and remarkably smooth. But there weren't any sheep there now. And no trees. Tracy peered out of the side window as Bernadette negotiated the gate and slid Lambo gently to a halt; from the house, a nearby window-frame rattled and jerked noisily downwards on its protesting sash. Then a man's face and shoulders appeared. A round, red face with a roughly trimmed moustache and an irritated expression.

"And what the hell happened to *you?*" Tommy Pope said.

He didn't sound like a friendly fellow at all.

CHAPTER 17

In fact it was at Bernadette that this courteous enquiry was directed; and during the touching marital reunion that immediately followed, Tracy found himself ignored completely. He occupied himself usefully in the meantime transporting Bernadette's luggage from the car through to the foot of the long staircase inside the hallway, while from the front room the raised voices of Mr. and Mrs. Pope bickered away anxiously at each other. Uncertain what to do next, he leaned against the wall and rubbed his left toecap against his right calf, surveying the grim mezzotint landscapes with which the hallway had unaccountably been furnished, until the growing audibility of the voices suggested a movement in his direction. ". . . I mean, look at it. What the hell of a mess."

"Well, you can't get anyone in to do the cleaning. It's eighty miles from anywhere." Pope now sounded aggrieved rather than annoyed; doubtless in the space of some four minutes Bernadette had contrived to put him irrevocably and irretrievably in the wrong. "You couldn't clean it up yourself," she now announced sarcastically. "I quite see that. Which is my room?"

"*Your* room? You're not staying here, are you?"

"Of course I am. I didn't come all this way just for the pleasure of a chat." And Bernadette emerged, huffily. She glanced briefly at Tracy and recognised him almost at once. "Oh, you've got the cases. Bring them upstairs, will you?"

Tote that barge. *Lift* that bale. "Yessuh, màm, Ah sho' will," Tracy said.

Pope came through the door to watch perplexedly as Tracy picked up the cases again, acknowledging this time his presence— or perhaps merely this surprising display of physical activity—with an abrupt upwards lift of the chin, hardly definite enough to be called a nod. "Come *on*," Bernadette said, from halfway up the stairs. Tracy, who in view of the steepness of the treads had thought it only gentlemanly to give her a good start, sighed to himself and plodded up the flight, head lowered, creaking thunderously. It wasn't all that *old* a house. Victorian, maybe. But strongly built, yes, that it was. The walls looked to be all of two feet thick. And dry, too, judging by the noise the floorboards made.

At the head of the stairs, a narrow passageway turning off at right angles and, on the left, a door that already stood open. "In here," Bernadette said; her voice booming oddly, as though heard from outside a cavern. Tracy went in and put the suitcases down on the floor. There was a Windsor chair beside the door; he sat down on it, breathing heavily. Bernadette was standing by the window and staring out of it; even from where Tracy sat, there was a spectacular view.

"How old is this house . . . ? I was just wondering."

"I suppose about a hundred years. My great-grandfather built it, or had it built. Being some kind of a nut."

"That's Mr. Greene's grandfather?"

"He was in the shipping business, or so I'm told. Barry docks. He could sit here and watch his ships come in and probably punch them in on a time clock, the old bastard. Yes, this is where it all started."

"I didn't know," Tracy said. "I'm not very well up in your family history."

"Oh, it's great stuff. Someone ought to do a television series. *The Bernadette Saga.*" She moved over to the dressing table and sat down in front of it, drawing a finger across its surface and examining the result with a grimace. "Of course the place has been modernised. It's filthy, but it's modernised throughout. I suppose you can't cook?"

"After a fashion," Tracy said cautiously.

"But naturally you can. I'd forgotten I was dealing with *der Übermensch.*"

"Eh?"

"Anything I can do, you can do better—isn't that it?"

Tracy rubbed his nose pensively. "I'd say my powers are rather limited, but I'm content with them, on the whole. Except," he said, "that I wouldn't mind some of that lil ol' X-ray vision once in a while. Come in handy, that would."

"If it's that blonde down there in the deckchair you're thinking of, it's hardly necessary. She's meeting you *more* than halfway."

"I wasn't thinking of that so much." But being so reminded, he rose and took, in his turn, a peek out of the window. You couldn't see the cottage from that angle, but you could certainly see an awful lot of sea; the house, he now realised, had to be perched almost on the edge of a substantial cliff. Galsworthy might have found that symbolical; Tracy found it only mildly terrifying. He didn't like heights. "Anyway, I'd rather be the Lone Ranger. Then you could be Silver. His horse, of course."

"Our tastes in literature clearly differ widely."

"There ought to be room for agreement on other topics. You coolum down now, smokum pipe of peace?"

"Better drinkum pint of beer, if you ask me. You go on downstairs and Tommy'll give you one. I want to get changed."

"Okay," Tracy said affably.

". . . Tracy?"

He paused with one hand on the doorknob. "What?"

"Don't worry. I'll coolum down all right."

"Good."

"It's just that I'm in for a sticky spell with Tommy. I can see that. But I can handle it. Really I can."

"Yes," Tracy said. "I'm sure of it."

Pope had put on a good deal of weight since Tracy had last seen him, and his cheeks—marked, as Tracy had remembered, with prominent red veins—seemed heavier and looser. Otherwise, he wasn't greatly changed. "Sure you wouldn't fancy something a little stronger?"

"No, thanks."

"Please yourself. It's tinned beer, I'm afraid. Every bloody thing's tinned in this place."

Tracy sampled the proferred beverage. "It's cold, anyway."

"Oh yes," Pope said glumly. "It's cold all right."

He himself was taking his refreshment out of a gin bottle and seemed already to have downed a considerable quantity. The effects of it weren't specially noticeable in his movement or in his speech, but he seemed to have a little difficulty in focussing on Tracy's face when, as now, he levelled towards it one of his childishly puzzled stares. "So you work for old man Greene? He's my father-in-law."

"I know."

"Well, you would. Of course you would. But where?"

"Where what?"

"Where d'you *work*, I mean, dash it."

"I run a repair shop for him. In Brighton."

"Ah, then *that's* where I've seen you before."

"That's it. With the Alvis."

"The Alvis, Good Lord, yes, the dear old Alvis. Traded it in a while back. Got a Bentley now. Suppose you must be pretty much in the old boy's confidence these days, if he entrusts you with these delicate missions . . ."

That was one way of looking at it. "He asked it as a favour," Tracy said guardedly, "and I'm hardly in a position to refuse."

"I wanted to thank you, anyway. For bringin' along the squaw."

"That's all right," Tracy said, taken aback both by this unexpected magnanimity and by this incursion into his own Lone Ranger idiom. "It was a pleasure." Perhaps, he thought, it was ill-advised to put it in quite that way, even to so broadly permissive a husband as Pope appeared to be; but Pope seemed to be paying little attention to what he was saying, anyway.

"How does that thing go? Squaw on the hippopotamus, what? Damn clever, really, how he worked it out. That feller."

"What feller?"

"*You* know. Euclid. Or rather that other one. Pythagoras. Couldn't've been easy for him, not at all easy, with all the other buggers countin' backwards."

"How do you mean, backwards?"

"The Greeks. They *all* did, dincha know? Sheer bloody ignorance but there it is. Same with the Persians, that Cyrus or whatever his name was. Seized the throne by force at the age of sixteen and came to grief in a pitched battle thirty years earlier. That's what makes Classical history so bloody tricky, far as I'm concerned. Never quite got the hang of it myself. Do any Classical history at *your* school?"

"I believe we did, but I can't say I remember—"

"They make quite a thing of it at Eton, quite a thing of it. And I passed, mind you. I passed the exam all right. I took twelve O levels at Eton, believe it or not. That's me all over. When I set out to do something, I usually manage it. I'm not stupid."

"Twelve O levels, eh?" At a loss for words, Tracy shook his head in awestruck admiration.

"Rather goes to prove my point, don't you think so? You got a *brain* in there, Pope, m'tutor used to say. What's more, the dodderin' old sod was right for once. That's why I know, d'you see?—I *know* what those fellers went through. I know just how they felt. Euclid and Pymonidas and all that lot. It's just the same today. Sheer bloody ignorance, that's what you're up against. Ignorance, stupidity—it's all the same. But I'll tell you something, you, what's your name—you know what still wins out? What wins out all the time . . . ? No, listen, will you? *Listen.* I'm tellin' you. *Brains* what's still wins out. Brains. The old grey matter. Every time."

"Yes. Like with Ulysses," Tracy said, happily conscious of having now caught on.

"Look, Ulysses . . . Listen. No. *Listen.*"

"I am."

"I mean, tell me now. Man to man. What d'you think of him? Of that feller?"

No. He'd lost it again. He'd certainly need something stronger than beer if this went on. "Who? Ulysses?"

But this afforded Pope no end of amusement. "That's it! Ulysses Schmulysses! Old Leopold Bloomysses himself, you got it in one!" He doubled himself up in a paroxysm of mirth, somehow contriving at the same time to retain in his right hand his glass of gin-and-lime unspilt—indeed, virtually unrippled. "Old Jew-boy Leo. No, honestly though, what d'you make of him? A tough cookie, would you say? A real little know-it-all? Hard man to cross . . . ? Go on and give me your honest opinion. *I* won't mind."

"It's Lewis you're talking about?" Tracy wanted to be sure.

"He and no other."

"Well, but since he's a friend of yours—"

"And of Bernie's, *and* of Bernie's."

"Yes, *and* of Bernie's, it's a little difficult—"

"Well now, look. Old Jew-boy Leo, I got him right *here*." Pope indicated with his index finger an imaginary spot on the table where the gin bottle stood, ground down on it fiercely with his thumb. "That's where I got him. *There*. I mean, *friend*, he'd cut my throat for ninepence, that little mother would. To be more exact, he'd cut *anyone's* throat for ninepence. He'd do mine for free. Why doesn't he, then . . . ? Good question. I'm glad you asked me that. I'll tell you why he doesn't. He doesn't because he doesn't dare—*that's* why he doesn't. That's why not. And why doesn't he dare? Because I've got him—"

Tracy nodded. "There."

"And nowhere else but. Just givin' you an example, you see, to prove my point. It's a tough old world, I'm not denyin' it. But if you got brains an' can use 'em, there's always a way. You want to remember that, er . . . er . . ."

"Tracy."

"Tracy, Tracy, of course, yes, me old friend Tracy, well, just remember what I'm tellin' you, Tracy. Good advice and I wouldn't give it to anyone, I really wouldn't, except to me dear friend . . . Tracy . . . Did you say, by the way, your name was *Tracy?*"

"It was and is. T–r–a–c–y. Tracy."

"No E?"

"Without an E."

"Without an E, you say? Unusual, that. 'Cidedly unusual."

He peered suspiciously into his now empty glass, as though in hopes of discovering there this mysteriously missing vowel; then, giving up the search, darted a swift glance at Tracy's necktie. He had probably tried for Tracy's face again and missed.

". . . The thing is, Tracy boy, if so I may call you, you should have got here yesterday. Yesterday afternoon, to be exact. So what's it all about, eh . . . ? *That's* what I want to know."

"Yes," Tracy said. "Well, we had a slight mishap."

"I know, I know, she told me. But you ought to know better than to go round crashing cars all over the place. It's not the sort of—"

"It wasn't his fault," Bernadette said, entering unexpectedly but right on cue. "It was mine. And you'd best stay on the right side of Tracy, 'cos he's about to cook us all some lunch."

"Is he?" Pope thought about this for a while, swaying from one foot to the other and pouring himself out another glass of gin as he did so. "Ah. Yes, that's not such a bad idea."

CHAPTER 18

The kitchen was long and dark and stone-tiled and, like the other rooms of the house, in pretty much of a mess. The heavy table in the centre was littered with empty tins and with food packets, and someone had spilt onto it a good deal of sugar; there were, therefore, not surprisingly, a number of fat and contented flies buzzing lethargically around. A heterogeneous collection of conveniences had been installed along the far wall, and these no doubt would represent the modernisation to which Bernadette, in passing, had alluded: an electric cooker with heated cloth rail, a dishwasher, a gigantic refrigerator with a deep-freeze compartment—all these oddments were in working order. There didn't seem to be a pantry, but in the corner there was a large wooden cabinet in which the main food supply had been carelessly stashed; nearly all of it was in cans, so Pope had been right about that, at least. Tracy morosely inspected a few of the labels, which failed to infect him with their mood of frenetic optimism (*STEAK CHUNKY-LUNKS*, Dripping With Goodness), and then, leaving the cabinet door open to give the tins an airing, went back to the table and started to clear up.

The dustbins were in the outer courtyard, outside the kitchen door. Tracy, lifting the lid of the nearest, was mildly surprised that a certain amount of clearing up had been done already; the bin was half full, at any rate, of an odd miscellany of articles in which tins, again, and empty bottles predominated. Beer bottles, mostly. Tracy added his own modest contribution, replaced the lid and turned to look thoughtfully about him. The grey stone outbuilding—stable, garage, whatever it was—was now directly in front of him; the door was closed, but leaning drunkenly inwards on a parted hinge. Tracy crossed the yard, which wasn't very wide, and contrived with some effort to lift the latch and pull the door open. Inside, it was very nearly dark. He could make out nothing, initially, but a few feet of grey concrete floor. There was no smell of petrol or of hay or of anything else that he could determine. If there were windows, they had been boarded up. Tracy struck a match. It sputtered and went out. He tried again.

This time the flame stayed alive long enough for him to glimpse bare cobwebby walls, a bare floor completely empty; to his right, however, there was another door that, unlike the wall, seemed clear of cobwebs. He shuffled cautiously towards it, the match dying in his fingers as he moved, and, fumbling in the darkness, found the door handle. The door wasn't locked and the hinges seemed, indeed, to have been recently oiled. He edged it open. Bright light shafted through the crack.

A very definite smell now. Tobacco smoke. But still no sound. Tracy pushed the door wider open, looked in. Another room, smaller as far as he could judge, again with bare walls and concrete floor but not dark at all; sunlight was flooding in through two tall westward-facing windows. There were chairs, shelves, and a trestle table covered with an oilcloth; on the table, magazines, a newspaper, a confusion of playing cards. A man sat at the table, reading a comic. A cigarette burned between his lips, the smoke spiralling straight up into the air in a thin blue-grey tendril. Someone tapped Tracy lightly on the shoulder.

"Don't just stand there, Mr. Tracy. Go on in."

Tracy's reactions weren't as fast as, in a rather similar situation, Bony Wright's had been. He didn't even look round. He stepped, instead, into the room, and the other man followed him, closing the door silently behind him. The other man was tall and well dressed; the corners of his mouth were pulled down, deepening the creases that ran from nostril to chin. This gave him a sad expression. He probably wasn't sad, though; he always looked like that. His name was Starshine. The man sitting at the table looked up briefly, nodded, then went on reading.

"Looking for us, were you?"

"Not really," Tracy said. "Wondering where you were, that's all."

The tall man rubbed his chin. His name wasn't *really* Starshine; it was Stashin. But people had called him Starshine for years and years. He had served under that name—or so they said—in some obscure cloak-and-dagger branch of the British Army, and what was good enough for the British Army had to be good enough, surely, for everyone else. Where he came from didn't much matter. He had light grey Baltic eyes and wide Slavonic cheekbones and certain unimportant difficulties with his consonants; none of that mattered at all. He was Starshine, and had been Starshine since the war, and was now a famous man, in his way. "You knew we were here?"

"I knew someone was somewhere," Tracy said. "There's a lot of beer bottles in those dustbins. And Pope doesn't seem to be a beer man."

"Ah," Starshine said, and went on fondling his chin.

"Besides, I saw the talent. Down there in the cottage."

"The talent?"

"Jenny the Benny. She's quite a long way from home."

"You *know* Jenny?"

"By sight, yes. And there's certainly plenty to see. Kind of attracting attention, isn't she?—stuck out there in a deckchair? Or is she opening up a local branch?"

Starshine lowered his hand, clicked his fingers irresolutely. "Yes —the urban amenities. How can we get by without them? Life in the country gets boring after a while. Don't you find?"

The man with the comic snorted, by way of sufficient comment. Starshine glanced towards him, a quick, calculating flick of the eyes devoid of implication. "That's Tony. You won't know Tony. He's from the smoke."

"Good morning, Tony," Tracy said. Tony nodded again without looking up. He was a fellow who took his reading seriously. Starshine, with both hands now at his sides, moved his weight to his left foot, back to his right, a little weaving movement like a boxer's. "Boring. Yes. Very boring. If Jenny feels like taking the sun, I don't see why that need worry you. Or concern you at all."

"It doesn't," Tracy said. "Anyway, things may get a bit livelier for you now I've delivered the goods."

"The goods?"

"Bernadette."

"Ah. Bernadette."

"Who did you think I meant?"

"I didn't really know what you meant at all," Starshine said. "You express yourself very obscurely, Mr. Tracy, at times. Mr. Pope, he's just the same. You public school chentlemen, you really have a language of your own."

"You knew what I meant all right," Tracy said. "So what's with chummy?"

"With *chummy?*"

"The rest of the goods you've been expecting. He's due in any time now. He's been right behind us all the way."

"Take a seat," Starshine said. "Make yourself at home. Perhaps I should get to the bottom of your remarks."

He pulled out a chair from the table with a courtly and somewhat head-waiterish gesture. His hand—large and white and furred with dark hairs—rested for a moment on the bar of the chair, then dropped again to his side. Tracy sat down, staring at the copy of *Penthouse* on the table in front of him; the girl on the cover looked very like Jenny, but then all these overdeveloped bits of crumpet look alike anyway. He hadn't been *sure* it was Jenny; with those giant sunglasses on, her face had been effectively masked. It had just been another good guess.

"It sounds like there are things I ought to know," Starshine said. "Such as how far you're in on this deal."

"Mr. Greene wasn't very exact."

"Now that surprises me. Mr. Greene is a very exact man. His instructions to me, they were very exact."

It's all right when the guesses are good guesses, but you can get overconfident and that's dangerous. Because sooner or later you'll make a bad one, and a bad guess is a mistake, and a mistake with people like Starshine . . . Yes. That's dangerous. So why, Tracy asked himself, am I making guesses at all? "I can imagine that they would be."

"A very fine thing, is imagination. I admire it. That's because I'm a practical man myself, and being practical I like things cut and dried—as they say. Cards on the table. So I know where I stand. You know what I mean . . . ? more or less?"

You mean you think I'm making a lot of good guesses. "I understand you perfectly," Tracy said.

"Let me put it this way. *You* haven't been told to kill anybody, I take it?"

"No. Neither have you."

Starshine clicked his tongue. "A form of words. A form of words. We're not talking about words—at least, *I* am not. I am talking of practical realities. Try and remember."

He had been standing directly behind Tracy; now he moved round, unhurriedly, and seated himself not at, but on, the table, thrusting his hands deep into his pockets where they played with unascertainable objects, possibly loose change. "All right," Tracy said. "Let's name names." Why not, after all? He wasn't selling or bargaining for anything. Or he didn't think so.

"By all means."

"Bony Wright. Would *that* name have figured in your instructions?"

"Would it have figured in yours?"

"No," Tracy said. "But like I said, they weren't exact."

"Yet you say we should shortly expect a visit?"

"That was a guess."

"An informed guess?"

"Yes."

"Yes. You've seen him, perhaps?"

"He's been following us," Tracy said. "All the way from London.

Last night we stopped at a hotel and he caught up with us there—
or with Bernadette, since it's Bernadette he's after. That's not
a guess, that's obvious. Then the day before yesterday I called at
Bernadette's flat and there was a dead man there. His name was
Rusty Keyes. Wright probably killed him, but I don't know why.
And I don't know what he wants with Bernadette. Do you?"

Starshine ignored this last question. "When you say he caught
up with you last night . . . what happened exactly?"

"He tried to get into Bernadette's room. I sort of intervened, not
very successfully, and he went away."

"Yes, but how did you know who it was? You've never seen him
before."

"I've seen his photograph. In the papers."

"And Bernadette?"

"She hasn't seen him yet. She thinks it was a prowler or something like that. I don't really know *what* she thinks."

"I see," Starshine said.

He unhitched himself from the table and went over to the window. His head and broad shoulders were silhouetted for a moment against the sunlight before he turned into profile, head
lowered in thought. "It's sensible of you to tell me all this, Mr.
Tracy. But I can't trade information with you. You have to know
that."

"You could say it was none of my business."

"I could. And I will. If I were you, I'd go back to Brighton. Now.
Right away. To imagine things, to suppose things . . . Yes, that's
natural. But curiosity—"

"I know what curiosity did. That's the trouble. I'm worried."

"Why?"

"I've told you what I know. It isn't much. But it could be too much
from Mr. Greene's point of view."

Starshine shook his head slowly. "That's nothing to do with me."

"Indirectly, yes. It all depends on what's going to happen to Bony
Wright, if and when he gets here."

"That, too, you can imagine. But guesses, as such, do no harm.
You won't be able to *prove* anything, will you . . . ? I don't think
Mr. Greene is worried by guesses. He's a practical johnny like me.
Of course, if you were thinking of asking him for a little more
money, I've no doubt he'd be reasonable. But I wouldn't, in your
place, be greedy. I really wouldn't."

"I'm not a greedy man," Tracy said. "I don't want any more
money."

"I'm glad to hear it. It's so easy to give way to temchation . . . Oh, I know, I've been through it all myself. Having been involved in quite a large number of what you might call professional secrets. But then one learns to be discreet. It's best."

"It's different for you, though. You're a professional. You've got your ethics, and your reputation."

"Exactly so," Starshine said. "Exactly so."

"Bony Wright's a professional, too. You think you can take him? Just the two of you?"

"I think so. So does Mr. Greene, which is more to the point. And in fact there are three of us. We work in shifts."

"But you can't cover the whole house from here."

"Take a look," Starshine said.

Tracy got up and stood beside him at the window. The outlook was westwards, over the barren moor and down the approach road to the distant cottage; a mile-wide sweep of downwards-sloping and close-cropped grass and heather. Tommy Pope was leaning on the low stone wall by the iron gate talking earnestly to Bernadette, who was sitting on the wall, shoulders hunched and feet dangling; they were perhaps some twenty yards away. It'll certainly be difficult, if not impossible—Tracy thought—to come up the road or walk over the moor without being spotted. "What about the other side, though?"

"There *is* no other side," Starshine said. "You haven't yet grasped the geography of this place. The house is built on a promontory. On the other three sides there are cliffs. Very steep. Too steep to climb. No, it's up the road or across the moor. There isn't any other way."

"Yes, but once it gets dark—"

"At night we have other arrangements. You'll forgive me if I don't discuss them with you. The point about the cliffs is that they are otherwise convenient. There's a substantial depth of water at the base, even at low tide. Believe me," Starshine said, "it's a great convenience when one can arrange these details beforehand. People think that in my profession you just go bang-bang, and that's *it*. Nothing of the kind. It's when you've *gone* bang-bang that the difficulties really begin. That's what the Krays never really understood."

"They took Rusty Keyes off in a laundry basket."

"Who did?"

"Bernadette's boy friend fixed it. Lewis, his name is."

"Yes. I've met him. Well, there you are. I expect he had to arrange things very quickly, but even so . . . Keyes'll be found, of course. Soon. Very soon. Not very satisfactory. But here, you see, they have what is called the rip tide. A local phenomenon. A suitably weighted object will be sucked out to sea and won't appear again for weeks, possibly months . . . perhaps never. You see now what I meant about there being no proof, Mr. Tracy, that might support your guesses. There won't be any at all. That's all part of the service."

"Maybe after all you're telling me a bit too much."

"No. Just enough. Enough to convince you that discretion is really your only course. Go back to Brighton and mend your motor-cars—that's a sensible, rational occupation, and one that I'm told you do well. I very much envy you. Mine is really a sad and stupid business. Have no part in it. Not even as a favour to Mr. Greene. I'm giving you good advice now. In fact, the best."

"Everyone's giving me advice this morning. But I don't really need it. I'm convinced."

"Good," Starshine said. "I'm glad that you don't. And are."

CHAPTER 19

The bus stop was a couple of hundred yards down the road from the cottage. There seemed to be no special reason for its being so situated, or indeed any reason for there being a bus stop there at all. There was only the moor and the grey ribbon of the road and a very faint smoky haze rising over the Vale of Glamorgan; in the other direction, looking south, the sea, the Somerset coastline and high above England, stretched out across the sky, great torn pillars of broken cumulus with dark edges. Overhead the sun still shone, but there was a heavy stickiness to the air; the barometer had fallen since the morning. It was going to rain, and probably hard.

Lambo was parked just beyond the bus stop. Bernadette sat in the driver's seat and Tracy sat beside her.

"You didn't eat all yours, either," Tracy said.

"I'm not fond of carrots."

It was ten past four. The Cardiff bus was due along in five minutes' time.

"And I wasn't all that hungry, anyway."

"You're a good eater, usually," Tracy said.

"You noticed that, did you . . . ? That's the thing about the country. It isn't restful at all, like people say. It makes me nervous."

"All this emptiness."

"Yes."

She tapped her fingertips against the steering wheel, then took her hands away and folded them in her lap. Tracy stared out through the windscreen at the yellowing grass, the long purplish-brown crests of the slopes, at the blue-grey sea. There were no trees. That was why it seemed so empty. No trees, no people.

"I suppose you'd really like to have him back."

"Who? Tommy?"

"Yes."

"I'd be a fool."

She didn't deny it, though.

"I don't know," Tracy said. "It all depends."

"But what makes you say . . . ?"

"Oh, just a feeling I had. Besides, girls who really *want* to ditch their husbands don't usually find it necessary to talk to them about it first. They just go ahead and do it. I mean, why not?"

"But I explained all that. It's not as easy as you think."

Probably it wasn't. Always there were wheels within wheels. "Maybe not," Tracy admitted.

"Was that what *your* wife did?"

"Eh?"

"Just up sticks and left?"

"Well, yes. In a way."

"You should be grateful to her. That's the kindest thing, as well as the easiest. But then why the hell," Bernadette demanded, "should I be kind to that bastard? When has he been kind to *me?* It's never been like that between us. Never."

"No. All the same, if I were you I'd pick my fight some place else and at some other time. Don't push him right now. Get out of here as quick as you can."

"But I only just got here."

"I know."

"There's something wrong," Bernadette said. "Isn't there?"

"Wrong about what?"

"About Tommy. About this place. He's hiding from something, I'm sure of it. Not that there's anything unusual about that, he's always disappearing for one reason or another. Vanishing, popping up again . . . Now that I'm here I don't even know why I came. He's behaving damned oddly. What was it he was talking to you about?"

"When?"

"While I was getting changed?"

"Oh . . . Pythagoras. Euclid. All kinds of things."

"You'd think he was a bit mental. But he isn't. *I* probably am. I don't know what I want, that's the truth of the matter. Well, maybe *that's* what I came for."

"To make up your mind?"

"Yes. Or to have it made up for me. But now that I'm here, it all seems so silly."

Tracy went on staring out of the windscreen. He could see now a quiver of rising dust, down in the valley. "Here comes the bus," he said. And, as an afterthought:

"It's empty, all right."

He might have meant the bus. But Bernadette didn't think so.

It came rumbling to a halt and Tracy, carrying his suitcase, clambered aboard. There were indeed plenty of vacant seats; Tracy swung his case up onto the luggage rack, sat down and turned to look out of the window. Bernadette waved. He waved back. Goodbye, goodbye. Lambo moved off with a throaty snarl from the exhaust pipes, headed back to the house; the bus, with a derisively arthritic cough, lumbered forwards in the opposite direction. Tracy sat back in the seat and closed his eyes briefly.

"Cardiff, sir? All the way?"

"All the way," Tracy said.

The telephone line to Cardiff wasn't a good one.

"I can't hear you."

"Weapon to tracer."

"What?"

"I said, what *happened* to—"

"He's just left. She's taken him down to the bus stop. The *bus stop*."

"What about Bernie?"

"Yes."

"What d'you mean, yes?"

"Yes, *what* about her?"

"When's she leaving?"

"I don't know. It isn't so easy."

"What?"

"It isn't so *easy*."

"Well, you got to do something about it, old sport. We want her" (mumble) (click) "as soon as possible."

"All right. You want her, you come and get her."

"That'd be damned silly."

"What?"

"Be *damned silly* if I showed up there now. Well, wouldn't it?"

"You really think he's here? I don't see how—"

"We have to assume he is, don't we?—or there's not much point in the whole bloody exercise."

"Hey," Pope said. "I could hear you quite clearly just then."

"Yes, it sort of comes and goes. The thing to do now is just sit tight and play it cool. Leave everything to Starshine. And get Bernie out the way as soon as you can, now she's done her bit."

"Freesian crumbs."

"*What?*"

"*Here she comes.* I'll call you back later."

There was a good chance—Tracy thought—that he'd be home by midnight, or shortly after. Back home in his pad off the Steyne, with an old Glenn Miller record turning on the pick-up and the familiar growl of a late returner revving up outside on the corner and, when he opened the window, a warm damp breeze coming in from the sea. He wouldn't, presumably, have to go in to work tomorrow; he could go to the bank instead and deposit the best part of five hundred pounds and see his account move out of the red for once. It wasn't all that large a sum, but it wasn't bad for three days' work—if you could call it work. And as he'd said, he wasn't a greedy man. Lazy—yes, certainly. But greedy, no.

Starshine, after all, had said nothing but the truth. Running a garage, that was Tracy's job. Running a garage you meet all kinds of people. Some of them aren't very pleasant and many of them aren't very honest, but you learn how to deal with them and you get along with them somehow. But not with people like Starshine. People like Starshine you don't learn how to deal with, not if you're wise; you don't deal with them at all. Still less with people like Bony Wright—not that there could be very many like *him.* Tommy Pope was another matter; there were plenty of people like Pope. You heard this about him and that about him, but it was all rumour; you can't judge a man on rumour. Not that it was a matter of making judgements, exactly. It was a matter of comparing the rumour to the reality.

The difference could be rather terrifying. Like now, for instance. Down in Brighton you often got the buzz—as Deason put it; that so-and-so had the word out for somebody else, that Skinny Woods was "out of town," while the fellow with the heavy gambling debts was conveniently "gone to the health farm," oh, all kinds of rumours were constantly flying, they all helped to make life interesting and to keep the competition lively. Of course it wasn't like in the old race-gang days of *Brighton Rock* that Tracy couldn't anyway have remembered, still less like those weird places in the States where you talked all the time about "connections" and "contracts"; when all was said and done, this was *England,* dammit. Now and again, it was true, people did get killed, but then what had happened was an "accident"; there'd been a sad misunderstanding somewhere along the line, just a friendly warning was what had been intended, someone had lost his head, gone a little bit too far. Nobody liked accidents, nobody wanted them. The red-haze merchants were out. That was why nobody wanted Bony Wright. That was why everybody wanted Starshine. Bony wasn't booked for an accident; he was going to escape abroad, simply to disappear; in a few weeks' time he'd be "reported" as having been seen in Australia, in Canada, in Italy, it didn't matter where, then the trail would peter out and everyone would forget it. That was the decent English way of doing things. Bony killed, and didn't tidy up; he might as well have been a foreigner, or even an American; he rocked the jolly old boat, that was the point. He just *had* to be unpopular.

All this Tracy knew about—in theory. In other words, he knew about the rumours. But now he'd come up against the reality. He'd been to a health farm, had cooked lunch there; a perfectly ordinary building—what else was to be expected?—and a perfectly ordinary lunch. Starshine had talked to him there about killing a man, and this had been part of a perfectly ordinary conversation—and again, why not? Tracy, listening to him, had been frightened. Now, thinking about it, he was more frightened still—though without being at all sure what he was frightened *of.* He wasn't in any particular danger himself. Starshine had been reassuring on that point. Nevertheless he was frightened, the way he'd often been at the beginning of a race. Only there wasn't any race. He was going home.

All the way.

Or there again, perhaps he wouldn't. Because what was the hurry? He could stay overnight in a Cardiff hotel, then maybe spend a couple of days just drifting around. Mr. Greene had said a holiday, hadn't he? It was years since he'd been to the West country, he'd forgotten how it was and driving through it that morning he'd liked it. He could take a nice long walk across the Quantocks and listen to the skylarks singing. Of course, the weather looked like breaking; but then if it rained he'd have the hills to himself, without summer trippers surging everywhere. Not, to be fair, that there seemed to be very many tourists in *these* parts; the bus had been rattling along now for all of five minutes and so far he hadn't seen a single car parked at the roadside, with or without its nigh-inevitable accompaniment of picnickers. Except for that one there, on the high slopes . . .

His gaze ceased, of a sudden, to be reflective and became acutely attentive. He stared hard out of the window for maybe ten seconds; then stood up, bracing himself against the chassis sway, reaching for his suitcase.

The conductor seemed surprised.

"You want to get *off* here, sir?"

"Please," Tracy said. "I've changed my mind."

He wondered afterwards if the great swelling emptiness of the moors hadn't somehow hypnotised him into making an absurd decision—one that in Brighton or in London he would never have made. Of course there had to be hundreds, if not thousands, of navy blue Minis in Brighton and in London, but then there had to be plenty of them in Glamorgan, too. And there was nothing odd or unusual about this one, except that it was parked in the lee of a stone wall and had been left there unattended. But it was also parked well above the road, high up on the spur of land that, ever since leaving Y Bannau behind, the bus had been effortfully mounting; from that crest half-a-mile or so to the east there had to be a spectacular view, and included in that view, quite certainly, would be Y Bannau itself. Even so, he didn't know quite why he'd thought it necessary to get down from the bus. It hadn't been a very *intelligent* thing to do.

Anyway, he'd done it. He put his suitcase down in the dry brackeny ditch beside the wall, where it was, though not hidden from view, at least inconspicuous, and walked over to the Mini. There seemed to be nothing very distinctive about the interior; there were folded newspapers on the passenger seat and a tartan rug, also folded, in the back, but nothing in any way revelatory of the owner's identity or character. The bodywork was heavily filmed with dust, a fact that might be consonant with the car's having been recently driven a long way (from London, say), but equally well with its having been chuffing round South Wales for a week or so without benefit of a wash. Tracy didn't try the door to see if it opened; he couldn't see any point in doing so. Instead he turned away, climbed over the stone wall and began to make his way towards the litter of brown rocks marking the summit of the crest.

There was, he soon saw, a man there, sitting on one of the rocks and watching him approach; this was presumably the owner, or anyway the driver, of the Mini. The crouched position in which the man sat made it difficult to assess his height or build, but he didn't seem to have a moustache. Tracy stopped at some fifty paces distance and waited. The other man watched him and also waited. After a pause of some thirty seconds, Tracy continued his advance, since it seemed ridiculous to have come all this way for nothing. When the distance between them had shortened to about ten paces:

"You better stop there," Bony Wright said.

Tracy stopped.

"You still got that gun?"

"No. Not on me."

"So what's it you want?"

"I want to talk to you," Tracy said.

"*Talk* to me?"

"Yes."

"All right. So talk to me."

"I said talk. Not shout."

"Fold your arms across your chest."

Tracy did so.

"Keep 'em that way. Okay. Come on over."

Tracy moved forwards again and sat himself down—not very comfortably—on another projecting lump of rock facing Bony, who didn't move but went on holding the knife, limply, in his right hand, the blade open and slanting downwards at forty-five degrees, sharp edge outwards. He wore a pair of binoculars on a strap round his neck and the binocular case, Tracy saw, was at his feet. Without the moustache, he looked younger and somehow paler.

"How did you know I was here?"

"I saw the Mini."

"And you knew it was mine?"

"No. But I thought it might be. Because I saw one go past us yesterday after the shunt."

"You know who I am?"

"Yes."

"Well, I know who *you* are, now. That chick was saying Tracy, Tracy, but it didn't sort of click—not at the time. Then I was sitting up here thinking about it, and it all came back to me. Funny."

"It doesn't much matter who I am, does it?"

"The coroner," Bony said, "might want to know."

He had one of the strangest accents Tracy had ever heard and quite unlike anything he had expected; the vowels flattened and nasalised—as it seemed, deliberately—and the enunciation oddly overprecise, like that of an old-fashioned schoolmaster, while the phrases were spoken very fast and with a chanting disc-jockey slur. It didn't sound like the form of speech of a man with a highly developed sense of humour; Tracy hoped that this last comment could be taken as a joke, but he wasn't any too sure.

"Saw you drive at Brands Hatch three years running. And Silverstone, that time you spun off. Used to watch you on the box, too. Le Mans '64 is the one I always remember. Tell me, though—d'you reckon it keeps the audiences away?"

"What, me spinning off?"

"No, no—the box. The telly. I mean, it gives you a better view an' all. With helicopters and such. So why go to a meeting when you can see it all from an armchair? That's what I wonder."

"Yes," Tracy said. "You could be right."

"But then where's it all going to end? They'll be televising bank snatches before you know where you are. Kidnappings, shootings. Like that Munich thing. And Kennedy. They'll use them satellite things with telephoto lenses. You got to think of these things, you know, before they happen. Move with the times."

"I suppose one must."

"That's the one I remember, '64. You and that other geezer."

"Michael Andrews."

"Andrews, yes. He was good, too. But what I liked was the way you kept taking the others on that corner where all the pine trees were—took me a while to work out how you were doing it. Oh, I picked up a tip or two from you on *that* one."

"You'd have done better watching Graham Hill that year. Or Clarkie."

"I got a theory about that," Bony said. "I don't feel it's much use watching the geniuses. They do things no one else can do. If you want to learn something, you want to watch someone who's better than you are but not all that much better. Likely as not, what makes him better is he knows a few tricks—like that one of yours for moving inside on the corners. Know what I mean? What d'you think of this bloke Fittipaldi?"

Tracy's eyes were beginning to glaze over with the effort of concentrating intently on total irrelevancies; it's always pleasant, of course, to mull over matters with a fellow motoring enthusiast, but a conversation of this kind, he couldn't help thinking, wasn't what the situation demanded. This man was almost as bad as Tommy

Pope. "Yes, that's just the trouble. Other people learn the tricks, or at least know how to deal with them. And then—"

"Then you're *through*, no need to tell me. That's what I mean about moving with the times. Same thing happens on what you might call a broader spectrum."

If it came to that, it had been an awful long time since Tracy had had *control* of a conversation. People just seemed to be talking *at* him these days; Bernadette, Pope, Starshine, and now this knife-wielding weirdie. "What sort of a broader spectrum?"

"Ah, that's *it*, you wouldn't understand. The thing is when the tricks stop working, you have to retire, you're finished, right? That's motor racing for you. And the way I see it, the same thing happens with people. I mean, you and your sort, you're *through*. Dead as the dodo. Because all the tricks you used—too many people are on to them, they can see through you. I don't know if I'm making my-self clear," Bony said, "but then the way I see it, that's one of the tricks. Glibness, I'd call it. That's how your lot got up on top, by be-ing glib. Well, I don't have the trick myself, but it's just like you said . . . When I meet up with someone who's glib, I know how to deal with him."

"*I'm* not glib," Tracy said hurriedly. "Not at all. Not the least bit."

"I wasn't being personal. That was what's called a generalisation."

"What," Tracy asked, in something like desperation, "what about Rusty Keyes?"

"What about him?"

"You got a bit personal with him, didn't you?"

Bony gave a little thought to this allegation before replying; he had the slightly pained air of a molecular biologist being asked what the DNA double helix could do for Mrs. Henderson's Billy's nasty cough. "Well now, that was different, wasn't it? Did you *know* Rusty?"

"No."

"Ah. I didn't think you did."

To know him, Bony's tone implied, would inevitably involve ap-plauding his demise. Tracy's question was hence answered, at least to Bony's satisfaction. Tracy, however, having roughly grasped the initiative, wasn't yet ready to surrender it again. "I know Berna-dette Pope, though."

"Yes," Bony said.

"Not in the way you probably think, though."

"Look, mate. I don't think at all about *that* side of things. I don't have to. It's a waste of time."

"It isn't her you're really after."

"I got nothing against her," Bony said. The biologist was now an expert witness conceding an unimportant point in court. "Or against you, neither. Not personal, that is. Reason why we had that little up-and-a-downer last night—"

"You wanted to find Pope."

"An' now I have. He's down there." Bony touched with his long thin fingers the adjusting screw of the binoculars. "I've seen him. Seen 'em both together."

"You're supposed to have seen him."

"How d'you mean?"

"He's waiting for you. You're expected."

Bony smiled faintly, as though enjoying this little play upon words. "Maybe. In a manner of speaking. Otherwise he wouldn't be hiding away like that, would he? If he'd had the sense not to tell his missus, or if she'd had the sense—"

"He's got protection."

"Protection?"

"Ever heard of a man called Starshine?"

There was a short hiatus in the conversation, during which—and for the first time—Bony removed his gaze from Tracy's face for long enough to survey the countryside to Tracy's rear; it didn't take him long; maybe one and a half seconds. "I heard of Starshine."

"He's down there, too. Look, they laid a trail for you. You followed it. So you're expected."

"You mean, you and the girl?"

"Yes."

Bony sucked his teeth.

"I don't think the girl knows about it. I'm not sure."

"And you?"

"Me . . . ? No. I just sort of worked out what was happening."

"Tricks," Bony said. "Tricks. Like I said. He *knows* I been following you?"

"Starshine . . . ? Oh yes. He knows."

"Because you told him about last night?"

"Yes."

"How did you know who I was?"

"I recognised you from the photographs. In the papers. You're a famous man these days."

"*When* did you recognise me?"

"That time I first saw you. Outside Bernadette's flat. But it was a bit like me with you—it didn't click, I mean, until a little bit later. When I saw a newspaper."

"I see," Bony said.

"Then when I realised—"

"Shut up," Bony said. "I'm thinking."

Tracy obligingly closed his mouth and there was silence. Except, he noticed, for the sound of a thrush singing, a liquid and seemingly endless judder of notes from no easily determinable location. He hadn't till that moment been fully aware of the extent of his own concentration upon Bony Wright and their conversation, which had clearly been such as to exclude virtually the whole of their external surroundings from his consideration. Now he looked up at the sky and the gathering masses of dark-edged cloud and he took, quite inadvertently, a deep breath. The bird went on chippering away. He thought it was a missel thrush. There was going to be a storm.

A couple of minutes had passed. The collar and sleeves of his shirt were damp with perspiration. It was hot on the open hillside, very hot and sticky.

"They'll never catch him this year," Bony said. "Not with the start he's got."

"Who?"

"That Fittipaldi."

"Jes—!" Tracy said, and stopped abruptly. Losing his temper certainly wouldn't help. "Is *that* what you've been thinking about?"

"No business of yours, what I'm thinking about."

"None of all this," Tracy said, "is any business of mine."

"Ah. *That's* what I was thinking. So why've you come to tell me all this?"

"So you'll go away."

"Go *away?*"

. . . Utter incredulity.

"Yes."

"All right. So I go away. Or maybe I don't. What's it to *you*, whatever I do?"

Tracy sighed, the result of having taken another too deep a breath. "If you go down there," he said, "looking for Pope, someone's going to get hurt. Killed. Starshine's planning on its being you. But from what I've read in the papers, it may not be as easy as he thinks. Other people might get hurt as well."

"You mean the girl?"

"Yes."

"I got nothing against the girl. I told you that."

"She might get in the way. It often happens."

"Yes." Bony nodded. "She might."

"Much better if you just don't go in. That way you make them look pretty stupid, don't you? Sitting round waiting for nothing. You can settle up with Pope some other time, when he hasn't got half the heavies in Brighton looking after him. Or better yet, forget the whole damned thing. That's the sensible thing to do when the odds aren't right."

It was true, though. He wasn't glib. It was rather a pity.

"The odds are never right," Bony said, "from where I'm standing. They never have been. That's what you sods can't understand."

"All right. You still don't have to bet against professionals."

"That's what *I* don't understand."

". . . Sorry?"

"Tommy Pope's no professional. Inside man, that's about his mark. All he does is set 'em up. Outside of that, he's nothing. He couldn't even turn me in without getting Rusty to do the grassing for him. He's really *nothing*. So where does he get all this weight from? Someone like Starshine . . . ? It doesn't make sense."

"Starshine's for hire."

"Not to anyone, he isn't. Not to amateurs. And not to Pope, never in a month of Sundays."

"Mr. Greene must have sent him."

"Who?"

"The man I work for. Bernadette's father."

"And why would he do that?"

"Maybe he owes Pope a favour."

"You say you've come to tip me off because you're worried about the girl?"

"Yes," Tracy said.

"Then why isn't the old man worried? He's her father."

These were certainly very pertinent questions. Dinky Fox had been right about Bony. He wasn't stupid.

"Well, he *was* worried. That's why he told me to carry that gun."

"Yahhhh," Bony said, a sound expressive of derision. "Since when have you been in the protection game? You're another like Tommy Pope. Not even amateur class."

An unflattering estimate, but accurate enough. "What else could he have done? You know all the iron boys by sight. If you'd seen any of *them* with Bernadette, you'd have smelt a rat. No, he just wanted her to have some company while she ran you into the trap. I don't suppose—"

"But now she's in the trap herself. So there we go again. How come that you're worried and he's not?"

"*I* don't know," Tracy said. "Maybe she was supposed to leave again. At once. But I'll admit that's not what he said to me. He said . . . I don't know. It's funny."

"Maybe he's got a lot of faith in Starshine."

"Or maybe somebody's forcing his hand somehow."

"All kinds of maybes. I can think of another. Maybe you're kind of not telling me everything."

"Oh, I'm telling everything," Tracy said. "But I'm not pretending I *know* everything. And what I don't know, I have to guess."

"Me, I don't like maybes. I could say, maybe there's no one down there at all except for you and Pope and his missus. I been watching the place ever since you got here, and I seen no one there but the three of you. Well, so maybe you three have thought up a story that'll make me go away. Sort of a farfetched story, you might think, but I just might be mug enough to swallow it. And who'd be looking stupid then, Tracy? You or me? I mean, I was stupid once when I let Tommy Pope and Rusty shop me—why shouldn't I be stupid again? Would *that* have been your line of thought?"

"No."

"We've been talking about maybes, up to now. But you're not much of an actor either, are you? You're beginning to look worried. Not to say scared."

"Of course I'm scared," Tracy said. "You *kill* people. So does Starshine. I'm scared of both of you. I wouldn't try to hide it. I'm scared all right. Wasn't Rusty Keyes?"

"He had reason to be. He turned me in. Admitted as much. But *you* got no reason to be scared of me. Have you?"

"It doesn't work like that. You're not scared because of reasons. At least, I'm not. Just the opposite."

Bony thought about this for a little while. In the end, he clicked the knife shut and slipped it into his pocket. "That's true," he admitted. "That's true. You mean you do things because you're scared and for no other reason. Like you're sitting here talking to me when you could have stayed on that bus and been halfway to Cardiff. Yes. It's true. That happens to me, too. Only I never thought about it that way before."

"You never raced cars."

"But I could've."

"Yes," Tracy said. "I think you could have."

"People say I'm impulsive. But it's not that. Not exactly that."

"No. It just looks that way. You could say the reason I'm here now is because I was so damned scared when you pulled that knife out last night—I wanted to see you again and *not* be scared. Racing's just like that. You want to go out there again and *not* be scared—but you always are."

"The knife? But you had a gun, for Crissake."

"It was just something I was holding in my hand. You've killed people. I never have. And I don't want to start now, either."

"You know something?" Bony said. "*I* was scared, too."

He laughed. It was a surprisingly pleasant laugh, communicating a genuine amusement. Possibly out of nervous tension, Tracy laughed, too. Perhaps the oddest thing in this whole damned business was that while he was still scared of Bony Wright, now that they'd met he found him strangely likeable. Or what was perhaps even odder . . . somehow he didn't find this at all surprising.

And as though he himself had simultaneously recognised this fact, Bony leaned a little forwards and started talking.

". . . It's the same with me, it's exactly the same. I know they say I'm a nutter. But I'm not. They just don't understand it, that's all. Listen to that stonefaced old bastard of a judge I had when I was up, you'd think I *enjoyed* killing people. Well, I don't. Honest, I don't. If I got half the kick out of croaking someone that that old judge got out of clamping me in bird for the rest of my natural, then I *would* be some sort of a kink. But I don't and I'm not. That's where all the *real* psychos are, if you ask me—up there on the Bench. You can't kid me he didn't enjoy it. Satisfaction written all over his face. Know what they call it . . . ? Sadism. That's what. Pleasure of inflicting pain. Oh, I've met a few of 'em around, no doubt about that. But I'm not a sadist. That's all newspaper talk. That's what *they* are, all those reporters and . . . Sadists. They don't care a damn what they say just so long as it hurts. Bastards. I mean, here we are, aren't we . . . ? you and me . . . enjoying a bit of a chat up, exchange of views you might call it, and all the time you're *scared* of me because of all that cock you've read in the papers. I haven't threatened you, have I? I got nothing at all against you—I told you that, I meant it. So what you got to be scared about? It's always the same. It was the same back in Strangeways. Everyone scared of me. It makes you want to puke. People read a lot in bird, you know. Did you know that . . . ? They read a lot. What else they got to do? And what the books feed 'em is a lot of lies. Newspapers and books, it's all the same. Just a load of crap. If they put all them reporters and writers in bird for a spell, maybe they'd write the truth. Like the *Pilgrim's Progress*. Bloke wrote that in the old flowery dell—I'll bet you never knew that? Lots of people don't. Well, someone else ought to write a book from inside, and put the truth in it. About all them lawyers and psychiatrists and company directors and the like. The truth isn't what they say it is. They don't tell the truth about *me*—that's how I know. If they don't tell the truth about people like me, chances are they don't tell the truth about anyone else. Stands to reason, doesn't it? It's not the truth, it's tricks. That's how they fool you till you catch on. All that paranoia stuff—oh, I've read the books, it *sounds* all right. But before that they had that phrenosis stuff, reading your bumps, and before that they threw you into the river to see if you drowned, and of course it all made sense at the time because there were all those people to *say* that it did. They may even believe in it themselves—psychology and that—and the due process of law—and sending people to the moon—but it's all *tricks* is what I'm saying, it's just not the *truth* . . ."

An altogether extraordinary monologue. Of course, Tracy thought, he probably hasn't spoken to anyone for days and days; he's been on the run, completely alone. But even so. He sounded a shade obsessive, but perfectly coherent; he certainly wasn't stupid and he certainly didn't *seem* to be mad. He sounded mostly like a man who'd been very, very lonely. And of that, too, Tracy understood a little something.

All the same, he had to be checked or he'd go on forever. Tracy said abruptly, interrupting the other in mid-sentence:

"Why are you after Pope?"

"Pope?"

"Yes."

"Oh *him*, that's another matter. I got my pride, haven't I? If I didn't come back hard on the buggers who shopped me, people'd think . . . They'd say . . . And there again, I haven't much choice. I owe people money. Tommy owes *me* money. It's as simple as that."

"Perhaps he'd pay you off. Just to get you off his back."

"Not him."

"Why not?"

"It's simple and it's not so simple. I mean, I *got* to do him and he knows it. If I don't, people just won't respect me. You can see that, can't you?"

Tracy clicked his tongue. "They won't respect you if you get dead, either."

"It may not break that way. And you still haven't proved that Starshine's there at all. So far it's all been a lot of talk."

"Only one way you can prove it."

"That's right," Bony said.

"Unless . . . You've been watching the house?"

"I said so."

"You wouldn't have had a look at that cottage down the end of the track?"

"The one with the bird in the bikini? Sitting in the garden?"

"Well, in that case you might have wondered what a piece like that's doing out here, a hundred miles from nowhere. Jenny's her name. Used to be a stripper. Right now she's doing Starshine and the boys a favour."

"Never heard of her," Bony said. "Means nothing to me."

"I doubt if Mr. Greene knows she's here, either. You don't think she looks the country-cottage type, though, do you? So what else'd she be doing—"

"I wouldn't know about that," Bony said. He sounded now almost sullen.

"Then take it from me."

"I might and I might not." Bony stood up. "Just sit still for a while. Don't go away."

In fact he'd have been ill-advised to take Tracy's word on the matter. Tracy knew very little about girls and next to nothing about strippers. Jenny was a country-cottage girl, all right; she'd lived in one for fourteen years—the first two-thirds of her life—on the outskirts of a diminutive Sussex village called, not inappropriately, Balls Cross. Then she'd run away from home. She'd done this by walking eight miles and taking the Brighton bus. Unlike Tracy, she hadn't got off it.

Being a country girl, however, didn't mean that she wasn't finding her present situation boring. She'd been agonisingly bored in Balls Cross, and this dump seemed to be a bloody sight worse. There was nobody to talk to. Not even cows. She couldn't talk to the tall one called Henry; he was asleep upstairs. He spent the night up at the big house, and during the day he slept. He'd leave a quarter of an hour before midnight, and half an hour later the other one'd be back, the London boy. Tony. And guess what he'd want to do . . . ? Yes. Right. But after that, *he'd* go to sleep, too. There wasn't much time laid aside for a meeting of minds. And Jenny liked talking. She enjoyed an intelligent conversation, or a good long gossip. Starshine, now, was a brainy bloke. She could talk to Starshine, usually; it wasn't like talking to a human being, but it was better than nothing and he was, after all, the big butter-and-egg man. But right now daddy was up at the big house, too, and he'd been there ever since they'd arrived, and it didn't look as though at any time he'd be back. Well, it wasn't really what she was contracted *for*. She wasn't, in her opinion, giving value for money; she'd asked for rather a lot when she'd been told there'd be three of them, but it hadn't worked out like that at all. A couple of quick bangs a day, that was like, nothing. Jenny was a friendly girl and she enjoyed that part of it, too. Why not? It was the only damned thing she was any good at. So it was all proving rather a tragedy, in a way.

She went upstairs, in search of something to do. The bedroom door, as usual, was open, showing most of the big double bed and a confused tangle of blankets in the middle of it. The tangle didn't move. Jenny sighed plaintively and went over to the dressing table and seated herself at it, studying her own face in the tilted mirror.

On the whole, she wasn't best pleased with it. When she was fourteen, she'd looked to be eighteen at least. Fine. But now that she was twenty-one she looked to be all of thirty. The morning's sunbathe hadn't given her, as she'd hoped, a nice even tan; it had merely left her cheeks unbecomingly flushed, as from an incipient fever. She wasn't used to sunshine, of course. In her dancing days she'd never been allowed to sit out in it; nobody wants a stripey stripper, or so the theory runs. Starshine and the boys weren't so fussy. Jenny sighed again, rather more profoundly, and took off her blond wig and tried the chestnut one instead. There was no noticeable improvement.

Country holidays. Starshine could have 'em.

Watching Bony Wright return, Tracy realised that he was tired; the high-shouldered military lope had stiffened, so that his legs moved mechanically, unnaturally rhythmically, as though powered by clockwork. Of course, if he was tired that was hardly surprising. "Nothing stirring," Bony said. "No action."

Tracy was stirring, as far as he was able. He wasn't all that tired, but he was very uncomfortable. For the last twenty minutes he'd been wriggling about on his bumpy seat of rain-eroded rock, not daring at any time to get up in case Bony should misinterpret the movement. "She's probably darning Starshine's socks. Or having a nice cup of tea. I could do," he added, "with one myself."

Bony ignored the hint. "I don't see her anywhere."

"What d'you want to see her for? You've seen her already."

"Reckon I might drop by for a little chat," Bony said. "Chances are I'd do better talking to her than I would've done talking to Tommy's missus. It was just an idea."

Not, Tracy thought, a particularly good one. But one that at least promised a change of location, and almost anything would be preferable to another twenty minutes on his hard-edged granite gridiron. Bony's patience, he now had to concede, was altogether extraordinary, and could probably be in some part debited to hindquarters of leather, rubber, or some similarly durable material; Bony could—as was now demonstrated—sit unmoving on a jagged boulder for seemingly interminable periods, gazing the while—and without a moment's let-up in his concentration—through high-powered field glasses at a house four miles away, and do this without ever evincing the slightest sign of bodily discomfort. Tracy considered that from the cockpits of racing cars he had learnt a certain amount of stoicism, but compared to Bony he had to be accounted a proper nancy. He was, and he admitted himself, impressed.

"All right," Bony said. "Let's go."

He put the binoculars away in their case. Tracy thankfully stood up, surreptitiously massaging his rear. They made their way down to where the Mini was parked, Bony walking a pace or two behind him. The breeze blowing from the sea had strengthened and seemed perceptibly colder now; the collar of Tracy's shirt felt damp and sticky at the back of his neck.

"Perhaps," he said diffidently, "you wouldn't mind giving me a lift."

"A lift?"

"Just back to the bus stop. It's almost opposite—"

"I was thinking you might like to come calling, too. Seeing as you're such a man for the ladies."

"Oh, well, no, I don't really—"

"That your case over there?"

"Yes."

"Fetch it."

Tracy fetched it.

"Open it."

Tracy took the keys from his trousers pocket and opened it.

"You keep that gun loaded?"

"No."

"Very wise. I'll look after it for you, if you don't mind."

"I don't mind," Tracy said.

"I'll take the ammo as well. Not much use to you, is it, without the iron?"

"No use at all," Tracy said.

"Okay. Get in the car."

Out at sea the clouds were building up fast. There was rather more than a drop of rain coming along, Tracy thought, easing himself into the minuscule passenger seat. The pressure was dropping very fast. It was blowing up a storm.

She brightened up a little when she heard the knock on the door. Someone to talk to, maybe. At worst, something *happening*. She checked up on herself quickly yet again, crossing the bedroom, this time in the long wardrobe mirror opposite the bed; white blouse, black slacks, black sneakers, and the blond wig back in place. Henry went on sleeping, snoring faintly and mellifluously. She went downstairs, trippety-trip, trippety-trip, all light and fairy-like, if you can imagine a fairy with a forty-inch bust line; she opened the front door. *Two* men. Better yet. "Yes?" she said.

"Starshine in?"

The question didn't surprise her in the least; this was exactly the kind of man who always asked for Starshine. It was getting so she could spot them in the street, and at middle distance. The other one she wasn't so sure about. "No, he's not here."

"He sent for us."

"He's up at the big house. You go up this road—"

"He told us not to go there."

"Oh yes, that's right." She couldn't go up there, either. Big secret and all that jazz, only she wasn't in on it and didn't want to be. "But he's expecting you?"

"So I'm told," the smaller one said.

"You'd better come in."

Smaller One strolls in as fresh as paint, as though he owns the joint. Bigger One more cautiously, as though ill at ease about something. "He hasn't been down here at all, not since we got here. He's up at that house all the time."

"You mean you're left here all on your own?"

She didn't fancy Smaller One, but she found his surprise gratifying. "Sure. Except for Henry, but he sleeps all day. And Tony. Tony's different. He sleeps all night."

"So Henry's here now, is he? Sleeping?"

"That's right."

"Then I'll just creep quietly upstairs and give Henry a big surprise," Smaller One said. ". . . Not you. You stay here. You wouldn't have anything to eat around the place?"

"Well, there's some—"

"See what you can find. Me, I'm hungry."

Smaller One padded through the door and turned up the stairs. A tread creaked once, and then there was silence. She turned her head to look at Bigger One, who was staring, though with no great show of interest, through the latticed panes of the window towards the garden lawn, where the coloured canvas of the deckchair was lifted by the gathering wind.

"Hey, don't *you* talk?"

"Yes." But he still didn't look at her. "I talk."

"What's your name, then?"

"Tracy."

"Tracy? What kind of name is *that?*"

"*My* name," Bigger One said.

"Well, I'm Jenny."

"I know."

"We haven't met before, have we . . . ? Or you mean someone told you?"

"I'm from Brighton, too."

"No kidding? What you do there?"

"I run a garage."

"Oh." It didn't help her much. "Well, go on and sit down. Make yourself at home."

He sat down and she perched on the arm of the sofa opposite, though she already had the feeling that this one wasn't the conversational sort. Still, no harm in trying.

"Who's your pal?"

"His name's Wright. He's not my pal, though."

"He just brought you along?"

"Yes, that sums it up rather well."

"Hey." She pointed one finger at him. "You're not a friend of that Tommy Pope?"

"Not that, either. But I know him. Why?"

"Nothing. Just a guess. You talk like he does."

"Insofar as I talk at all."

"Yes, insofar as . . ." He had rather a nice smile, when he could be persuaded to use it. But the girl'd have to work at it. He seemed

to have things on his mind. "What do you want to eat? We got loads
of stuff. You know, eggs, ham, beans, stuff like that. But I'm not
much of a cook."

"I'll give you a hand," Tracy said.

"*You* can cook?"

"Yes," Tracy said. He sighed heavily. "I should be a bloody good
cook, before I've finished."

The cottage had been renovated, probably, at the same time as
the big house up the road. The kitchen was small; there was no
deep freeze or dishwasher, but half-tiles had been put in to replace
the peeling plaster and there was a gas cooker, a refrigerator and a
hot plate. The layout was handier, Tracy thought, than the one up
at Y Bannau. He fried eggs and bacon and chipped potatoes, while
Jenny—nominally supervising the operation of the electric toaster—
sat at the table and watched him, smoking a filter cigarette. While
he was draining the oil from the chips, Bony Wright came through
from the hallway; he, too, pulled a chair up to the table and
watched. "You're a man of many talents."

Tracy grunted.

"Smells good, that does. Smells very good indeed."

"I'm having some, too," Jenny said.

And after a pause:

"What about Henry?"

"*He's* all right," Bony said. "He's gone back to sleep. He enjoys a
good kip, does Henry. Don't you worry your head about old Henry."

"I wasn't *worried*, I just—"

"Yes, that smells pretty good. But how about tomatoes? I just
about fancy some tomatoes."

"There's some at the bottom of the fridge," Tracy said.

"Fried, I think. Yes, I really fancy some fried tomatoes."

Tracy put the frying pan back on the cooker and got out the tomatoes and started slicing. "I'll have some, too," Jenny said.

"All right, all *right*."

"No need to be querulous, cocker. Don't," Bony said to the girl,
"take any notice of my friend when he's querulous. He's inclined
to be querulous, that's all. He's the querulous sort."

"He says you're not his friend."

"Me? Not his friend? Now that's what I mean, you see. That's
what I'm talking about. Imagine him saying a thing like that." He
picked up his fork and bounced the prongs eagerly on the table.
"Ready, isn't it? The eggs and bacon? Right, let's be having it."

"The tomatoes aren't finished yet."

"Eggs and bacon I said."

Tracy brought the eggs and bacon and the chips over from the hot plate and put them on the table. Bony heaped up his plate and began, ravenously, to tuck in. So, a little more hesitantly, did Jenny.

"Hey, Tracy," she said, with her mouth full.

"Yes?"

"You *always* do what the little feller tells you? Just like that?"

"Just like that," Tracy said. "What's more, I'd advise you to do the same."

"Me? Why?"

"That way, maybe he won't kill us both later."

Jenny choked on a laugh, inadvertently spattering the table with half-chewed crumbs of toast. Elegant she wasn't. Then her gaze grew gradually reflective, eventually almost petrified, though her lower jaw continued its firm rotatory motion; her resemblance, at all times apparent, to a large, placid Sussex cow became so marked as to verge on caricature. "Wright," she said indistinctly, swallowing whole the entire enormous mouthful long before it could possibly have been reduced to cud. "Wright, you said. Not Bo . . . But not Bony . . . ?"

"Bony Wright, yes. That's just a nickname, mind. What people call me. My real name's Albert."

"But Bony Wright, wow, you're *hot*."

"Most people are, some time or other."

"But Starshine never works with people who're hot. He told me himself. Not ever."

"I didn't say I was working with him. I said he was expecting me."

Jenny's lower jaw had now become unnaturally motionless. She found it necessary to move it up and down once or twice before next she spoke. "You mean," she said, looking at Tracy, "you mean you weren't . . . ?"

"Tomatoes," Tracy said, tilting them straight from the frying pan onto Bony's plate. "Fried tomatoes, as ordered. I wasn't joking, no."

"Come off it," Bony said, with some good humour. "Don't get worried, love. He's putting you on. You do just what you're told like a good girl and you won't get hurt. I'll leave you as right as rain, not even poked, and I can't say fairer than that, can I now? Here, have some fried tomatoes."

"I've changed my mind," Jenny said. "I don't want no fried tomatoes. What you going to . . . ? Hey, and what about Henry? What you *done* to Henry?"

"You keep saying, *What about Henry*. Gets a bit tedious, you know that . . . ? I haven't done anything to Henry. He's just finishing his kip, like I said. In the wardrobe. I locked him in, to be on the safe side, but he won't cause any trouble. Gave him quite a shock to wake up and find me sitting on the side of the bed with a shiv up against his neck. You should've seen his face." Bony, transfixed with amusement at this recollection, broke once more into his pleasantly boyish laugh, which the tiles of the kitchen, however, re-echoed hollowly. Jenny seemed in no way relieved to hear it.

"It's all got nothing to do with me." She frowned in the effort to render her thoughts coherent and to express them intelligibly, something she rarely found it necessary to take the trouble to do. "I'm not his bird—Starshine's, I mean—I don't care what they told you. I'm just on a visit, like. I look after the three of 'em, you see, I just have to keep them happy, that's all there is to it. For the rest, I don't know anything. Honest I don't."

"You don't have to tell me that," Bony said. "I know what you're here for. I'm not stupid."

This doesn't much lessen her alarm. All the same, she thought, he's got no reason to hurt me; maybe I'll be all right, after all. If only he'd stop smiling away to himself . . . He had a nice smile, the other one. Tracy. But this one hadn't. No, this one most certainly hadn't . . .

"What's for afters?" He pushed away his plate.

"There's bread and cheese. And biscuits."

"Bread and cheese, eh? Good. Nothing wrong with bread and cheese." And turning to Tracy: "You still feel like a nice cop of char, Tracy boy?"

"I wouldn't mind one."

"Right," Bony said. "Put the kettle on."

CHAPTER 20

The line to Cardiff was clearer that evening. Sitting in the fast-darkening room with his eyes closed and the receiver held to his ear, Pope could imagine the words he heard as coming from someone in the armchair opposite him or, possibly, as originating inside his own head, like the words he spoke. Curious, he thought, you never mix them up—the words you hear and the words you speak.

You can always tell the difference. Except maybe sometimes when you're drunk. He was drunk tonight, but not drunk enough for that.

". . . All this stuff about divorce. She's getting on my nerves. She always did go on and on, and now she's worse than ever."

And the other voice, the other flat clipped voice with the slightest suspicion of a lisp,

"She's got to go."

"I know she's got to go. But she won't."

"Look, I told you how to explain it to her. You two are alone there—as far as she knows. If she stays there tonight, it's cohabitation. So if she wants a divorce—"

"*You* try explaining it to her. She won't go, and that's all there is to it. Why don't you come here and fetch her? See if with your well-known powers of persuasion—"

"How the hell can I do that? It might spoil everything." A pause. "D'you think she suspects?"

"Suspects what?"

"Any thing. About . . . what's going on."

"No," Pope said. "How can she?" He rubbed lightly, with one finger, at the soft skin just beneath one closed eyelid; it felt hot and dry to his touch. "Why don't you just talk to her, Leo? Talk to her on the phone. Say you're waiting for her in Cardiff, say anything you like—"

"She knows that already."

"Yes, but . . . Oh, for God's sake, *talk* to her."

"I don't think I'd better, Tommy. After all, she's safe enough there with you. She's just as safe as you are. All you have to do is sit tight and leave everything to Starshine."

"But you just this moment said—"

"I changed my mind."

"That's all very well," Pope said.

"Protection is what you asked for, protection is what you're getting. So if Bernie . . . I mean, dammit, I should be worried about Bernie as much as you are—I'm going to marry her, aren't I?"

"Are you?"

"That was the agreement."

"You didn't agree it with *me*." Pope clicked his tongue. "Oh, you're welcome, I assure you. You're welcome. I'm not worried about Bernie, either. It's entirely her own damned—"

"Yes. That's all right, then."

The receiver, unexpectedly, clicked. The line went dead. Pope continued to hold the black plastic mushroom-head of the auricular against his left ear, listening to silence. Then, when the dialling tone started again, he put the telephone back on the cradle, fumbling it slightly because his eyes were still closed. As he did so, a sudden gust of wind shook the windowpanes behind him, rattling the sashes. He suppressed a shudder.

It had become quite cold.

Opening his eyes at last, he stared across the empty room and thought for a while about Rusty Keyes; then got up to pour himself another gin-and-lime, having decided that it would be better at this juncture if he didn't think about Rusty Keyes but about something or somebody else. He trickled the gin and the lime-juice carefully into his glass, as though measuring out a prescription. The clouds had hung so heavy a pall over the evening as to filter out most of the dying daylight, and he found it difficult to see just how full the glass was; through long practice, luckily, he knew precisely when to stop. Luckily, unluckily; it didn't really matter. He didn't want to switch the lights on. Not yet. He liked the semidarkness; it was cosy. And finding his way around the sideboard was no problem. Finding his way anywhere else, yes, that'd be more difficult. But he didn't want to find his way anywhere else. Not yet. He took a long, thoughtful sip and sat down again, resting the glass on the arm of the chair.

He was drinking rather heavily. That had to be admitted. Later, when all this was over, he wouldn't drink any more; or not so much. He'd go abroad. He'd go to India. Stopping off maybe in Rome; Bernie had liked Rome that time before. At least, he thought she had. Well, maybe it wouldn't be Bernie this time, it rather looked as though it wouldn't be Bernie. After all, he'd promised. Sort of. And a gentleman's word is his bond. Still, if it wasn't Bernie, it'd be somebody else. He'd relax, anyway, and cut down on his drinking. Get the stuff through to Bombay, and cash in. Later on there'd be openings in Rome. He knew a few people there and quite a few girls. He was sure there'd be something for him there. There are always openings in Rome, for a feller with a modest capital.

Suppose there wasn't? Suppose the luck ran out?

You heard of that happening.

You sometimes got unlucky.

Bony Wright's breaking out of jail—now *that* was unlucky. You could call it an omen. It shouldn't have happened. But it had. And maybe when it happened, he'd have done better to have gone abroad right away. Italy, India, Australia, any damned place. Why hadn't he?

Money, that was why. All that gold stored away in London. Nothing anywhere else. He should have had some of the greenstuff over there somewhere, Switzerland, South America, somewhere like that, the way old man Greene almost certainly had. You had to admire old Greene. He diversified his interests. He was cautious, he played it cool. But then when all was said and done, it was only money. Old Greene was just that—old. What he had, he had to look after. When you're young, it's different. You make a packet, you lose it —so what if you lose it? You can always make another packet. If you're Tommy Pope. If you know the right people. And a few of the girls.

He rubbed again, tiredly, at the loose skin under his eyes and finished his gin-and-lime. He put the glass down on the table and made his way, with no more than the anticipated degree of waggle in his wake, across the room and up the stairs. Bernadette was lying on the bed in her room. She wasn't asleep. The standard lamp in the corner was turned on.

"Who was that on the phone?"

"When?"

"Just now. I heard it ring."

"Oh. Only Leo. He's still in Cardiff." He sat down rather heavily on the foot of the bed. "Waiting for you."

Bernadette turned her head on the pillow, looked at the darkened window. The far shore of the estuary was now invisible, the grey sea a blur, the sky aswirl with smudges of torn black cloud. "We're in for a storm."

"Yes. Well?"

"Well, what?"

"Leo. What are we going to do about him?"

"What did you tell him?"

Tommy shrugged. "That you wouldn't go. And that I can't very well make you."

"I never *said* I would."

". . . Are you really going to marry him? I mean, is that what . . . ?"

She turned her head again towards him but looking straight through him, as if at something beyond; moving her gaze from the window, she had left the focus of her eyes unchanged. "Why not?"

"You could have married him before, couldn't you? I mean, instead of me. If that was what you really wanted."

"What I want's got nothing to do with it. It's all part of the deal."

"Deals, deals—everybody talks deals."

"It's the family tradition." Her eyes had picked him up now, but impassively, neither imposing nor rejecting any relationship. A new trick, he thought, she'd picked up somewhere; it was as though he were something on a television screen; he found it irritating. "What sort of a deal are *you* talking, Tommy? Or have you cooked it up already?"

"With Leo, you mean?"

"I don't know, do I? I'm asking."

"Well, *I'm* not being difficult. If you're sure it's what you . . . Only thing is, Leo's not like me. He's kind of vulnerable. You can hurt him."

"Like now? By staying here?"

"Yes. Like now."

"He enjoys it. He likes being hurt. He's a Yid, isn't he? Well, there you are."

"Nice sort of a bloody little bitch *you* are," Pope said, but not with heat; indeed, almost good-humouredly. "I suppose you'll have made the running on the way down here with that other chappie. I'd've thought you'd be dying to tell Leo *all* about that."

"With Tracy . . . ? No, I didn't make the running, as you so elegantly express it. I don't fancy him, anyway."

"Oh yes, you do. I can tell."

"He's not my sort, though. Or *our* sort. He doesn't talk deals."

"He'll learn all right. You could teach him."

She moved her head sideways, once. "No."

"So what *did* you do with him?"

"We went for a walk. We looked at some ducks. I watched him fix the car. He doesn't need anyone, he really doesn't." She started to sigh, let the sigh change into a yawn. "I envy him. I'd like to be like that."

The windowpanes vibrated to another great gust of wind. She stared up at the ceiling, then rolled ungracefully off the bed.

"Where are you going?"

"To fix us up something to eat. I'm hungry if you're not."

From the cliff-edge the rocks tumbled downwards in roughly eroded layers, each tilted slab of blue-grey granite overlaying the next like cards in a pack; on the beach beneath were more rocks, fallen boulders, pebbles, and shallow seaweed-laden pools. An innocuous sea lapped gently at the sand, tentacling an occasional inquiring inlet towards the base of the cliff but threatening nothing. Farther out there were waves, but seeming from the height where Tracy stood no fiercer than ripples, merging into the greyness of oncoming night. There, earlier in the day, had been the sun dazzle, a shoal of brilliant light-splashes, and the hills of Somerset; to the west, where the cliffs lost their forbidding altitude and climbed less steeply, there had been other distant metallic glints and a heat haze rising over serried rows of cars, baking in the glare of afternoon. Now the cars were gone, all but a few, and between Tracy and the beach park was nothing but four miles of space, of slowly flattening ground, empty of all but cropped grass and a crisscross of low stone walls. Beyond the car park the ground rose again, and again emptily, to an unbroken skyline where the clouds stood massed. It was a beach all right, Tracy thought, but it wasn't very much like Brighton. Not like Brighton at all. And now, in the gathering dusk, it wasn't as it had seemed that afternoon, but looked another place entirely. It was odd if cliffs and rocks and moors should also be subject to the vagaries of time and space, when measured not in millennia but in minutes; that wasn't, surely, what the geologists taught?

A heavy raindrop struck him in the face, so smartly that he jerked his head back; following the raindrop, a long, slow breath of wind. He turned away and crossed the lawn, picked up the deckchair, folded it, stacked it away in the shelter of the porch. Thunder crashed as he did so, almost overhead, and lightning blinked furiously to the south.

Bony opened the door, peered out. "Took you a long time. Where you been?"

"Just taking a look at the weather," Tracy said mildly, stepping inside. "It's coming over pretty dark."

"I can see that."

Bony's earlier mood of euphoria had changed to irritability. It thundered again as they went through into the kitchen; inside the cottage the reverberations seemed to be magnified, and the effect was almost that of a sonic boom; the empty teacups on the table shivered on their saucers. The drumroll seemed to be prolonging itself indefinitely, then ended with a whickering rattle like that of a loose flapping blind on a railway train. How long had it lasted? Fifteen, twenty seconds? Probably not more than five. The silence that followed seemed to be full of echoes; Tracy noticed that Jenny's knuckles were white where she gripped the arm of her chair. "It's all right. Only thunder."

"I'm scared," Jenny said. Her voice, strangely enough, carried very little conviction.

"It's been building up all day, so it'll come down heavy. But it'll blow itself out pretty quickly. You'll see."

"What time is it?"

Tracy looked at his wristwatch. "Half-past eight."

"How much longer are you going to *stay* here?"

"Ahhhh, come on," Bony said. "You wouldn't send us out in this lot, would you? It's going to come down in bloody buckets." He narrowly failed to recapture, somehow, his former bantering tone; maybe he didn't much like thunder, either. Lots of people don't.

"That's all very well. But Henry's got to be up at the house by twelve o'clock, and if he doesn't show up they'll know something's happened, and then they'll come down here and . . . Oh gosh, there doesn't *have* to be trouble, does there?"

Bony said nothing. Instead, and as if confirming his words rather than answering Jenny's, the rain arrived and the kitchen seemed to tremble to its impact. Lightning crackled again across the sky, showing the windowpanes aswirl with running water, and a few seconds later the thunder hit the roof like a falling hammer. Jenny made a faint whimpering noise, *ooooo-oooooohhhh,* jumped out of her chair and scuttled across the floor to sit down again, almost cowering, in the corner of the room, her hands pressed tightly over her ears; if she'd had an apron, Tracy reflected, she'd certainly have flung it over her head, and possibly she was sorry that she hadn't. She wasn't nearly as *modern* a girl as he'd supposed. He looked at Bony, who was gazing morosely at the floor. "Well," he said. "Does there?"

"Eh?"

"She asked you a question."

"No trouble. Not for her. Nor you, either. They won't be coming down. I'll be going up."

He wiped his mouth, for no apparent reason, with the back of his hand. "Not the cliff way, you won't," Tracy said. "I've just had a look and it's hopeless, it isn't *on*. Up the road or across the moor is the only way. And Starshine knows that, too."

"That's my problem. Not yours."

"Except we're part of it."

"No, you're not. No problem at all. You and the girl, you can stay here. I'll lock you up nice and cosy. You can't complain about *that,* can you?—with her being scared of storms an' all. There's lots as'd pay for the privilege."

Again, he'd just missed the right intonation for the comment to pass as a joke. It was like listening to a record rotating at fraction-

ally less than the proper speed. Tracy fetched the teapot from the
hot plate and poured out more tea; the sound of its trickling into
the cups was lost now in the steady, though irrhythmic, rush of water down the outside gutters, the loud whisper of the rain on the
walls and windows. Going in tonight didn't make sense, but Bony
knew that already. The hour before the race begins—that's when
you always ask yourself why the hell you have to go through with
it, and the time when you can least bear having someone else ask
you that same question. You say you haven't any choice, but that's
never true. You always have a choice. Why not tell me what it's
all about?"

"What's what about?"

"What did Tommy Pope have to do with it, anyway?"

"The Bond Street job, you mean?"

". . . If that's where it started."

"That's where it started all right. Tommy set it up. I thought you
knew."

"For you and Rusty?"

"Tommy put it up to me. And I brought Rusty into it. Ironical,
that, when you think about it. But someone had to do the safe,
y'see . . . Otherwise it looked a right old doddle. It *was* a doddle.
I'm damned if I know," Bony said, "why they had to go and grass
on me and spoil the whole pretty picture. Greedy, I reckon. That's
the trouble with amateurs like Tommy Pope. They're greedy."

The vice of greed, Tracy decided, had to be held in particular
reprobation by the criminal element; this was the second time today
that he'd heard it expressly condemned. A little surprising, maybe,
but there it was. "He wasn't actually in on the job with you, then?"

"God, no. Not likely. No, there was just me and Rusty. 'Course,
if we'd had someone else in, we needn't ever have croaked that
Peabody bloke. We didn't have anyone to watch him, that was the
trouble, so I had to put him out and I hit him too hard. It happens.
An accident, really."

"Except it was murder."

"I should've had a better lawyer. But then I shouldn't ever've
been in the dock at all. They didn't have to grass on me. Stupid,
that was."

"Maybe they panicked."

"What, because of that Peabody . . . ? If we'd all sat tight and
waited, nothing would have happened. But he may have got nervous . . . That Tommy Pope. An amateur, see? Like I said."

"You must have known that before you went in with him."

"Oh, sure. But it seemed a fair risk. Besides, if you take on an inside job, nine times out of ten there's an amateur setting it up. Or anyway, giving you the info. Nothing wrong, mind you, with Tommy's griff. Everything was just as he said it'd be. It was easy. Too bloody easy."

"How did *he* know how everything would be?"

Bony shrugged. "He'd got the connections, hadn't he?"

"I suppose he had," Tracy said.

He drank some tea, which had cooled to luke-warmness. The windows were still vibrating to the beat of the rain, the water still surged down the gutters, but the storm front had now moved past them; the thunder was now a deep, ominous murmur in the distance. In the warm and well-lit kitchen, seated at the table, he and Bony were enjoying again a certain intimacy; outside the domesticity of their surroundings, only the passing storm existed; nothing else seemed entirely real. Jenny still sat in the corner, but alone, unnoticed. "It was gold you got, wasn't it?"

"Gold, banknotes, papers, all kind of stuff. We left it all in the car, and Tommy picked it up. I don't know *what* we got, exactly. But gold, yes. Weighed about a ton."

"So you don't even know what the loot was worth?"

"Nope. I came in for twenty-five thousand, guaranteed. Tommy got the rest. Rusty was in for ten, but that was out of my split. Fair enough—since I brought him in."

"Then he never got paid?"

"*I* never paid him. I never got paid myself. Except for a few hundred nicker Tommy gave me to cover expenses. What happened, though, he and Rusty got together to cut me out. Clear as daylight."

"Is that what Rusty said? When you . . . talked to him?"

Bony shook his head, as though in regret. "Ah, he was such a liar. Always was. Told a lot of lies, Rusty did."

"It's what you reckon, then?"

"Yes. That's what I reckon. Fact is, I'm not specially interested in the *why* of it all. They shopped me, fine—I just don't *care* why. I didn't ask Rusty about that and I won't ask Tommy, either, when I catch up with him. People do funny things, Tracy—you can't go round asking them *why* all the time. I mean, it's a waste of energy. No, I'm concerned just to set the matter to rights. That's all."

"Funny you should say that. It's what *I* do all the time."

"What is?"

"Ask people *why*. Or not so much ask other people as ask myself.

Wonder about it, sort of. I think you're right. It's a bad habit. But I just can't seem to help it."

"It's the way you been educated."

"Yes. Very likely."

"That's what they teach you at school, isn't it . . . ? To ask why everything's the way it is. It's not a good thing. I mean, everything *is* the way it is, know what I mean? So who cares why? And this education business, it creates a social gulf—that's what it does—between people like you and me. And that's a pity. Otherwise you and me, we could get on fine."

"We *do* get on fine. Up to a point."

"Ah! There it is! Up to a point—that's the trouble, isn't it? Pity about that *point*, wouldn't you say?"

"Yes. But it's there. There's no denying it."

Again Bony shook his head, but this time vehemently, as a spaniel shakes water from its floppy ears. Then he pushed his chair back, stood up and went to stand by the window. Out of the direct circle of the light of the overhead bulb, his face looked more pallid than ever; faintly phosphorescent, even, like the face of a corpse. "Look at it this way. You tipped me off, you done me a good turn, I owe you a favour—there's no denying *that*, either. And I don't owe many people favours. I don't *like* owing favours. Well, if it weren't for that point—as you call it—and if you were a different sort of person to what you are . . . Know what I'd do? I'd call you in on the show. Fifty fifty. Well, why not? We'd screw that twenty five grand out of Tommy Pope and we'd split it down the middle. Because I could use some help with that Starshine, I'm not saying I couldn't. Only thing is . . ." He turned back towards the table. "No, you don't have to shake your head. It isn't on."

"Sorry," Tracy said. "No. You couldn't trust me."

"Too right, I couldn't. Not if it's a matter of a trigger that has to be pulled. Because you couldn't pull it. And it *is* that kind of a matter and you know it." He sat down, planking his elbows on the table. "No. You couldn't pull it. You'd just stand there and ask yourself *why*."

"I would, yes. I couldn't kill someone without a reason. And a better reason than it seems to me you've got."

"Reasons," Bony said. Thoughtfully, not contemptuously. "Well, there you are. It's a pity."

He rested his chin on his hands. Then he said:

". . . You never told me what you thought about Fittipaldi."

CHAPTER 21

The rain came now out of the southwest with a heavy, nagging persistence; Starshine raised his head as he crossed the courtyard, peering up from under the slanted brim of his hat, and even under the shadow of the eaves where, as of habit, he walked, the windy impact of the rain against his face forced him, for a moment, to narrow his eyes. He could see no break in the great lead curtain of the thunderclouds, but the light burning in the nearby porch and the occasional ragged flicker of distant lightning had dulled the edge of keenness of his night vision; just as the splashing drip of the rain against the cobbles, the gurgle of water down the shallow runnels had blunted his hearing, making it difficult for his ear to pick up small sounds and impossible for him to distinguish them as familiar or as out of the ordinary. It was a bad night for bodyguards. But at least the thunderclaps seemed to have ceased. In the darkness behind the open door of the outhouse, Tony was sitting, the shotgun held loosely across his knees.

"What a night," Starshine said. He took off his hat and slapped it lightly against the door lintel; tiny slivers of flying water impacted against his hand and wrist.

"You said it."

"You can see damn-all from inside the house. Black as a duck's arse."

"He won't come in this," Tony said.

"He'll come in this if he comes at all. You better get up the top of that staircase and stay there. You can cover the front door that way, as well."

Tony nodded invisibly, stood up and leaned the shotgun against the wall; then was gone. Not a great talker, Tony. Nor was Henry, for that matter; Starshine didn't much favour talkers. Though tonight, in the beat and scurry of the falling rain, it wouldn't have greatly mattered; no low-pitched conversation could possibly have been overheard. Maybe hot coffee had been uppermost in Tony's mind; that was understandable. It wasn't warm, out here in the outhouse. But at least it was dry. Bony Wright, if he was crossing the moor in this downpour, would be cold and wet. Cold and wet slow you up. It was a bad night for bodyguards, yes, but a bad night for intruders, too. It worked out about even.

Starshine sat in the chair, his weight tilting it back on its rear legs. He picked up and broke the shotgun, checked the dryness of the cartridges; then rested the gun against the wall again. Henry, his relief guard, would be arriving in an hour's time; he hoped Henry'd have the sense to keep off the road when he walked up from the cottage, to use the grass track behind the skirting wall. There'd be an inch or two of mud on that track, so he might well be tempted to use the road. But then so might Bony Wright. Bony wouldn't know about the track; and he'd use the road, on a night like this, rather than run the risk of getting lost on the moors, with an unfenced cliff edge yawning a few hundred feet away. He'd come quietly up the road until he could see the light conveniently burning in the porch; then he'd climb the wall beside the gate and circle the outer rim of that pool of light and come in across the courtyard, keeping, no doubt, to the far wall. Starshine had worked it all out. There wasn't very much, he thought, that could go wrong.

He felt, all the same, a little uneasy. He wished that he knew why.

CHAPTER 22

Motor racing, that source of endless anecdote. The tracks, the shunts, the winners, the losers, the quick and the dead, the maimed and the lucky, the breakdowns, the spin-offs, the lame dogs and the squirt jobs; Ford, Ferrari, Maserati, and Aston-Martin; Clarkie, Graham Hill and Surtees, Hawthorn and Jackie Stewart. "He was a wonder on the corners, Hawthorn. Him and Stirling. Nobody to touch them when they were getting hot."

"Ah, it's the key to style, cornering. The key to style. Sorts out the men from the boys, I always say."

"You never knew where they'd strike, on a wet track. Could come from the left or the right or even from right behind you. While someone like Rinty . . . Lovely driver, mind you, but he'd always strike from the right. Always gave you the chance to cut him off. Oh, sometimes it'd be a feint, he had a trick or two, but I always reckoned to have old Rinty's number once I was in front of him. Trouble was getting there in the first place."

Jenny in the corner armchair, seemingly asleep. The two men at the kitchen table, talking quietly, the overhead light flicking shadows across the table's surface as their hands moved, gesticulated, mimed caution, aggression, joy, sudden disaster. And outside, the ceaseless murmur of the falling rain. ". . . Lost me a race though, once. Rinty did."

"Spun you off, you mean?"

"No. Did it without ever even coming near me. Right on the last lap, too, when I was sitting on a nice long lead—which wasn't something that happened all that often. There I was, tooling along nicely, when up from behind comes old Rin-Tin-Tin, cornering like smoke and all tucked up over the wheel as usual and moving out right to take me, sure enough. I'm not worried because if I can edge out to hold him back on the corners, I know I've got enough squirt to hold him on the straights. And that's just the way it is, all the way round —creeping out, falling back again, no kind of problem. Up to the last straight, that is. I take a quick look on the final bend and there he is, edging outside me again in a resigned sort of way, so I think, *Good, he knows he can't take me now,* I take the corner wide to pin him back and buggered if he doesn't come left and take me like I'm standing still—wham! Like, squirt . . . ? He's got *bags* of it. Shoots up that damned last straight like an electric bloody hare. Well, and then, *then* I realise it wasn't Rinty at all. It was bloody Graham. Having me on like a good 'un."

"What you might call a bit of an impersonation, was it? I'm surprised," Bony said, "you fell for it."

"I never fell for it again. But you're right. Just the once is once too often."

"You mean he *tried* it again?"

"Not the same trick, no. But he had a different bluff for each day of the week. There was the great tyre-changing gimmick, for example. That was the time—"

"Yes," Bony said. ". . . Wait a moment."

"That was the time he . . ." Tracy, in full flow of reminiscence, had a moment's difficulty in finding the brake pedal. Bony's right hand, raised abruptly like a policeman's, helped him to discover and apply it; following the new direction of Bony's gaze, he turned and stared back at Jenny the Benny, who, slumped in her armchair with her eyes closed, was clearly taking no interest in their conversation whatsoever. He couldn't quite fathom the reason for Bony's interruption. ". . . No, *she's* all right. She's asleep."

"I wasn't thinking about that," Bony said.

"What *were* you thinking about, then?"

"I was thinking, that's a wig she's wearing. Noticed it before, but it didn't . . . Now I'm *thinking* about it. Know what I mean?"

"No," Tracy said.

"Danny LaRue wears a wig like that."

"*What?*"

"He's an impersonator, too. Haven't you ever seen him . . . ?
Very popular, he is. Specially at Strangeways."

"Ah!" Tracy blew out his cheeks. "Now I follow you. Yes. *Now*
I see the connection. Rather a different sort of a—"

"No. Just the same thing, really. If it only works once, that's
enough. It's just the same principle."

Tracy stared at the snoozing Jenny in considerable puzzlement.
He was being, he couldn't help feeling, slow in the uptake. *What*
had to work once? What was the connection, if it wasn't . . . ? The
thing was so annoyingly elusive. He could see it, and then he
couldn't. He saw it. And then he didn't . . .

And *then* he saw . . .

Bernadette: "What's that man doing on the stairs?"

She didn't sound angry or frightened. Curious, chiefly.

"That," Pope said, "is Tony. He's there to keep an eye on things."

"What things?"

"It's Leo's idea, really."

"But *what* things?"

"Well, on us, I suppose. There has to be someone else here because of the divorce. Otherwise it's co-operation or whatever they
call it."

"If you think I'll swallow that, you think I'll swallow anything."

"Then let's just say it's none of your business."

"Yes," Bernadette said. She still didn't get cross. "*That* explanation I can accept. How am I supposed to treat him . . . ? Like one
of the servants?"

"Like he isn't here."

"How many other people aren't here?"

"You don't *really* want to know," Pope said.

CHAPTER 23

The little bulb glowed smokily, hanging from a length of dilapi-
dated flex at just above Tracy's eye level; from time to time it
flickered off and on, a kind of token strike action that seemed only
too likely to end in a permanent dismissal. Even when it was working properly it had barely the power to illumine dimly the farther
wall of the cellar, some six feet distant from where Tracy stood.
Bony Wright, his hand still resting on the switch, looked about him

with apparent favour: "Nice secluded little nook," he said cosily. "You'll be very comfortable down here, I should think."

Tracy couldn't share his optimism. There was a rickety bench in the far corner just big enough for two people to sit on, but the furniture otherwise fell very short of his not very exacting standards; it wasn't, in fact, furniture so much as a pile of miscellaneous junk, much of which seemed to be rotting away. It was damp enough, of course, down in the cellar for this not to be wondered at. The door, on the other hand, was, as far as he could tell, depressingly solid.

It was secured with a nine-inch iron bar which slid into a hole in the brickwork on the far side. This bar Bony now tested, rattling it cheerfully to and fro. "You won't get past this in a hurry."

"No," Tracy said. "At least, I don't see how."

"Well . . . So long, then."

The door closed, this time behind him, and the bolt rattled again in its groove of cement, this time with finality. Not, Tracy thought, the most prolonged or affectionate of farewells, but then time, for Bony, was getting short. It was half-past eleven. He gave the closed door an experimental push (really with no purpose in mind other than that of giving the door an experimental push) and, when it didn't open obligingly, turned to walk the length of the cellar (a total distance of four short paces) and sat down on the cobweb-fringed bench, which creaked alarmingly. He felt dispirited.

"What you going to do?" Jenny said.

"Nothing much we can do, until he's left. Then we'll try and get ourselves out of here."

"You reckon we can?"

"We certainly have to try. He's the only one who knows where we are."

"And he won't be coming back? To let us out?"

"I don't suppose so for a moment."

"Lummy," Jenny said. She managed to invest this quaint and rather old-fashioned expletive with a good deal of contemporary significance. "There's a nice thought."

Tracy had turned half sideways on the bench to rest his head against the undressed bricks of the wall. "Don't talk for a moment. I'm listening."

The cellar walls, under ground level, echoed the ceaseless splashing of the raindrops on the earth as a monotonous, whispering boom, clearly audible yet, after the first few seconds, so easily assimilable by the ear as to pass unnoticed. There were other sounds, most of them indirectly caused by the rain and the sudden increase in humidity; the occasional sighing murmur of expanding timbers, the rattle of tiny pebbles washing down the gutters, the gurgling slither of rainwater flowing down narrow and doubtless badly rusted pipes. Behind this steady screening rumble of inanimate movement there were other sounds, the sounds that Tracy was listening for; sounds of indeterminate human activity, the more definite and rhythmic thud of footsteps, the grunt of complaining stairtreads, once—he was almost sure—the sound of a man's voice, either Wright's or Henry's. Tracy was listening to the cottage with the same fastidious ear he was accustomed to attune to the varying pitch of a racing engine—with a delicate instrument carefully trained and developed; he turned away and relaxed only when, some eight minutes later and loudly enough for Jonny also to hear it and to look upwards towards the flaking ceiling, the front door slammed. ". . . There. They've gone."

"*They* have?"

"Yes. Henry as well. Before that he was doing something . . . What's on the left-hand side of the passageway? At the foot of the stairs? A cupboard, or something like that?"

"Yes. Where we keep the raincoats and things."

Tracy clicked his tongue. "Well, of course. Stupid of me."

Now that he wasn't concentrating, he could feel the beginnings of pain, a nagging ache around the eye muscles and behind the base of his nose; it wasn't a bad pain, not as yet, but he knew that now it had started it would get worse. It always did. Already it seemed to have affected the clarity of his thinking; raincoats of course they'd have needed, and probably hats. What else, on a night like this? Anyway, Bony was gone, taking Henry with him. That was what mattered.

"There was this thing I saw on the telly," Jenny said. "They dug a tunnel."

"Who did?"

"It was in the war, like, and there were all these prisoners and they dug this tunnel. Then they all escaped down it and ran away."

"Ah yes. I think," Tracy said, "I'll have a look at that door again."

But the door still promised nothing. Certainly there was a crack at the bottom wide enough to permit the insertion of a crowbar, and the stone floor beneath offered excellent leverage; but they didn't have a crowbar or anything like one. "I've got a nail file," Jenny said. "I'm afraid that won't be much use," said Tracy. He reached up to probe with his fingers at the plaster ceiling, no more than nine inches above his upturned face; this seemed very much more hopeful. There were damp patches there where the plaster flaked away almost at a touch. "I don't know, though. It might be. Let's try it and see." The point of the file sank easily into the plaster to a depth of perhaps an inch, halted against the harder-packed material above. Tracy began to scrape; evil-smelling yellow powder descended in clouds onto his hair, his shoulders, and to the floor; Jenny retreated hastily as far as she could, which wasn't very far. "Puh," she said.

"Yes. But it's pretty soft, isn't it? The trouble's going to be when we get through to the floorboards."

"What happens if it all comes down on top of us?"

"That's not very likely to happen." All the same, the idea occasioned Tracy some disquiet; he paused, and spat out a mouthful of mould. If possible, the stuff tasted even worse than it smelt. "Have a look round and see if you can find anything better to poke with. A bit of stick would do. Or a hammer and chisel." Smiling bitterly at his own savage irony, he resumed his painful scratching and scraping, while Jenny investigated, not without some trepidation, the heap of useless lumber piled up by the far wall. "Here you are, then," she observed eventually. "A hammer and chisel."

"A *what?*"

"A hammer and chisel. That was what you wanted, wasn't it?"

Tracy gaped at her in silence, wondering whether under the strain her tiny little mind had given way or whether, alternatively, he had been incarcerated with a woman whose sense of humour was so hideously perverted as to verge on the psychotic. Neither prospect encouraged him very greatly. Then he tottered across the cellar to find that, incredibly enough, there was no mistake. She'd found not merely a hammer and chisel, but a whole bloody toolbox. It looked as though someone had been carrying out some kind of repairs on the cellar brickwork, or possibly interring a cadaver; there was a recess where the plaster looked comparatively fresh and where the bricks, clearly, were new. The toolbox was in the recess. It was of metal and there were specks of rust on the outside of it, but the tools within were apparently in perfect condition. Hammer, chisel, brace and set of bits, screwdrivers, screws and nails in plastic containers, a nine-inch handsaw . . . "Good God," Tracy said. "A Do-It-Yourself Housebreaking Kit. I can't believe it. I mean, I thought you were joking."

"Me?"

"They wouldn't have dared to put this in your television script, I'll tell you that."

Jenny seemed no more than moderately pleased at having thus rendered the kind gentleman a signal service. "Can you get through the ceiling with that lot, then?"

"Through the ceiling? God, no. Whatever for? We'll have that door down in a jiffy." Tracy slapped at the front of his jacket, and another pungent yellowish cloud rose sulkily into the air. "I wish," he said, in a momentary display of unjust irritation, "you'd found that box five minutes ago, before . . . However."

"Well, I wasn't looking, was I?"

"No, but then who'd have thought . . . Never mind."

He took off his jacket, tossed it over the bench and, seizing the toolbox, carried it energetically over to the door. Hammer, chisel, who *would* have thought of it, indeed? Bony Wright obviously hadn't. He knelt before the door, probing its defences with the edge of the chisel; then, selecting his spot, began to wield the hammer with vigour and precision. The cellar resounded to the vehemence of his attack. *Bang, bang, bang.* Dust drifted from the heavy wooden panels.

CHAPTER 24

Starshine heard them coming through the gate; first the creak and rattle of the gate itself, moving painfully back on its rusty hinges, a sharp click of metal against stone and then the sound of a voice, recognisably Henry's, uplifted in brief expostulation. He heard it, but he couldn't believe it. He stood up, leaning forwards to peer into the swinging palm fronds of the pouring rain, and there they were, coming straight across the courtyard, Henry and that bloody Jenny, his hand tucked solicitously under her elbow to guide her as she moved awkwardly over the loose cobbles; the chestnut-coloured wig, tucked inadequately under the hood of her light blue raincoat, gleamed in the lamplight as she turned her head—like a signal, he thought, like a flaming signal. What the hell she thought she was doing . . . and what the hell Henry thought he was doing, bringing her up here . . . His fury was such that at first he couldn't find the words he needed, not in English. Stupidity of this kind he hadn't expected, *nobody* could have expected. "What in . . . God's name are you doing here?" It wasn't what he'd wanted to say; it was the best he could manage. When, by way of reply, Jenny waved her hand at him, he could barely repress the urge to leap forwards and hit her in the face; he felt his fingers curling up into fists, relaxed them with a deliberate effort of concentration. "Listen, Henry, I'm going to, I'm going to . . ." Raindrops glistening on Henry's long face, above the turned-up raincoat collar; Starshine glanced from Henry to Jenny and saw that it wasn't Jenny and knew what had happened and by then they were only five paces away from him and it was too late; he turned, one hand extended towards the shotgun, but changed his mind, knowing he'd left it too late, and he turned back and knew, seeing Bony's narrowed eyes under the incongruous shining curls of the chestnut wig, above the broad slash of the heavily lipsticked mouth, that he had changed his mind just in time to save—at least for the time being—his life. The blue steel barrel of the pistol was also regarding him incuriously; he looked down at it, then away. He didn't want to see that small dark hollow eye dimmed by the blossoming flash of the bullet; he had faced pistols before and he wasn't afraid, he had control, if it had to happen it would happen but if it happened he didn't want to see it happen, he'd feel the blow, the searing impact, the pain, and that would be all. He stared instead into Bony Wright's calm, curiously unseeing eyes and Bony Wright gazed evenly back at him.

"No," Bony said. "Don't back up. Just turn round. Slowly."

That was really all there was to it. It was simple.

Starshine turned, thinking *She'd never have worn the wig. Not in this rain* and, while he was turning, Bony struck at him with the pistol barrel and Starshine fell, his shoulder striking the wall and twisting him round so that he pitched, in the end, face upwards into a long black puddle of rainpocked water, mouth open in an unconscious recollection of pain and of surprise. Bony looked down at him with cautious satisfaction; he didn't think he'd hit too hard this time. Though if he had, this time it wouldn't very much have mattered.

"Drag him inside."

Henry hesitated for a moment; then stooped, got his hands under Starshine's shoulders and, with Bony stepping daintily alongside, lugged the dead weight through the outhouse door. He didn't have the chance to straighten up again; Bony was fast gaining in expertise. Henry's knees buckled and he slid straight forwards to pillow his head on Starshine's recumbent body. The angled lamplight showed only his muddy shoes.

Bony pushed the pistol back into the pocket of his, of Jenny's raincoat and took out a handkerchief to wipe the smeared lipstick from his mouth. He pulled off the wig and threw it, with a gesture of infantile triumph, down at the prostrate figures on the floor; it had worked, he thought—worked once, and that had been enough. He'd have been great on the racetrack, one of the great ones; he'd always thought so, and now he knew.

He swung the outhouse door soundlessly to, fastened it securely with the padlock and chain. Then he checked his wristwatch. Twelve o'clock exactly. Time to get on with the job.

CHAPTER 25

. . . While seated once more at the table in the cottage kitchen, Tracy held against his forehead a folded handkerchief full of fast-melting ice cubes. Even with the help of the hammer and chisel, breaking down the cellar door had involved him in considerable physical exertion, and at one point his head had seemed to be splintering to the blows faster than the wood itself. He wasn't surprised that his habitual migraine had chosen this moment to return; he'd been having, by any standards, a harrowing time lately and it was odd, indeed, that it hadn't returned before. "It'll clear up all right," he said, knowing that it wouldn't. "I went a bit short of sleep last night. That's probably the cause of it."

"You ought to lie down if you're feeling bad."

"Lying down doesn't do much good."

"Well, where's it hurt?"

"It's sort of a headache, really."

She stooped over his chair from behind, and he felt her fingers touch his temples, then move down to press gently on the muscles at each side of his neck. "Sometimes you think it's a headache and it's really your neck where it's at. I had a good doctor told me that once."

"No," Tracy said. "It's my head all right."

Her fingers moved up again behind his ears and stopped there, motionless. He sensed her sudden consternation. "Cor luvvaduck. What you got here?"

"It's just a bit of metal. They took a bit of my skull out, you see, and put a metal plate there instead. It's nothing to worry about."

"No wonder your head aches." Her fingers went away; he heard her moving round to the far side of the table. He opened his eyes effortfully; she was leaning on the back of a chair and watching him dubiously. She was scared, he thought. If so, she wasn't the first;

there's something about men with stainless steel heads that young girls find very off-putting, and Jenny was a good deal younger than he'd at first supposed. She was opening her handbag. He wondered why. Pain creased his eyes, and he screwed them shut again.

". . . Here. Try a couple of these."

Small red pills on the table. And a glass of water. "What are they?"

"They'll give you a lift."

He pushed two of the pills into his mouth and sipped at the glass, clumsily sloshing water over the table as he set it down again. "So that's why they call you that."

"Call me what?"

"The Benny."

"Ah, that's silly. Those aren't bennies. Nobody takes bennies any more. Those are . . . phenosomething. Nothing wrong with *them*, I got them from my doctor."

"The one who massages your neck?"

"They all do that."

"I'll bet."

Tracy pushed his chair back and stood up. "Is it still raining?"

"Bloody pouring. Can't you hear it?"

He could, yes. It was just that he'd forgotten you could tell by listening. "I'll need a coat, then."

"You're never going out?"

"I can clear my head that way sometimes. A nice long walk in the fresh country air. Try and find a coat for me, there's a love."

"All right."

A nice, obedient girl, Jenny. Or maybe that metal plate was still worrying her. Tracy didn't really blame her; he wasn't sure that he'd much care to be left all alone with himself in a deserted cottage by the edge of a cliff on a wild and stormy midnight. And she'd had a pretty harrowing evening, if it came to that, being locked up in cellars by jailbreaking murderers and escaping only to find Frankenstein Junior starting one of his headachy spells; once out of doors he'd no doubt conveniently transmute into a werewolf. Really she'd behaved with remarkable aplomb. And here she was back again with somebody's brown check burberry; Starshine's, most likely. It was rather too wide at the waist, but that didn't matter; he could belt it in, and did. It was also much too short in the sleeves. There was nothing he could do about that.

"Are you coming back?"

"I don't know," Tracy said.

"I'm locking the doors, anyway. Soon as you're gone."

"A very sensible plan."

He walked out into the hallway. The image came to him, as he thumbed the heavy latch of the front door, of two men sitting on a hilltop in sultry afternoon sunlight; Bony Wright with the field glasses in his hands, the other with his arms folded and knees pressed primly together, seated on a hard hot rock (a sure means, according to his mother, of developing piles). The recollection was of hallucinatory intensity; it was possible, he thought, that in fact he'd taken too much sun. Certainly the skin of his face and neck seemed now to be burning hot, and the coldness of the wind that pressed against him when he swung the door open took him by surprise. Buttoning down the skirts of the raincoat, he wondered if he mightn't again be doing the wrong, as well as a stupid, thing; the chances were high that he was running a temperature. He looked back at Jenny, standing silhouetted in the kitchen doorway; the kitchen seemed indeed to be a warm, well-lighted place, her silhouette an obviously pleasing—not to say promising—one. "Well," he said uncertainly. He thought that he rather liked Jenny. She seemed a placid, good-tempered girl; except in thunderstorms, of course.

"If you're going up to the house . . ."

"What?"

But his present uncertainty seemed to be affecting her, also. ". . . Nothing."

He looked away, and rain spattered sharply into his face. "Keep the doors locked," he said. "You'll be all right."

He closed the door behind him without looking back and set off in what he took to be the general direction of the garden gate, though initially he was aware only of darkness, of the wind, of the blustering rain and of mud underfoot; the mud was sticky rather than slippery, adhering grimly to the heels of his shoes so that he had to wrench his feet free at every step. The thump of the raindrops on his bare head was at first actively painful, but then invigorating as a shower—unless, as he walked, the phenobarbitone was taking a hold on him and inducing an artificial euphoria. He missed the gate, but by the filtered light from the kitchen window he found the stone wall that circled the garden; it was no more than four feet high and he surmounted it without any difficulty. The mournful strain of a Cat Stevens number followed him across the wall; Jenny had turned on the radio.

On the road, progress was much easier. He covered some fifty yards before discovering—in fact, almost bumping into—Bony's Mini parked where they had left it and before realising, in consequence, that he was walking along the main road on a course that might eventually, if he scaled a number of varied mountains and coaltips, bring him out somewhere north of Merthyr Tydfil. He retraced his steps, recovered his bearings, found the side turning and trudged off down the driveway, still wondering whether Merthyr mightn't be, after all, quite a *good* place to end up in after a pleasant forty-mile stroll. A dip, a rise, and then in the distance the dim lights of Y Bannau burning in the swirling rain; he stopped and gazed at them vaguely. Nothing was moving. Nothing was happening. Or maybe something was, but he couldn't see it. He still had a full half mile to go. Another ten minutes of teeming dampness. The rain had been falling for three hours now and seemed likely never to stop.

He couldn't get much wetter, that was for sure. Marching stolidly forwards again, he could feel the clammy pressure of his trouser legs against his calves, where the raincoat skirts were diverting streams of water, and he could hear the squelch of the moisture in his shoes. The noise didn't much matter; the night was full of the sound of the gurgling rain, a sound oddly distorted and magnified by he didn't know what. Puzzling it out, he realised eventually that his ears, too, were collecting the water that dripped down from his hair; he tried to expel it with the tips of his little fingers, and that helped things a little but not much. The odd auditory effects were softened, but continued. Squelch, squelch, squelch. Left, right, left, right.

He was covering the ground splendidly now, with long, steady, unhesitant, manly strides; he quickened his pace a little, squilp-squilp-squilp, then slowed it down again. Perfect control, perfect. Almost his whole body was wet now and getting cold, rivulets having worked their way down inside his collar and between his shoulderblades to make a sodden mass of shirt-cloth around his waist. The only comparatively dry part of his anatomy was that which still ached unpleasantly from Bony's kick; everywhere else it was wet, it was cold and it itched. Tracy giggled to himself and looked up.

The gate was no more than fifty yards distant; the lamp in the sheltered porch was no longer a pale speck but cast now a warm, inviting glow. As he surveyed it, a brighter, sharper light leapt at him from the courtyard, a little to his left, annihilating the intervening space and stabbing cruelly at the pupils of his eyes; Tracy doubled up, half-crouching, as though heavily struck in the solar plexus, and staggered in this position a few paces sideways, hearing as he did so the bumbling mutter of a high-capacity car engine starting up. *Off the road*, he thought, *get out of the road*, and reaching the wall, toppled over, raincoat skirts flying and ripping, his hands thrusting downwards into cold and greasy mud; he lay on the grass, snorting unamusedly to himself, as the moor behind him became alive to the headlamp beams, a vast heaving glitter of raindrops, the moisture rising from it in smokelike wraiths. Recovering his feet and, to some extent, his balance, he peered cautiously over the wall as the car went by. It was Tommy Pope's Bentley. There were two people in it, but he couldn't see their faces clearly. He clambered back over the wall, wiping his hands on the sleeves of his raincoat. The tail lights of the Bentley winked and disappeared, returned briefly to view as it mounted the slope by the cottage, finally vanished as it swung right onto the main road. Tracy turned, stared back at the house. The glare of the headlamps had dazzled him; now, outside the fan of light radiating from the porch, he could see nothing at all. But beneath the centre of that hazy circle there was a rectangular circle; the front door, it seemed, had been left open. Tracy started to run; his feet slipping here, there, everywhere, his former control of their movements apparently lost. The raincoat kept catching irritatingly at his knees.

All the same, he got there somehow.

The lights were on in the hallway and the man called Tony was lying at the foot of the stairs, one leg thrown up against the banisters, in a position that suggested he'd fallen while descending; this one, however, couldn't have been an accident. Blood had stained and was still staining the carpet where his head lay; some of it had come out of his mouth, but most from the thin knife slit at the base of his neck. Rusty Keyes's mottled face had been bad enough, but this was worse. This was obscene and horrible. Tracy gave it no more than a glance, then went on through to the sitting room, where Bernadette was trying, without much success, to push herself up from the floor where for the last two or three minutes she'd obviously been lying. Tracy picked her up and planked her down in the nearest armchair. *She* was all right. As he might have guessed.

"Tracy . . . ? What the hell are you doing here?"

"Looking for trouble," Tracy bragged. "You got any?" He leaned forwards, leering up into her face, which was disfigured—he now saw—by the beginnings of a magnificent black eye. "Yes, I see you have. Where d'you get the shiner?"

"The shin . . . ? Never mind that now. Wasn't that a car I just heard?"

"Yes. The Bentley."

"Tommy and that . . . another man?"

"Two men, anyway. I couldn't see."

She stood up, pushing him back in order to do so. He didn't quite fall over. "Where've they gone?"

"I don't know," Tracy said. "London, maybe."

"Come on. Come *on*. Hurry up."

"But come on where?"

"I want you to drive."

"Why?"

"Because you drive better than me. Even when I haven't got one eye bunged up." Half pushing, half helping him through the door back into the hallway. She paid no attention to Tony's corpse. She had to have seen it before.

"You want us to *follow* them?"

"Well, of course."

"He's a pretty fast driver."

"Tommy? He can't drive for nuts."

"It won't be him. No. The other chap."

"You're supposed to be fast, too, aren't you . . . ? I'll say one thing for you, Tracy. You show up damned opportunely."

CHAPTER 26

It was odd how, once in the driving seat of the Lamborghini, everything became very simple. Walking had been difficult, thinking had been difficult, making plans almost impossible. Arguing with Bernadette . . . you're joking, of course. But driving—yes, that as always was easy. That was the trouble. Driving, you didn't have to think about anything else. And a little forethought is sometimes a good thing to take. But not now. Now it was too late. Because Tracy was driving now and driving was easy. Lambo purred out of the gate and down the driveway, windscreen wipers flicking greedily, competently at the streaming rain. "Which road'll he have taken?"

"I don't know. Probably straight up to the Cowbridge Road and then he'll turn right for Cardiff. That's if he's headed for London. Well, we have to assume he is, because if he's not we won't catch him, anyway."

Out onto the road in a fast screw turn, the tyres biting into the soft mud to find the hard undersurface. A glimpse in the rear view mirror of a dimly lit window, of the blurred outline of the cottage; a sharp, unexpected recollection of a slim silhouette in a narrow hallway; goodbye, Jenny. Fourth gear, and Lambo sliding exhilaratingly forwards down the long slope of the moor, toboganning in a hissing stillness along the silver-flecked blackness of the road; there wouldn't, Tracy thought, be much other traffic abroad tonight. There had to be a chance of his picking the Bentley up, though unless he did it before they reached Cardiff the chance had to be accounted very thin. He glanced sideways at Bernadette and saw, by the phantasmal dashboard light, that her cheeks were wet. And not, as he thought, with rain.

"Painful," he said, "a smack in the eye. I know. I've had one."

"It's not that. Or not only that. I'm frightened."

"Yes. That I can understand, too."

"He killed somebody back there."

"I was afraid he might have to," Tracy said. "In fact I was afraid he'd kill *you*. But you seem to have got lucky."

"Why would he . . . I mean, who *is* he? What's he want?"

"His name's Bony Wright. And he wants Tommy."

"That's the one who . . . ?"

"That's the one."

". . . Was in all the papers? What's he want with *Tommy*?"

"It's a long story," Tracy said.

"But you know it?"

"Some of it. Tommy owes him money, is what it all boils down to."

"I owe lots of people money. They don't chase after me with guns and things and . . . slit other people's throats. It doesn't make sense."

"It's rather a lot of money," Tracy said. "Not by your standards, maybe, but Bony Wright thinks so. And Tommy got him sent to prison, you see, so as not to have to pay him. It's all gone to give him rather a jaundiced view."

"But he was sent to prison for murder."

"And for robbery. But it's a long story, like I said."

"And now he's killed someone else. It's different when you see it done. To reading about it in the papers."

"I imagine it is. *Did* you see it done?"

"Oh yes. It wasn't very nice."

"No," Tracy said. "Not nice. No."

Bernadette was all right, though, except for a black eye and maybe a bump on the back of the head. That was the important thing. He was driving fast, now, but well within himself; he couldn't see a lot of point in this pursuit, and if he didn't catch up with the Bentley too quickly she might change her mind about it.

She had to have time, though, to make the decision for herself; it'd be no good trying to persuade her. Maybe (Tracy thought) from my brief contacts with Bernadette I'm beginning to gain some inkling of feminine psychology, a subject I never knew very much about before. And there again, maybe I'm not.

(The car running now between grassy banks topped with high hedges; the road narrow, winding and with a watersplash at every dip. The rain was showing no sign of stopping.)

". . . Robbery," Bernadette said. Her voice was this time raised little above a whisper; in almost any car but Lambo, it would have been inaudible. "But it was Leo's place he did. The Bond Street one. I remember about it now. It makes sense after all." The tears had left dark smudgy tracks across her cheeks, but she wasn't crying now. "You're telling me, aren't you, that Tommy . . . Was it Tommy who set it up?"

"You ought to ask Tommy about that. Not me."

"I don't have to ask him. I can remember his asking *me*, I remember our talking . . ." She stopped, suddenly and, Tracy felt, deliberately. "Why didn't you tell me about all this before? And how are *you* in on it?"

"I'm not. I didn't know about it before."

"Then how do you . . . ?"

"Bony Wright told me."

She shook her head. "I don't understand."

"I've been with him ever since I left your place. Talking to him. I thought maybe I could talk him out of it. Going in after Tommy, I mean. But no. I couldn't."

"Not exactly your strong point, is it? Your command of rhetoric."

"No, and besides, he's a little bit obsessed."

"You mean off his rocker."

"Well, I wouldn't say so. Not exactly. He just has a funny way of looking at things. But we got on all right, on the whole. In fact I rather like him."

"Yes, you would."

"He likes me, too. He didn't kill me. He locked me up in a cellar instead. The thing is he wanted once to be a racing driver, so we had something to talk about. Or a point in common, sort of. Of course, he'd kill me if I got in his way. But then I didn't do that. I was careful not to."

"The man on the staircase did."

"Quite so. I wonder what happened to the others. Well, better not to wonder, perhaps."

"There *were* others, then? I thought as much."

At last, the Bonvilston crossroads; and the wide three-track highway, running east to Cardiff. They were higher now than on the coast, and turning, Tracy felt the shuddering drag of the wind; it would have to be blowing a force eight gale, at least, for Lambo to feel it. Perhaps this was the warm front, following the eye of the storm. ". . . Tommy didn't say anything about them?"

"Oh, just some stupid story."

"There were two others in the outhouse. A hard boy and the bloke in charge. A man called Starchino."

"That's . . . I've heard that name."

"He works for your father sometimes. Unless I should say, *worked*. Anyway, Mr. Greene sent him."

"Sent him to help Tommy?"

"Well . . . As a bodyguard."

After a long pause, she said,

"That I don't understand, either."

Here on the heights Lambo was running into pockets of mist, long trailers of streamy moisture hanging at eye-level and lower, fanning out across the road in the angled headlights. Tracy couldn't make it out; the combination of mist and a raging gale seemed to him a bit much. Often, he found, these cloudy tendrils were the prelude to a fierce whipping *whooooshhh* from the spinning tyres as they slashed across puddles of standing water. "They won't be going too bloody fast in this," Tracy said. "Not till they're on the motorway." Of course there was the chance they weren't headed back to London after all; but it seemed the most likely bet. London was Bony's home patch, and much the most likely place for Pope to have stashed the loot. Getting his hands on all that gold was still going to be something of a problem for Bony; even when Pope had talked, he still had to collect it and transport it somewhere else. Tracy raised his left hand to squeeze the bridge of his nose. Driving was easy, but thinking still wasn't. His thoughts still circled, collided, bounced off at a tangent. The words wouldn't come.

"What are we going to do?"

"Eh?"

". . . When we catch them up?"

A good question. Tracy didn't know the answer. "Well," he said. "I'm open to suggestions."

"I thought we might just follow them and see where they're going."

"That's about all we *can* do."

"But he'll know he's being followed. He'll see our headlights, won't he . . . ? He's bound to."

"Yes, that's true."

"D'you think he'd do anything? If he thought there was someone after him?"

"He'd certainly do *something*."

"Yes, but I meant . . . dangerous . . . ?"

"For us?"

"Yes, for us."

"Almost anything he did," Tracy said, "would be dangerous for us. Even if it was just try to run away. This isn't the weather for chasing after people." And there wasn't any prospect of its clearing up; in fact, by driving eastwards they were probably moving back into the centre of the storm. The petrol tank, he had noticed, was almost full; their fuel supply wouldn't outlast his, and in these conditions the extra weight wouldn't slow him down all that much. His own energy drain was another matter; he didn't think that the effect of the phenobarbitone tablets would stay with him for more than an hour or so. But then, he didn't really know. And calculations, these were all calculations; he wasn't in the mood. Drive, yes. That he could do; at least, for a while. But nothing else.

"So maybe it's not very sensible. Going after them."

"Probably not."

"But what else can we do?"

"Yes. That's been the trouble all along."

"I don't know what the hell you mean by that."

"Nor do I," Tracy said. "Not really."

Starshine, when he came to, could hear the telephone ringing distantly in the house, the faint shrilling of the bell at odds with the rhythmic, hurtful thumping inside his skull. Mr. Lewis, no doubt, would be calling from Cardiff, checking up on how things were going; now that things had quite certainly gone, there didn't seem to be much that Starshine could do about it. He massaged his head, nonetheless, and started to crawl on his hands and knees towards the door; which shook, as he approached, to a great tearing gust of rain-spattered wind. Then, abruptly, the telephone stopped ringing.

. . . While Bony drove, fast and competently, down the long hill towards Culverhouse Cross, the storm-dimmed lights of Cardiff spread out in front of him against a dark backcloth of unbroken cloud. Now that his operation was almost completed, he, too, was beginning to feel tired; the long drive back to town would demand his last resources of energy and concentration and he was trying— in this its initial stage—consciously to relax; but to do so without surrendering to the waves of weariness that were threatening to overcome him. The right mood of comfortable alertness was hard to find; his mind kept seesawing awkwardly from one extreme to the other. He had silenced Tommy Pope's earlier attempts to open a conversation and Tommy had, since then, been a very good boy indeed, sitting motionless in the passenger seat and gazing lugubri- ously out through the swimming windscreen; but a bit of a chat, Bony now thought, might be a good idea. It would help to steady his nerves and to distract Tommy Pope's attention from the un- palatable future. (Though the truth of the matter, he now realised, was that he was missing Tracy. It's agreeable sometimes to have someone you can talk to. It was almost like a discovery he had made.)

". . . You want to talk?"

"I thought *you* didn't want to," Tommy said, without turning his head.

"I was a bit jumpy when we started off. It's all right now."

"Could you untie me, then?"

"No," Bony said. "No point in it."

Pope was brave, if you counted that a point in his favour. At least, he didn't now seem very obviously to be afraid. And it wasn't en- tirely Dutch courage, either; he'd been drinking all right, but he wasn't being belligerent. He was being a very good boy. Exercising, in other words, a tight control; Bony admired that. Though even now Pope maybe had some small hope of being able to talk up a deal; they're always optimistic, that kind, and he couldn't yet be sure that he was going to be killed. Not *completely* sure. And it was better, from Bony's point of view, that he should remain uncertain, at least until the journey to London was over.

"Look," Tommy said. "Really the situation's very simple. You want money. I want to stay alive. We ought to be able to come to some arrangement."

"Yes, we can. That's the whole idea. You're going to tell me where you've unloaded the stuff. I'm going to collect it. You're going to sit tight while I'm collecting it. Then I'll let you go."

"The snag is, how do I know you'll let me go?"

"It's a snag from your point of view, yes. Not from mine. Because the other things you're going to do, anyway."

"I'm no use to you dead," Tommy said.

It wasn't altogether true, but Bony nodded equably. They had passed the crossroads now and were driving into Ely; pavements, lampposts, comfortable white-fronted houses to either side; civilisation. But the road empty of cars; at one o'clock on a Sunday night with the rain still whipping down in a frenzy, they had the whole place to themselves. "It's not letting up," he said. "The weather, I mean."

"Where are we going?"

"I told you. London."

"But where in London?"

"Just a place I know," Bony said.

Bernadette staring, tight-lipped, through the side window. The ordered lights of Llandaff, the warm orange and the yellow, the long rows of blinkered houses, all argued a return to normality, imposed a sensible pattern on their former windy rushing through a vast nothingness. But with this sense of normality, a return of fear; the possibility recurring of a warm well-furnished room, of a door opening and of a man entering, looking at her, of a bubble of blood bursting from his mouth in place of the expected words of greeting. An image of nightmare; she closed her eyes; it had been, it *was* horrible. She had been, and still was, frightened. She had tried not to admit it, to close her mind to horror, to be brave. But all that had entered her mind in place of fear was a cold unreality, a jumble of disconnected memories and thoughts through which the obvious need for immediate action had struck a random path, had taken her out to the car and into the storm and now to this maze of lights and houses. But wasn't that madness? Or something very like it? Now that the patterns of reality were re-forming about her, she had no choice but to recognise her own irrationality of behaviour and to see that its source lay in terror. "I'm frightened again," she said suddenly.

A huddle of road signs in the steaming haze of rain; a roundabout; Lambo taking the turn at speed, effortlessly, with no more than the softest sigh from the outside tyres. A dual carriageway now, the houses falling back, giving way to trees and open fields, arc-lamps high overhead; a lorry in front of them, its own shadow chasing it, catching it, reappearing and recommencing the chase; Lambo swung out to pass and brought the tail lights of another car or lorry, a mile or so ahead, briefly into view.

"Let's go back."

Tracy didn't look at her, didn't say anything. She might as well have spoken to the car and expected it to obey her. Rain slammed at the windscreen in a sudden spurt of venom; she shivered, though Lambo's internal heater was functioning perfectly and it wasn't cold. Tracy said:

"We *are* going back."

"I meant back to . . . You know what I meant."

"We've come this far," Tracy said, not very distinctly. Then, instead of adding the usual obvious corollary,

". . . Someone else made the mess back there. Someone else can clear it up."

"A dead man isn't a mess."

Slim concrete bridges spanning the road, the mutter of their exhaust pipes whiplashing back as they passed beneath. And again, twin tail lights in front. "That's them," Tracy said. "Or could be."

"Let's stop here. This is Cardiff, isn't it? Let's stop and ring Leo. Leo'll know what to do."

"I doubt it."

Lambo was gathering speed, as if by way of reply. The other car, a long way ahead, took on shape and colour for a fleeting second where the overhead lights seemed to be congregated, then became once more a dark low shape fleeing before its tail lights, dull but steady. Tracy, unexpectedly, began to swear. She stared at him, open-mouthed, taken totally by surprise; he went on as though she weren't there, muttering monotonously to himself, long unbroken strings of hideous profanity unwinding from him as from the spinning spool of a tape recorder while his face remained expressionless, completely disassociated. It was all extremely odd; it wasn't *like* Tracy. But then perhaps it wasn't Tracy. Tracy was doing the driving; another man inside him was doing the swearing. Inside him or outside him . . . Bony Wright, maybe. Or someone like that. Would he have acted like this, she wondered, when he'd been on the racing circuits? It seemed very likely. Maybe every calm, outwardly imperturbable bastard has an angry little man tucked away inside him, yelling to be let out. Unless he has someone in the pits to do the job for him. Tracy hadn't. Or hadn't now. It was no good his asking anything of *her*; she'd let him down tonight in that respect. She didn't seem to have any anger left. It had all gone down the drain. All that remained to her was fear.

"He's going to go fast," Tracy said. "He's going to go fast." His mode of intonation hadn't varied in the slightest, so it wasn't till he'd repeated the phrase that Bernadette realised it had been addressed to her; or, if not, was at least intended to be separate from the preceding rhodomontade. "He's picked up our lights. I was afraid he would. Now he's going to give it a bit of stick."

"This car's faster than his, isn't it?"

"Shut your gob," Tracy said.

It was true that they were going faster, much faster. The width and smoothness of the Eastern Bypass had masked their increase in speed, and Lambo's superbly disciplined engine had taken the acceleration in its stride, with a change of tempo barely discernible to Bernadette's inexperienced ears. The speedo needle had moved up to eighty and was still rising; yet in spite of this the tiny twin lights in front were slowly receding from them. "No need to be rude," Bernadette said, feeling no indignation. Perhaps he hadn't been; perhaps his idea had been simply to provoke her into anger, to reacquaint her with some emotion other than this stomach-turning, brain-dulling sense of dread. A good idea, if so. But it hadn't worked.

"He's got a Bentley," Tracy said, now with unanticipated mildness. "It's faster than most things on the road, so he's bound to think he can get away easily. Of course he can't know it's us behind him. That's the last thing he'd expect."

"He knows the car, doesn't he?"

"Yes, but he can't have recognised it yet. Not with all this spray coming up behind him. And we're still a long way back."

"Dropping back farther, too. He's getting away from us."

"He's going too fast, that's why."

"But Christ, you're a *racing* driver."

"I was once," Tracy said grimly. "That's the trouble. No one in his senses'd keep the pedal down in *these* conditions." Though it wasn't really a matter of being in one's senses; it was a matter of being a professional, as opposed to a good amateur. The difference is one of knowledge, rather than of skill. You can't rely on amateurs; Bony, ironically enough, had said that himself.

"Then if we can't keep up, why not turn back?" But there wasn't any force to her question; it was just a querulous semiobjection, a meaningless grumble. No good talking to Tracy, no good talking to Lambo; Tracy, indeed, might have become integrally a part of the car, a guiding intelligence at the steering wheel, impervious to everything but the machine's unspoken demands. The new intimacy of their relationship was quite startling; the thought came to her, for the first time (and as the impossible echo to Tracy's own earlier meditation), that Tracy's idea of driving and her own were different not merely in degree but also in kind—that the difference in their abilities wasn't one of technical skill and of practical experience but chiefly of empathy, of a mental attitude, not dedication, intuition, determination, anything describable like that, but of the assimilation by a machine of the totality of a certain human being's powers and of the imposition on the machine itself of a similar demand. That was what being a racing driver had to mean; it had nothing to do with speed, as she'd always supposed; speed was only an external aspect, one very small part of that uncompromising mutual demand. Whether the Bentley was well or badly driven, whether it was Bony Wright or anyone else at the Bentley's wheel . . . This, she now realised, hardly mattered to Tracy; he wasn't worried at the Bentley's seizing an initial advantage, any more than Nicklaus would be worried at losing three opening holes to a good weekender. His real struggle was with the course, and Tracy's, as always, with the road. Following now this line of thought rather than her previous remark—implying, indeed, the latter's negation—she said:

"We're only just doing ninety. Is that dangerous?"

"Yes," Tracy said. "Tonight it is. And what he's doing, that's more dangerous still."

The end of the Eastern Bypass was coming now towards them, bringing with it an appallingly direct confirmation of Tracy's opinion; Lambo, shortening slightly the rhythm of its stride to accommodate the approaching roundabout, first shuddered, suddenly and with tremendous violence; then swung slowly, but with an irrevocably increasing velocity, across the road and into a near-broadside position—this without any of the expected dramatic accompaniment of screaming tyres, complaining brakes, protesting metalwork, but in what seemed a complete and businesslike silence through which the rasp of Bernadette's intaken breath tore like a scream. They slid sideways in this way for about three-quarters of an hour, the brightly lit island at the centre of the roundabout skating towards them, also in silence, with viciously evident intent, until Lambo, whipped by a fierce cross-gust of wind and with an incredible tilting of its axes like that of a banking aeroplane, seemed not so much to straighten out as to adjust within its vector the outwards curve of the roundabout and to be proceeding, the next second, on its way as impeccably as before. Bernadette looked at Tracy, whose left eyebrow had risen very slightly. After a while, she said:

"I think it's easing up."

"A little, yes. But the rain isn't really the problem."

"What is?"

"The water on the road. And these crosswinds. We'll be sliding about a lot if we have to keep these speeds up."

"What they call aquaplaning?"

"Exactly."

"I've heard about it," Bernadette said.

"Not a hell of a lot you can do, when it happens."

"Did it happen back there?"

"Yes."

"It wasn't much fun."

The long, low bonnet tilting before them to descend a hill; at the bottom of the slope a cluster of houses, a church, a garage, grouped to either side of the dual carriageway, and the rhythmic flick of an indicator light as a car pulled out of a side road; it was the first car they'd seen since leaving Cardiff and the driver—no doubt equally accustomed to solitude—couldn't have seen them coming up behind. Bernadette bit her lower lip; but Lambo's control of sway and swerve were as perfectly balanced and timed as the evasive jink of a top-class rugby forward, taking them past the possible disaster of the tackle in the blinking of an eye. She looked at the speedometer; again on eighty, and rising. The Bentley was now a thousand yards or so in front, or so she reckoned; it was hard to estimate distances accurately, though, with visibility varying—as it now was— from minute to minute. The rain wasn't really easing up; it was just that there were times when it was less intense. The sky, everywhere she looked, was as black as pitch.

"Where are we now?"

"Coming up to Newport. But he'll take the motorway for sure."

"To London, then."

"Yes. But if he hasn't dropped us before he gets to the Severn Bridge, he'll know he can't just outrun us. He may try something else. Turn off at Chepstow, maybe, and start dodging."

"You'd rather he did that?"

"If he does, it'll show he's worried."

"About us?"

"That's the whole point. He can't *know* it's us. All he can really know is, he's being chased. And he won't be happy about it."

High stone walls and a glare of road signs, black and white and blue and yellow, blurry letters, arrows, M-4; the motorway. Then pools of watery orange light spread over the dark fields and the flat straight road, and Lambo seeming to settle itself down on its well-cushioned monocoque chassis, as though in anticipation of a fine unrestrained gallop along the bank of the Severn. The Bentley, too, with its thirty-second lead already augmented, was accelerating fast, its metallic glitter lost in the fan of spray thrown up by the furious drive of its rear tyres; he'll have seen our lights, though, Tracy thought, turning after him onto the motorway, he'll be peering at the side mirror and cursing because he can't get a clear view of us, what with the spray and the drifting rain and the vibration . . . I know how it is, no one better . . .

So this is where I'll stay, tagging on behind, so far back he can't even recognise Lambo. And all my lines are going to be obvious and correct and unimaginative, the lines of a well-trained police driver; Bony knows my style, or says he does, and I don't want to betray myself by showing any of the old hallmarks. Psychological warfare is what I have to practise, to keep that niggle of worry working away at the back of his mind . . .

"I've got a gun," Bernadette said.

After all, if throughout the day I've made a lot of stupid and near-disastrous mistakes, well, maybe I *am* stupid, at least I've never claimed to be particularly clever. But throughout the day I've been standing and walking on my own two feet; on my feet, I'm not at my best. Now I'm on wheels, and that's different. Now I'm doing what I can do well, it's thinking but a different *kind* of thinking . . .

"You've got *what?*"

"A gun. I completely forgot about it. I've got it in my bag. I hate guns. You'd better have it."

"But where did you get it?"

"That man, the one who was killed. He dropped it. So I picked it up." She clicked her handbag open, took out a heavy-looking pistol. "Here you are. *You* take it."

They were coming up to the Newport tunnel at something just under a hundred miles an hour; not the best of times, Tracy considered, in which to have pistols waved at you by nervous young females. "For God's sake," he said. "Is the safety catch on?"

"What's it look like?"

"Look, don't touch *anything*. Just put it in my pocket. *Carefully.*" The hollow boom of the tunnel, the sudden and unbelievable withdrawal of the rain; he felt her fingers pulling at the edge of his raincoat, then the weight of a hard, heavy object against his left side. "A damned silly thing to do, go round picking up pistols, if you don't even know what the safety . . . I mean, what's the point of it?"

"*He's* got one."

"Yes. He's got mine. I had it before and it didn't help." It wasn't going to be a matter of having pistols; it was going to be a matter of brains, just as Tommy Pope had said. Of brains, and also of nerve. In fact, of psychological warfare. The Bentley, swinging away up the long slope, was now almost out of sight; Bony Wright was still crowding it on. Tracy hadn't thought him capable of holding his speed for any length of time under these appalling conditions, but he seemed if anything to be building up on his lead; he couldn't be driving any other way than flat out. "I think," Tracy said, "we'll try a change of tactics."

"How do you mean?"

. . . Because now would be the time, now that he thinks he's moved away into the clear, to show him that he really *has* to worry. Now, when he's driving flat out, is the right time to come up on him like a streak. "I want him to know it's me," Tracy said. "He fancies himself a bit as a driver, does Bony. We'll see what he does when he's got us tucked in right behind." A moral ascendancy, that was what he wanted. Or had to have. With a knife or a gun in his hand, Bony had always had the edge on him; now was the time for Tracy to turn the tables, because if he didn't, at the end of the run—and no matter how it ended—Bony would have the whip hand again. Tracy had had a gun before, and it hadn't helped; now what he had was Lambo, and that was different. What he had to do with Lambo was shake Bony's confidence and shake it badly, so that when it came to knives and guns he wouldn't be the same as before. "Let's go up and push him," Tracy said.

. . . Go up and push him, so he knows it's me. Lambo's got up to thirty miles an hour on his crummy old Bentley, there's no question of that. Whether *I* have is another matter. Of course I can't hold it for long; a hundred and fifty-plus on a swimming wet two-lane motorway with no banking and in a howling cross-gale is suicide. But it doesn't have to be for very long. I just have to pull him back as fast as I can, reel him in like a fish, so that he knows I can do it and can do it any time I choose, even when he's pushing the pedal through the floorboards. All right. Here's the downslope and beyond it the open country; no more overhead lights till the Severn Bridge. There's Bony all of a mile and a half ahead, his brake lights flaring as he slows for the curve at the bottom. Headlamps up then, *click*, so that he can see *me*, can see the radiance coming up on him from behind. Ninety on the clock now. A hundred. And Bony, slipping out of sight round the bend, he's lost us now in the mirror and so here we go . . .

But Lambo's response to the throttle surge was far too well-mannered to give an effect of violent acceleration; it wasn't until they, too, had reached the long curve at the bottom of the hill and the pull of centrifugal force edged her sideways that Bernadette realised that the stops—so to speak—had been pulled out. Even then it wasn't any sensation of tremendous speed that caused her to look down again at the speedometer, but awareness of a new watchfulness in Tracy's attitude, of the combined gentleness and caution of his hands as, coming out of the curve, he corrected an incipient snake. At first glance, she missed the needle; it was a full inch farther round the clock than she'd ever seen it before and, for the first time, not implacably steady; instead, juddering very slightly on the 140 mark. She looked up in surprise and—such is the impressionability of the human mind—froze at the sudden and overwhelming revelation of Lambo's howling speed; the headlamps seemed to be discarding the red marker cat's eyes at the side of the road as fast as they were picked up, so that they were blurred into a continuous unwinding ribbon of red on which the eye couldn't clearly focus. Time, similarly, had gone shapeless, had turned into something equally unmeasurable. Sitting absolutely still, she found that her toes had curled up inside her shoes so tightly as to hurt her; how long had she had them all screwed up like that? Five seconds? Ten? Twenty? She had no idea. Relaxing them required a deliberate and conscious effort. She made it, and they obeyed her, but slowly and as if reluctantly. They seemed to have moved off a very long way away.

"That's it," Tracy said. "Breathe slowly. And deeply. It takes a bit of getting used to."

It was odd that his voice sounded perfectly normal. She had expected it, for some reason, to sound deep and distorted, like a record played at half the proper speed. "It's all right," she said. "I'm not scared."

"I am," Tracy said. "No fooling."

She could see it was true. The skin of his forehead had gone pale and great globules of sweat were breaking through it; they shone in the dim reflected light with a feverish glint, echoed by darker streaks of moisture on his cheeks and chin. "Oh Tracy," she said, betrayed into at least the semblance of emotion, "what's it all *for*? What are you trying to *prove*?"

He didn't reply. The tail-drift had started again. She watched his hands on the steering wheel, motionless at first then suddenly exerting pressure, the tendons standing out in his left wrist as Lambo wandered peaceably across into the outside lane without the steering wheel, as far as she could see, moving in the slightest; they were going downhill again, faster than ever, pushing 150, and the misty spray from the Bentley was now a dense grey cloud on the rim of their headlights, moving steadily closer. Why in God's name, she thought, doesn't *he* slip, that bloody Bony? It could all end like that, and so easily. All the problems, all the trouble, over in a flash, in a jumping, careering tangle of twisted metal. "He's heavier," Tracy said, as though he'd read her thoughts. "It's a heavyish car, that Bentley. It'll skid like a bugger if he's rough on the brakes. But it ought not to slide."

"We're nearly up on him."

"Yes," Tracy said. He'd mastered the drift now, and the needle imperceptibly was dropping back; the Bentley was full in Lambo's headlights, a low dark scurrying bulk a hundred hazy yards away or less; the spindrift from its wheels was reaching their windscreen, mingling there with the streaky rain. "Now we drop in and take a tow."

"Do what?"

"You'll see."

Lambo's headlamps suddenly dipped, leaving the Bentley again running on the rim of a tight circle of foggy radiance. They were still closing in on Bony at 120, pulling him slowly deeper into the new diminished circle of light, but with the drop in their previous vertiginous speed Bernadette had—quite illogically—relaxed; she suddenly felt, indeed, extremely sleepy. The two cars were now rocketing along the motorway no more than ten yards apart, as though connected by a towing chain; the spray was sloshing heavily against Lambo's windscreen, but the buffeting of the wind had sensibly diminished. "Is this," Bernadette asked, "what you do in the races?"

"All the time."

The other car was now so close that she had to look up, rather than forwards, at its rear window; because Lambo was so low-built the chances were, as she now realised, that, from the driver's seat of the Bentley, Bony Wright couldn't see their headlamps in the mirror at all. He could be only aware of a vague glow radiating from the rear window and moving with him, ghostlike, wherever he went. "You'll worry him all right if you get any closer."

"No," Tracy said. "This is close enough."

His concentration was still intense, but his voice seemed a little more cheerful; she saw, too, that the normal colour had returned to his face. "You were doing a hundred and fifty back there."

"Or thereabouts."

"So you *can* do it, after all."

"Yes," Tracy said. "But it's not as simple as that."

"You told me you were—"

"Anyone can do it once in a while. When he's forced to. All through a racing season, that's another matter."

"Why do you say when you're forced to? Nobody's forcing you to."

"*He* is."

"That . . . Bony Wright?"

"Yes. Though maybe he thinks it's the other way round. God knows who's right."

For the first time since they had started out, she saw him smile. And as he did so, a pale white radiance showed against the dark horizon before them and to their right; the lights of the Severn Bridge. The clock showed that they were eight minutes out of Newport, which seemed ridiculous, at once impossibly fast and infinitely too slow; the run had lasted for an eternity. "There's the bridge," Bernadette said.

"He's going to turn off."

"There's some way to go yet. You can't be sure."

"He's going to turn off," Tracy said. "I can feel it."

As though intentionally to contradict him, the Bentley swerved suddenly across to the outside lane; Lambo followed easily, inexorably, as though Bony had steered both cars with a single movement of the wheel. When he changed, with equal suddenness, back to the inside lane, the same thing happened. "God," Bernadette said apprehensively. "What if he brakes?"

"He'd like to. But he has to dodge us first. That's what he's trying to do."

"But if he brakes anyway?"

"He daren't," Tracy said. "We're too close."

Again, the same manoeuvre; but undertaken this time to pass a trailer truck trundling somnolently back to Bristol. Sixty feet of lumbering metal flicked back like a whipcrack; the Bentley, the Lamborghini streaking past with barely ten feet of windy space between bumper and bumper, coming like twin bullets out of nowhere, their tail lights curving away like tracer and disappearing in a sheet of spray; a banshee howl, a double blur of metal and that was it. The Bentley coming back in fast, brake lights flaring, trying to duck in before the lorry and leave Lambo squeezed outside, committed to the outside lane; Lambo matching the move, Tracy letting the discs touch once, briefly, and then again, the two bumpers

touching in the gentlest imaginable of nudges, the Bentley starting to snake, Lambo falling back . . . The Bentley swinging, swinging badly, straightening out . . . Bernadette touched her lower lip, found blood where she'd bitten into it. "He won't do *that* again," Tracy said.

"Christ, you *touched* him."

"Yes, and he didn't like it."

"Nor did I."

The Bentley was rock-steady again now, racing along the inside track with what seemed like a new intentness, a rabbit headed incontinently for its burrow. "He's had enough," Tracy said, with some satisfaction. "He's going to turn off. Like I said." Lambo was back in its former position, loping easily along in pursuit some five or six yards behind, the speedometer needle now and at last down below the 100 mark; again, that feather-light touch on the brake pedal, that slightest discernible check in Lambo's already decreasing stride as the preliminary turn-off signs for Chepstow came up on the left and vanished on the instant in a blue-and-white flicker. The distance between the cars lengthened to ten, fifteen yards, then —as if in recognition of an imposed command—the Bentley's brake lights also flashed again. My God, Bernadette thought; he was right. It has to be some kind of high-speed hypnosis. Not telepathy, exactly, but . . . Ah, well, *experience*. Nothing but that. She could see now the swimming lights of the raised roundabout ahead and, above them and to the right, the orange glow of the lamps on the Severn Bridge approaches and the aircraft warning lights burning higher still, all smudged and kaleidoscoped by the spitting rain; Tracy was braking again, the needle dropping fast, the Bentley edging left and Lambo relentlessly following, the long bonnet lifting as they left the motorway and mounted the slope to the roundabout. A swing of the wheel, a sharp left turn and they were out on a wide double-lane road, a row of long-haulers drawn up to one side, the Bentley still a few yards in front and putting on speed again. The relaxation of tension was as sudden and as evident as the sharp snapping of an elastic band; Tracy felt the hot centre of pain between his eyes and rubbed at it with the back of his hand. It had been there all the time, but he hadn't noticed it.

"By the way, is he giving you your divorce?"

"What?"

"Your divorce. Wasn't that why you . . . ?"

"Oh yes. That. Yes."

"He could save you a whole lot of legal fees."

"Who could?"

"Bony Wright."

"Yes. I'm sorry," Bernadette said. "I'm not thinking very straight at the moment." Surely the Bentley was *crawling* along now? Was there something wrong with the car . . . ? She looked at the speedometer needle, which pointed to 60. She couldn't believe it.

"Or were you just stringing Leo along about that? So that he'd help?" Tracy's eyes were narrowed, as though in an endeavour to repulse a wave of tiredness. "I suppose you reckon all of us men are mugs. Well, I won't say you're wrong."

"Look, Tracy, what you can do is drive. So just drive."

With the withdrawal of nervous tension, a return of irritability. Or of something like it. Tracy, though, seemed to be feeling it too. "Yes, I can drive all right. I can keep up with him while the petrol lasts. Or till my head splits, whichever happens first. Or till the silly bugger goes off the road. What I can't do is get Tommy back for you. I can't even get my own wife back, let alone someone else's husband."

The Iceman, he'd called himself. And now she knew why. So what was this? A crack in the surface? Or a coming thaw? "What's the matter with your head? Does it hurt?"

"Yes, it does. I took some pills for it. But it's wearing off. I mean, d'you think he'll be *grateful*? Supposing by some miracle we . . . I mean, is *that* it? Because you rescued him in his hour of need? Is that the way it goes?"

"Oh, shut up." She was surprised to find herself again on the verge of tears—and this time, possibly, of hysteria. "What's it to you what I want or what I think? Assuming I know what I want, which I'm bloody sure I don't? Like, what do *you* want, Tracy?"

"Me? Nothing."

"Oh, come on. What was her name?"

"Anne."

"Don't you want Anne back, Tracy?"

The Bentley was diving down the long steep hill into Chepstow, Lambo pursuing shadow-like an insistent twenty yards to the rear, the mingled snarl of exhaust-pipes ricochetting back from the dark stone walls to either side. "It gets lonely, sometimes," Tracy said eventually.

This was the old Tracy. Quiet, calm, introspective. And Bernadette sighed.

"Yes," she said. "It does."

Chepstow. A dark, high, phantasmagoric street in the wind and the swirling rain. The Bentley rushing downwards between the tall buildings, ignoring the red imperative of the traffic signal and vanishing through the narrow central archway, Lambo nosing unhesitantly through a scant two seconds behind. No police to remonstrate, no pedestrians, no parked cars; a ghost town. "He's going for the bridge," Tracy said. They dived on endlessly through the vertiginously swooping canyon of the street, water hissing up from the tyres, the eye of a traffic light—green, this time—staring inimically at them; then they and the Bentley were fleeing across the Wye, the bridge beneath them vibrating to the combined pulsing of their motors and to the slow, shuddering gust of wind that came moaning out of the southwest as they crossed. Then the right-angled turn and the long uphill curve, the Bentley gaining speed and Lambo responding; above them, in light reflected from the wet mirror of the road, black leafy boughs swayed and swung against a grey-black sky. Now the loneliness of which they had just spoken lay all about them; apart from parked vehicles, they hadn't seen another car since they'd left the motorway, but only now did this fact strike Bernadette as obscurely significant. Because this was the old road, the river road, the true road, the road the motorway had made obsolete; a road that followed the windings of the Severn, that visited the little villages; a road made by men, not by technologists. The motorway, after all, carried in a peculiar way the town along with it; something about its width, its impersonal smoothness, its calculated camber had been reassuring. They weren't going fast now, or not so fast; but she was still frightened. She was frightened in a different way. She knew that somewhere on this road the chase would end. But how did she know . . . ? Not in the way that Tracy made his deductions—*he's going for the bridge, he's going to turn off*—from the observation of tiny details, virtual intangibles, that only combined intuition and experience could interpret with success. It wasn't like that. She didn't know how she knew; that was what was frightening. She was nonetheless quite sure. Sure enough to say to Tracy,

"Something's going to happen soon."

"What do you mean, something's going to happen?"

"I don't know. Maybe he's going to try something. I mean, something new."

"I expect he will," Tracy said equably. "He's bound to. But I don't know what—"

It wasn't Bony who did something new. It was—in a manner of speaking—the road. There was a sudden dip and a climbing curve;

there was water at the bottom of the dip, a pool, three or four inches deep; at the edges of the pool, there was mud. The Bentley hit the water and slewed, went into a violent skid; a great tidal wave of spray glared in Lambo's dipped headlamps as it hurled itself at the windscreen. The wipers flicked once, twice, desperately at nothing, then arced out a clear space through which the Bentley cavorted, sideways on, the dark hedges to the right scythed into silver by its swinging headlamps, its aristocratic bonnet nosing in towards the ditch and Lambo almost on top of it, sliding in hard and fast towards the near door. Tracy span the wheel to the left, stamping on, freeing, reapplying the brake pedal as the Bentley lurched, miraculously, out of ramming range and disappeared behind them. Lambo's brakes held, whining, clamping the tyres to the road's slithery surface; the engine stalled, picked up again, died as the locked tyres dragged them to a halt. Tracy switched off the ignition.

"You were right." His voice conveyed nothing but a mild astonishment.

"I didn't think—"

"Still, you could say it was a wonder it didn't happen earlier."

He ran down the side window, pushed his head out and peered backwards. All he could see was a rain-shot darkness. The Bentley's lights were off; it was somewhere there behind them, but he couldn't see where. "I can't see a thing."

"What's happened to them?"

Tracy clicked his tongue. "I told you. I can't see. But they're in the ditch, I think. I doubt if they're much hurt, but I'd better go and take a look." He swung open the door; cold wet air impacted on Bernadette's face. "You haven't got a torch?"

"No." He got out. Outside there was nothing but a spitting wetness. He reached back to the panel to switch off Lambo's lights. Then there was nothing inside, too. "Wait for me," Bernadette said. She was struggling with the clip of her safety harness. Her fingers felt heavy and stiff. When she got out, she found that her feet also had become disconnected from the rest of her; she had put them too close together, that was the trouble. She put a hand on Lambo's roof for support and levered them wider apart. Then it was all right. The gale was blowing great guns, full in her face as she turned to look back. The skirts of her raincoat flapped noisily. "Tracy?"

"Come on, then." His voice was comfortingly near at hand.

She walked round the car and he took her elbow. They went back along the road together. Their feet splashed through running water and the hedgerow to their left was alive with the sound of the wind and the bursting raindrops. She could see the Bentley now, but only as a dark bulk splayed half-on, half-off the edge of the road and listing over at an angle, like a torpedoed ship. "No damage," Tracy said. "Or I don't think so. They build 'em solid."

"I can't see anybody inside."

"Bony must be okay. Or he couldn't have cut the lights."

"I can't see anyone. Perhaps they've run off."

"Where would they run to?"

Certainly, beyond the road and the hedges there was nothing. There didn't seem to be a light showing anywhere. There was just the road, the hedges and darkness, the whistling wind and the rain. Miles away, probably on the far side of the river, there were tiny starlike pinpricks of light; but nothing any nearer. They reached the Bentley and Tracy opened the side door and the automatic interior light came on. Pope, at least, hadn't run anywhere. He was slumped forwards in the passenger seat with his head on the padded dashboard. He didn't look good. Tracy got a hand under his chin and lifted his head and saw the bluish-black bruise across his forehead.

"Is he . . . ?"

"No," Tracy said. "He's all right. Knocked cold is all."

"Look—he's got his hands tied together."

"That probably seemed to Bony a sensible precaution."

He straightened up and rubbed his own forehead. Pope didn't look good, but he looked a whole lot better than Tracy felt. Lambo's swift deceleration had pushed, as it seemed, his eyes right back inside his skull, and now they wouldn't come out again. Now that the light was on inside the car he could see Bony Wright. Bony was over on the far side of the car, the driver's seat, standing by the bonnet, leaning on it as though struggling to get back his breath; but Tracy couldn't see him clearly. His vision was blurred. His face was wet and tiny drops of rain were clinging to his eyelashes, but it wasn't just that; he didn't rub his eyes. It wouldn't do any good.

"Bony?"

"Yes," Bony said in exasperation. "It *would* be you."

"Well, you must have guessed."

"Couldn't've been anybody else. But I didn't see how . . . It doesn't matter. God, why are you so *stupid?*"

His hand was resting on the bonnet. His hand had the pistol in it. The rain was getting in his eyes, too. With his other hand he knuckled it away.

"You're not *that* good, Bony. It wasn't so difficult."

"You're all right in a car, mate. You should've stayed in the car. You should've gone on. Driven off. Why in hell's name d'you have to come back here?"

"I wanted to be sure you were all right," Tracy said pacifically.

"Oh, *I'm* all right. I'm fine. You just got in the way, that's all. I know what to do. I got no problems. You said it yourself, didn't you . . . ? I mean, you *knew*. It's all so bloody senseless."

"No, look, if you'll just wait a minute—"

"Stupid, that's what you are. Just stupid."

Tracy felt in his raincoat pocket for the gun Bernadette had given him. It was there all right. He took it out. From behind the car, Bony couldn't see clearly what he was doing, but anyway it didn't matter what he was doing because Bony wasn't going to wait a minute. Bony had run out of patience. Bony fired. He wasn't as good with the gun as he was with the knife and it wasn't a very good shot but he hit Tracy all right and Tracy knew that he'd been hit but didn't know where. There was pain, very violent pain, in his head and in the pit of his stomach, but otherwise unlocalised; he knew that he hadn't been hit in his head or his stomach because he was still standing up. So it didn't make sense. Time was moving very slowly again. Bernadette was screaming. Not a loud scream, but penetrating. He tried to raise the pistol, which had become enormously heavy, but this was difficult because for some reason he had to hold his elbow tucked in to his right side. He realised then that that was where the pain was. The pistol barrel wavered in the air, pointing towards where Bony had been but wasn't any more. Bony was coming round the car, half crouched, moving fast. Moving much too fast. Tracy tried to swing the pistol round to his left against the drag of his raincoat sleeve, but he couldn't do it. It just wasn't on. The barrel dropped downwards. Bernadette, beside him, was screaming. It was still the same scream. He tried to brace himself against the open door of the car, but the door gave way, sprawling him sideways. His free arm went over the door and he hung to it desperately, staring at Bony, who had halted some four feet in front of him.

". . . All bloody senseless," Bony said. His voice was distorted, as though he, too, were in some kind of agony. To Tracy, it was just a voice. He was looking past Bony now, far beyond Bony, at the dark and cloud-torn sky. Bernadette stooped to pull the pistol out of his hand, pushing him back against the door so that he almost overbalanced. She took the pistol from him and shot Bony Wright with it. It made a clean, sharp, cracking sound like snapping timber; a vehement sound. It made a vehement sound four times, in quick succession, then a fifth time; then, after a long pause, a sixth. After a while Tracy managed to bring his eyes down from their contemplation of the uttermost depths of the skies and to focus them, more or less, on the man lying on the ground almost at his feet. Bony had fallen face forwards into the shadows by the Bentley's canted wheels, his hands thrusting deep into the slimy mud, one black-shoed foot kicked out at an inconsequent angle. He didn't move at all. He seemed small, insignificant.

"He wasn't expecting that," Tracy said conversationally. Bernadette began to giggle.

He took the pistol from her and put it back in his pocket and she stopped giggling. She watched him in silence as he clambered into the driver's seat of the Bentley and turned the ignition key. The motor answered at once. He rocked the car to and fro and eventually rolled it backwards out of the ditch. Pope had come to with the movement of the car and was groaning quietly, under his breath. "You'll be all right," Tracy told him. He took out his penknife and cut the necktie that bound Pope's wrists, and Pope rubbed his wrists and then his head. "Where's that . . . ?"

"He's dead."

Tracy got out of the car.

"Can you drive?"

"I don't know. Oh, Lord. My head—"

"Drive," Tracy said.

"Where to?"

"Anywhere the hell out of here. Rest up for a while. Then take her back to the house."

"Okay," Pope said.

He looked past Tracy at Bernadette; a brief, questioning glance; he didn't say anything, though, and indeed barely seemed to recognise her. He'd taken a nasty knock, of course. Tracy slammed the door. Pope moved over to the driver's seat and switched on the lights and the Bentley moved off through the puddles on the way back to Chepstow—a little jerkily at first, which wasn't surprising. Tracy took Bernadette by the arm and walked her through the darkness back to Lambo. She moved jerkily, too, as though unable properly to coordinate the swing of her arms and legs. "Get in," Tracy said. She got in. Back again behind the wheel, he switched on the ignition and lights and rolled Lambo forwards. "What's happening?" Bernadette asked brightly.

"We're moving on. Before anyone comes by and sees us here."

He didn't think they'd be going very far. There was a grinding pain in his ribs, low down on the right side, and his head was splitting open. Spiders had spun cobwebs over the windscreen. Three hundred yards farther on there was a signpost that he couldn't read and a turning where there didn't seem too much risk of leaving tyre marks; a hard surface and plenty of water flowing. He braked and reversed in. Above the crest of the hill to his left there was a sharp eye-watering glow; headlights approaching along the main road. He backed Lambo another twenty yards, then turned off the lights and waited for the car to go by. He had a long wait. It turned out, in the end, to be a long-distance lorry, driving slowly. The driver didn't see them and wouldn't see Bony's body, down in the ditch. Nobody would see it there until the morning, and possibly not even then. Eventually there'd be headlines, ANOTHER GANGLAND KILLING: MURDERER'S BODY FOUND . . . something like that. But not for some time yet. It would be a messy one, after all; but that couldn't be helped. "You did the right thing," he said.

"What?"

"He'd've killed us all right. Both of us."

"But I never thought it'd . . . Honestly . . . I mean, we were *mad*, weren't we? Walking out there like that."

"Stupid, anyway. Like he said."

"I thought he'd hit you. The way you went back against that door."

"He *did* hit me," Tracy said.

"Where?"

He unbelted the raincoat. The wetness, where the fabric was loosened, was warmer and stickier than elsewhere, and when he probed with his fingers there the pain was sharp and sudden. "It's all right. Maybe you'd better drive, though. If you feel up to it."

"But where's the nearest doctor? Chepstow? I think there's a hospital—"

"I don't need a doctor. Just drive back to where we came from."

"But aren't you going to . . . ?"

"What?"

". . . Tell the police about it?"

"The *police*? What are you talking about? We just killed a man, for Crissake."

"But he shot at us first."

"You've got to be joking. I mean, the time for the police was long ago, it's too late now. What have the *police* got to do with anything . . . ? No, come on. Let's get back to where it's warm and dry."

"All right," Bernadette said. She swung open the door. "Move over."

. . . And then, before starting up the car again, "He *would* have killed us, wouldn't he?" she said. A comment, not a question; and one that carried, Tracy thought, an undertone of admiration. Why not . . . ? It's when they're dead, after all, that the Bonapartes of this world become legend.

CHAPTER 27

The body was gone from the staircase when they got back. Starshine was there, and Henry, and Leo; they were faces, as far as Tracy was concerned, with which he was vaguely familiar but faces that he couldn't be bothered to label. Tommy Pope had got back half an hour before them, so there weren't very many questions, or if there were, he wasn't understanding them very clearly. There was only one thing that Leo still wanted to know. Tracy gave him the empty pistol. Then someone helped him upstairs and put him to bed, but later he didn't remember that part of it.

Nor did he remember very much about the journey back from Chepstow, except that time and again they had thrown him over the edge of the cliff and he had watched, as from a circling seabird's vantage point, his weighted body plummeting downwards towards the foam-washed rocks until with the hungry impact of surging water he had rejoined himself, diving deep with his own body to the fronded bottom where the shells of crabs and other scuttling creatures lay scattered, ground to paper thinness by the friction of the sand against their surfaces, then moving with the slow pull of the undercurrent deeper yet, down past shelving ledges of naked rock, past the bare dark canyons and deeper yet, down to where the blackness of the uttermost depths was flecked with sparks and shoals of light, the starfire burning around him as he sank and sank and sank, deeper yet . . . The Lamborghini growling down the motorway, travelling fast, very fast, but still the prisoner of time and space, Bernadette at the wheel, squinting past the rhythmically beating windscreen wipers at the unwinding road with one open, one half-closed eye, while beside her he fell through the air again and struck and sank and went on sinking and the wind blew and the rain fell and the outflung lights of Cardiff grew steadily nearer . . .

When he woke up a little later, he found Bony sitting at the side of his bed. Bony looked the same, and then again he didn't. His face seemed younger than before. He wore oil-stained driver's overalls with scorch marks on the fabric and there was also a smear of oil on his left cheek. Tracy didn't feel afraid, not at all afraid; but it seemed to him that he ought to apologise.

"Sorry, Bony. It turned out to be a messy job after all. It's not the way we like to do things. It just all got out of hand, somehow."

When you're dead (Bony said) it's really all the same. It doesn't matter. Whether you lie in a grassy ditch or at the bottom of the whelming tide, whether they slide you into a furnace or lay you out in a dirty great pantheon, it's really all one. And anyway, marble tombs had never been his scene.

All the same (Tracy said) Starshine had planned things differently. "It's all right for you. You're dead. But Starshine knows I tipped you off and mucked everything up for him. That puts me in a spot, wouldn't you say?"

But Bony's view was that Starshine wouldn't do anything very much about it, unless of course someone paid him to. Starshine was a professional. He didn't allow himself little private luxuries, like enmity and revenge. Bony, of course, hadn't been like that. Bony had had pride. But now he was dead, things were different again. He hadn't any pride. He wasn't Bony any more. In fact, he'd never been Bony. He'd died quite a long while ago. "They gave me a run, Tracy. You know who gave me a run . . . ? Colin Chapman. No one else but. Let me take out one of the Lotuses. Well, I put in five good laps, but then I lost her on the corner and went right out into the sticks. Got a bit fraught, you know? Flames all over the shop. I tried to jump clear, but I didn't make it. *That* was when I died. Look at me, if you don't believe me. How old would you say I was . . . ? All right, I'll tell you. Nineteen, mate. I was just on nineteen when that happened. They didn't call me Bony till long after that, so I was never a Bonaparte at all. And anyway, that was all a mistake, too."

"What was?"

"Napoleon was. I mean, all those things they say, that Emperor stuff. It isn't true. I seen him, that's how I know, I've *talked* to him. Little chap with a pale face and a posh grey uniform, quite young he is—I doubt if he's turned thirty. Well, he got killed at a place called Mondovi, fell under his horse and that was it. First battle he was ever in charge of, and he blew it when he was winning it. Just like me."

"I don't understand," Tracy said.

"Of course not. You wouldn't. You're not dead yet."

Tracy wondered what it was like, being dead.

"Oh, it's great, just great. You'll like it. They got bloody good bananas."

"I never knew that you liked bananas."

"Me? I love 'em."

Yes, but this, Tracy thought, was simply ridiculous. They *couldn't* have bananas. "You can't eat things, surely? How can you possibly—"

"It's all possible. Everything. Ah, you don't understand."

"I know I don't. I was hoping you could explain. Because I'd like to know."

Supposing (Bony said) you're driving down a road. Well, driving down a road is like when you're alive. When you come to a fork, you have to take one turning or the other; you can't take both. But that's just how it seems to be while you're alive. When you're dead you see that you could take both, and you did, and you always did —not just once, but every time. Death is the realisation of every conceivable possibility that life presents you with, a trip down not one single road but down every road simultaneously. What you think of as your life is an illusion, or not quite an illusion because it's *there;* but so are all the other lives you've lived and somehow don't know about. Death is like life, but more so. It's being *more* alive. Much, much more.

"But look," Tracy said. "Taking a different turning to the one you think you took—that'd make you a different person. Things'd happen then in a different way."

"Of course. That's just what I was telling you. One of me died like I said, when I was nineteen, when old Chapman gave me a race instead of turning me down—but that wasn't the one of me you think *you* know, the one that girl of yours shot all to buggery. There have to be *millions* of me, mate. I mean, I'm infinite. Everybody's infinite. They just don't realise it. Look—you walk down to the beach tomorrow morning and pick up a pebble, any old pebble. Just pick it up and look at it. Say to yourself, *this one's me*. Then pick up another. It's the same but it's different. And then say to yourself, *this one's me, too*. After a while, you might get to see how it could be so."

Tracy, following in part this suggestion, stooped to pick up a hard pebble of fact from this rubble-heap of gibberish. "Why do you say *my* girl? She's not mine at all."

"Get away. You had her that night at the hotel."

Tracy shook his head. "You're wrong about that. I'll admit the thought—"

"Oh yes, you did. But you'll have to wait till you're dead to find out how it was. See what I mean now . . . ? It's great, boy. Of course, there may be another chance, another turning . . . but if there is, it'll be different. It doesn't matter. None of it matters. The possibilities, they're infinite once they've been set up."

"You mean the thought occurred to her, too?"

"Of course it did. You got the picture now?"

Tracy tried very hard; but no, he couldn't get the picture. He must, in concentrating, have closed his eyes; when he opened them, Bony was no longer there. A ghost, then. Ghosts could be comforting sometimes. That, too, he hadn't known before.

He could hear voices in the next room, and knew that he had been hearing them for some little time. It was just that the wraith of Bony had absorbed all his attention. These were material voices; at least, he thought so. A man's and a woman's; Tommy Pope's and Berna-dette's. Neither voice was notably raised in pitch; they weren't quarreling, for once, or even arguing. Indeed, they didn't appear to be conversing at all, in the ordinary sense. There would be brief snatches of words, a single phrase or two; sometimes an equally brief reply, and sometimes not; and for the rest, silence. It sounded like a consultation between two imperfectly tuned radio sets. Tracy closed his eyes once more, trying to go back to sleep. But he was too tired to sleep. That can happen. A million Tracys, all too tired to . . . No, that wasn't right. All the others had to be asleep already, because Bony hadn't talked to any of the others. Or had he . . . ? Sleep itself is a turning, anyway. Like death. You'd have of course an infinite number of deaths, and presumably only one of them was perfect—the one that rounded off the perfect life. For Bony, a flaming funeral pyre halfway through his first race; for the other, a sudden and violent end in the first battle in which he'd held supreme command. It made sense, in a way. For both of them, all that followed on the roads they'd subsequently driven might well have been inglorious anticlimax, all other turnings have led to crime and corruption. Had anybody ever actually *lived* that perfect life before dying that perfect death? There was supposed to be an answer to that one, wasn't there? That, when you thought about it, was the whole point about him. But then he was God. That had to be different.

Tracy turned his head on the damp pillow, listening to the strange gasping, moaning sounds coming from the other room. Strange . . . ? Well, yes. It was strange that that, too, had to be part of it. He hadn't been afraid while Bony was with him, but he was afraid now. And while he was being afraid, he fell asleep.

Then a little later Bernadette came in to see him. She stood beside the bed looking down at him, frowning slightly as though there were something important she couldn't remember. She was wearing the dressing robe she'd had on that night at the hotel. Her lips seemed a little fuller than usual, her cheeks a little puffier, and she had, Tracy thought, the narrow-eyed, faintly feline expression of a girl who has been recently and satisfactorily bedded. Or no, not of a girl. Of a woman. With the new gift of insight granted him by his interview with Bony's ghost (though of course it had been no such thing, but only a dream) Tracy was able to recognise the complexity of the motivations that had brought her now to his room; as a woman, no doubt, she was concerned to leave him with no illusions as to what he'd missed out on, while as a girl it was at least conceivable that she was grateful to him for helping to bring about what had after all to be accounted a marital reunion, of a kind . . . while as a child (and it was a child whose frown of perplexity underlay her outward façade of adult composure) she maybe didn't want to go to sleep until she'd said good night to her favourite uncle. An odd little creature, Bernadette, but probably no odder than most.

"How are you feeling?"

"All right," Tracy said.

"Does it hurt you much?"

"No. Not much."

"Nothing hurts you very much, does it?" She sat down, as Bony had, on the side of the bed, but this time Tracy felt the mattress subside under her weight. "That's the trouble with you. You don't feel any pain."

"I do, you know. I only said—"

"Not really. Oh, there's *some* things you feel. A little compassion, maybe. When you see a fox running, you feel sorry for him. You might even try to help him. But pain, no. Pain isn't for people like you. Only foxes know about that."

"I know about being afraid," Tracy said.

"We all know about that. I'm talking about being *hurt*. You're just not one of us, Tracy—you're not selfish enough. You have to be an egotist to be really hurt. Like me and Tommy and Leo. Starshine, even. *He* knows about pain. You thought you were putting yourself in the middle, but you weren't, you couldn't and that's why it all worked out the way it did. You were always outside. It wasn't your fault."

"But you weren't inside, either. Not in the way those others were."

"For God's sake, Tracy, I was *born* inside. The others just grew that way. If you thought any different, that was just another mistake."

"I didn't think any different," Tracy said. "I don't know that I ever really thought at all."

"It wasn't your fault," she said again. And stood up. "You were right about the doctor. You don't need one. Leo'll drive you down to the station in the morning."

"And that'll be that."

"Yes," Bernadette said. "Then that'll be that."

CHAPTER 28

By morning the storm had blown itself out, leaving a dull grey sky littered over with dark patches of leftover raincloud. Tracy couldn't see much of it through the bedroom window, which was small and at an angle to where he lay, but his eyes were still very sore and painful and before very long he closed them and left the weather to do whatever it wanted. It was warm and comfortable in bed, and it was quiet in the house; there was just the occasional sound of distant movement to reassure him that he hadn't been left completely alone, though he wouldn't much have minded if he had been. His ribs felt stiff and bruised on the side he wasn't lying on. After a while he remembered why. He rolled over onto his back and pulled back the blankets, but there wasn't very much to see; just a wide strip of sticking plaster stained, not very heavily, with dried blood and with some kind of disinfectant. A bullet burn, he supposed; he'd never seen one before, but he'd heard about them. Now he had one all of his own. Lucky old Tracy.

Twenty minutes or so later the door opened and Leo came in. Leo looked very tired, too.

"I want to get up," Tracy said.

"No reason why you shouldn't. I'll get you some clothes. Tommy's ought to fit you well enough."

"What happened to mine?"

"We burnt them."

"I bled a lot, did I?"

"Yes," Leo said.

"I've got a spare suit in my case."

"Where *is* your case?"

Tracy tried to remember. He couldn't. "It's somewhere around."
Leo nodded and went out again.

Tracy went on trying to think where the hell his case was, where
he'd left it. It was no good. His mind was confused. Things kept getting in the way. Not thoughts or memories, but *things;* the woollen
bedspread and the feel of it, the parchment lampshade and the
colour of it, the mirror on the dressing table and the way it reflected
the light. He was being distracted all the time by what he saw; it
was very frustrating. Closing his eyes again might solve the problem, but then he didn't want to do that. So in the end he lay quietly
with his knees half lifted, looking up at the white ceiling and thinking about nothing at all. Waiting for Leo to come back with the
clothes.

Leo didn't come back. Bernadette did.

"Hullo."

"Hullo," Tracy said.

She began to spread various oddments over the foot of the bed.
A blue shirt; cotton vest and pants; a rather jazzy pair of purple
socks; a grey suit on a hanger and a blue silk tie. "These ought to
fit you all right. Tommy's about your build."

"What about shoes?"

"Oh God, I forgot the shoes. They're drying in the kitchen."

"*My* shoes?"

"Yes."

"That's nice," Tracy said.

"I'll get them for you. Are you feeling all right?"

"No," Tracy said. "But I'll feel better when I'm up." He wasn't
sure that this was true, but he lifted his head from the pillow in case
it was and, finding matters no worse that way, propped himself up
in that position with his elbow. "How about you?"

"Me? I'm all right. Except they gave me some sleeping pills and
I'm sort of dopey."

"But didn't you come and see me? Late last night?"

"Did I? I expect I did, if you say so. I don't remember."

". . . So it's all tidied up," Leo said. "That's what I am. The tidier-
upper. Trouble is, what does the tidier-upper do when all the tidy-

ing's been upped? It makes me feel like one of those superannuated
empire-builders with nothing to do but twiddle an umbrella. Othel-
lo's occupation gone. Know what I mean?"

"I think so."

"Bernie and Tommy, you see—they're the ones who make the
mess. Careless people. Like Scott Fitzgerald used to write about.
You ever read Scott Fitzgerald . . . ? Well, the point is you have
the mess-makers and the tidier-uppers, sort of opposite poles, and
never the twain shall meet. You just have to recognise the fact."

"And what about me?"

"You? Oh, you're neither. Or maybe a little of both. Must make
things awkward for you, now I think about it."

Tracy nodded thoughtfully. It was probably true. It was certainly
true that the loose ends had now all been gathered together; his
case recovered from the Mini, the Mini driven off somewhere else
no doubt to be later competently disposed of; he himself, finally,
was being tidied up, travelling comfortably towards Cardiff Station
in the passenger seat of Leo's three-litre Rover, a car as neat and
efficiently functional as its owner. Leo might have been dispatching
a casual weekend guest or business acquaintance, with good humour and a ready flow of polite conversation.

"You don't fit in at all. There's a pattern to it, like to all games.
The careless people and the tidier-uppers . . . they can always talk
deals. We *need* each other. No arrangements are permanent. Right
now, okay, I've nothing to do. But before very long they'll be need-
ing me again. Or someone like me."

"And then you'll talk another deal."

"Then we'll talk another deal. That's the whole trouble with you,
soldier. You won't talk deals. You're more like Bony Wright in that
respect."

"In quite a few respects," Tracy said. "Or so I've got around to
thinking."

"Tell me something."

"What?"

". . . *Was* it you who shot Bony?"

"He tried to kill me," Tracy said.

"That doesn't answer the question."

"Of course I shot him. Who else could it have been?"

"Quite so," Leo said. "Quite so."

He drove for a little while in silence, then said:

"Better all round, of course, if it'd been Starshine."

"Much better," Tracy agreed.

"I'm glad that's how you see it. Because that's the way it happened—as far as Mr. Greene's concerned. Bony came in and Starshine got him, just the way we planned it. I say so. Starshine says so. And I've got another five hundred smackers that'll say so. They'll be in the registered post tomorrow morning. Then that'll be another little detail tidied up."

"And Bernadette?"

"Oh yes. You needn't worry about Bernadette. Bernadette most certainly will say so."

Tracy sighed. "It seems like I went to a hell of a lot of trouble, all for nothing."

"Five 'undred jimmy o'goblins ain't nothing, mate—not in my book. On top of the half a grand you got already."

"And if I said anything different, who'd believe me?"

"Not Mr. Greene. Not him. That's perfectly true. You can look on it as a nice little present, then. If it makes things any easier."

Certainly there'd be no point—Tracy thought—in refusing the offer. Honest money of course you couldn't call it, but taking it would at least be in earnest of his own good intentions. If he didn't take it, they wouldn't trust him. They'd worry about him. Tracy didn't want to have anyone worrying about him, least of all Starshine. So all right. A nice little present, then. "Suppose I asked you what Mr. Greene has to do with all this?"

"What he has to *do* with it?" Leo seemed surprised by the question. His long nose twitched.

"Yes. I wouldn't have thought that if Bony *had* taken Tommy Pope to the cleaners it'd have been any skin off Mr. Greene's nose. He's not overfond of Tommy, that's for sure. So why did he and you hire all the protection? Starshine costs money. He isn't cheap. Well, what's *your* interest?"

"It's like I said. There always has to be a deal."

"I don't see why. It'd suit you a whole lot better, wouldn't it, to have Pope dead rather than just divorced. And anyway, she's not going to divorce him. That's obvious. So what kind of a deal *was* it, anyway?"

Leo said eventually,

"You know something, sport . . . ? You're learning."

"They say it's never too late."

"You're right, of course. She's not getting a divorce. And yes, you could say I'm a little disappointed. But it wasn't that they set out to fool me—at least, I don't think so. What happened was that I fooled myself. So I'd be silly to bear anyone a grudge."

"Yes," Tracy said. "There'd be no percentage in it."

"No percentage at all."

They were going into Cardiff by the same road that Lambo had taken the night before, but there was very little that Tracy remembered. Hedges, fields, tussocky verges, a cluster of stone houses here and there; the dry ground had sucked up the deluge with surprising speed, or had diverted it down the hillside slopes, but pools of water still stood in the lower reaches of the fields and the road surface was still very wet. The air had a windy bite to it this morning that suggested that the long summer was over; Tracy wound up the side window another couple of inches.

". . . So," Leo said, "if I should tell you something that maybe I shouldn't, well, it's naturally with malice towards none. It's just that . . . perhaps you *are* learning. And who am I to discourage man's search for the truth? For knowledge? That's made us what we are today, wouldn't you agree?"

"Oh, I would, yes, I would."

"Good. Then we're on the same wavelength. The thing *is,* you see, me old china, that when Bony and Rusty Keyes bust open our safe in the Bond Street office, they didn't just help themselves to a whole lot of gold. There was other stuff in the safe as well. I won't say more valuable, but certainly . . . more embarrassing. To *us,* that is. We wouldn't've minded the hard stuff, it was all insured, but the other . . . You won't know what I'm talking about?"

"Drugs, maybe?"

"Drugs? *Drugs?* God, no." This time Leo seemed not so much surprised as shocked. "Who the hell d'you think we are? The Petersen brothers? Or the Mafia, maybe? *We* should get so lucky."

"Bony didn't say there was anything else."

"No. He couldn't have told you, because he didn't know about it. That's the irony—"

"Though he did say something about there being some papers."

"Ah. Yes. That's it. Papers. Ledgers. He handed the whole lot over to Tommy Pope and that's when it all *got* embarrassing. I wouldn't want to bore you with the details, but you'll realise that not everything a big firm like ours has to handle is as strictly legitimate as it might be. On the other hand, nothing that isn't strictly legitimate shows up in the company tax returns. There are discrepancies, so to speak. Well, the figures wouldn't have meant very much to Bony, but they meant something to Tommy Pope all right. Especially the payola file. He's done enough fiddling on his own account—"

"What payola file?"

"Oh, just a check on the money we've paid out for little unofficial services rendered. There are people in the Inland Revenue, you know, people in the police force, all *kinds* of people, not mentioned by name, of course—we're not *that* stupid. But you'll see what I mean. It was embarrassing. Very."

"Yes, I think I do see," Tracy said. "And for Mr. Greene as well?"

"Yes, indeed. He's very much involved in the matters I've just mentioned, and in any case he's a principal shareholder. So for some little while now keeping Tommy Pope happy and smiling has been our mutual concern. And when he calls on us for a spot of friendly protection in lieu of the usual monthly cheque—what can we do? He has us, as the saying goes, over a barrel."

"And I take it he uses the stuff as insurance against any nasty little accident that may chance to befall him."

Leo sighed heavily. "Indeed he does. If Bony *had* finished the bastard off last night, the old balloon would have gone up right away—so you did us a much more valuable service than you thought. Tommy alive . . . Well, he's a damned nuisance, but not much more than that; he's got sense enough to be reasonable in his demands. Greene and my father can carry him between them without even noticing, what's twelve or fifteen thousand a year to *them* . . . ? Tommy dead, though, that's another matter. There'd be a fat little packet posted to the Public Prosecutor within a week. Of course if we knew how he's arranged to get it sent . . . But that's wishful thinking. Tommy drinks too much sometimes, but he's no damned fool."

Ahead of them now, the junction of the Cardiff-Cowbridge road with a line of high-speed traffic tearing past. Leo braked and halted at the GIVE WAY sign to let them go by, his head turning nervously to the right, to the left, to the right; he was, Tracy had noticed, a jumpy driver.

". . . He's no fool, but one of these days he'll make a mistake. One of these days we'll send him up on a nice long sentence. That's the only answer—a good stretch at Parkhurst. He can't bother us while he's there, and on the other hand he won't use the stuff he's got on us—even if he susses it was us that put him down. Because that'd be killing the goose that lays the golden eggs." The car lurched abruptly forwards, swinging to the right; Tracy, who had anticipated the movement, had one hand pressed tightly against his ribs. "So that has to be the answer to dear old Tommy. It may take a long while yet, but I'm a patient sod. I can wait."

Tracy was thinking: Blackmail. I should have guessed. I was

stupid. Granted it's not my scene, all this talking of deals, this cross and double-cross, but I was stupid not to see it all the same. Bony said I was stupid and Bony was right. I've been thinking that maybe the Brighton garage, my frowsty little pad off the Steyne, that all that'd seem a little bit dull after all this chasing about and general excitement. But the truth is it's not my scene, I'm just too stupid. Machines, that's what I know about. That's what I'm happy with. Maybe at times in the future when I'm tinkering around with a high-powered engine I'll be disturbed (if that's the word) by this or that recollection . . . say of long, neat, nylon-clad legs stepping down the iron ladder of the inspection pit . . . but then I'm used to that. Memories I've always had. I know all about *them*, too.

"How did Tommy know about it in the first place?"

"Know about what?"

". . . What was in the safe?"

"Oh, that. He probably got it from Bernie."

"*She* knew?"

"Oh yes. She's old Greene's daughter, after all. And if it comes to that, I may have let something slip myself when I was . . . when we were . . . *You* know how it is."

"And she told Tommy."

"Inadvertently, no doubt. I like to think she probably talks in her sleep."

"You'd know if she did, wouldn't you?"

"Oddly enough, I wouldn't. I'm not surprised if you got the wrong idea; we've had rather an odd thing going, I suppose. But no, I wouldn't. What about you?"

"Me?" Tracy shook his head. "No."

"I didn't think so. But I wasn't sure. Of course it's a pity, really, about her and Tommy." And Leo, too, shook his head; in regret, not in negation. "But like I said, it's no good bearing grudges. They understand each other, those two."

Again the tree-lined curve and the long dip down to Culverhouse Cross; Cardiff once again outspread before them, no longer as a rain-swept gaggle of distant lights but as a sprawling, smoke-hazed city under a heavy grey sky; to the north the mountains and the steep cleft of the Rhondda gap; to the south, behind the hills, the river and the sea. She'd been an exhilarating companion, one way or another; but it wouldn't have done. What Tracy needed was someone as stupid as himself. He thought of that other dark and much ampler shape silhouetted in the hallway of the cottage . . .

Not her, not Starshine's girl, but someone like that. There had to be other ways of getting to meet them. And if it came to that,

"There have to be other ways of getting to be rich."

"Getting to be rich isn't the problem. It's keeping hold of it when you've got it and all the other buggers want it. *That's* the problem."

"Not mine," Tracy said.

Leo left him outside the Central Station some fifteen minutes later. The stairs from the booking hall to the platforms were very steep, and with his suitcase he found it heavy going; but he had plenty of time and didn't hurry. Who (of all people) should be standing on the up platform but Jenny the Benny.

"Yes, well, all good things must come to an end and I'd had about enough of that place anyway. So this morning I thought I might just as well pull out. A girl's got to look after herself these days, is the long and the short of it. I'm going back to Brighton. What about you?"

"Me, too. Perhaps I could buy you lunch . . . ? There's a dining car."

But the idea had no appeal. "I'd really rather not. No hard feelings."

Maybe it was the tin head she still found off-putting, or maybe on the basis of last night's experience she'd decided that Tracy meant trouble. Either way, it was a nice polite refusal. Tracy did in fact see her later in the dining car, sitting on the opposite side of the table to a burly London businessman in a pin-stripe suit, tucking into a plateful of roast lamb and conversing animatedly between mouthfuls. At another table, somewhat coincidentally, was seated an old acquaintance of Tracy's, a coming man in the car trade with all the outward appurtenances of considerable prosperity. So Tracy had someone to talk to after all. Desmond Davies was the old acquaintance's name; he liked, however, to be called D.D.

"British Railways, is it, boy? What happened to the wheels?"

"I had a bit of a shunt out west."

"Where you based now, then?"

"Brighton."

"Working for old man Greene, I seem to remember? Warm man, old Greene. Very warm. I could find you something in town, you know, or up in the Midlands, any time you feel you want a change."

"Thanks," Tracy said. "But not just yet."

"Well, bear it in mind, though. I mean, life gets boring at times, don't you find? Though I must say the most peculiar thing happened to me in Cardiff last night. You won't believe this, I don't suppose, but there was this bird, see, in one of the boozers . . ."

A change, Tracy thought (ceasing to listen) might not be a bad idea at that. Boring or interesting or whatever, life—as in spite of what Bony had said he had still to consider it—went on; there would always be D.D.'s around to remind you of the fact, and in so doing they served a useful purpose. Staring, and now quite absently, across at Jenny, he put a hand in his trousers pocket and fingered the small round black pebble he had carried there since that morning; he would carry it around with him always now, to perform just the opposite function . . . to remind him that just possibly another, a super-Tracy was somewhere about, a Tracy whose wife hadn't left him and never would, a Tracy who won all his races and kept all his money, a Tracy to whom the girls said yes, or a Tracy who maybe still climbed trees and lay on grassy hills and swung on five-barred gates in a cloudless summer. The odd thing was that had it been possible (and all things were possible—Bony had said so) he—this wifeless, friendless, impecunious, none-too-bright Tracy—wouldn't really have wanted to change places. He hadn't any regrets. In fact, he felt quite happy. A small black stone from a Welsh beach was all that he needed; a token that what had been, *had* been and could never be lost, and that what *hadn't* been just possibly had been, too.

Besides, he'd had another good idea. He could buy a dog.